POET ANDERSON

ANDERSON

...IN DARKNESS

TOM DELONGE
SUZANNE YOUNG

T● THE STARS⁚..

To The Stars, Inc.
1051 S. Coast Hwy 101 Suite B, Encinitas, CA 92024
ToTheStars.Media

To The Stars... and *Poet Anderson* are trademarks of To The Stars, Inc.

Written by Tom DeLonge & Suzanne Young
Cover © 2017 by Tom French

Editor: Michael Strother
Managing Editor: Kari DeLonge
Book Layout: Lamp Post Publishers

Published by To The Stars...
Distributed Worldwide by Simon & Schuster

Manufactured in the United States of America

ISBN 978-1-943272-32-7 (hc trade)
ISBN 978-1-943272-33-4 (eBook)

I would like to dedicate the next part of the Poet Anderson journey to my co-author, Suzanne. She is a joy to work with and enormously talented.

ACKNOWLEDGMENTS

Tom—Thank you to my family for supporting me and my own personal dreams. I also would like to acknowledge all the To The Stars employees, because none of this would work without their passionate dedication and work.

Suzanne—Thank you to my agent Jim McCarthy. And as always, this is for my grandmother Josephine Parzych.

POET
ANDERSON

...IN DARKNESS

PART 1

FROM THE SHADOWS . . .

CHAPTER ONE

POET JONAS ANDERSON ADJUSTED THE brim of his bowler hat and stepped inside the tunnel toward the Dream World. Air whooshed around him in a high arc, blowing open the lapels of his suit jacket, pulling him forward with an electric gravity that sent sparks over his skin, energy into his eyes—turning them bright white, brimming with power. He loved this feeling.

As he reached the other side, Poet stepped through. The heels of his shiny black shoes crunched on gravel, and Poet stopped to look around, surprised to find himself in a seedy alleyway of Genesis. The surrounding brick walls were gray with age and a metal dumpster seeped something rotten from its corners. Plumes of smoke rose from the grates of the sewer, the air noxious.

Genesis had this duplicity—at once filled with the dark shadows of nightmares and the bright lights of fantastical dreams. Above Poet, the night sky teemed with flying cars, airbikes, zooming in and out of focus. The sweet smell of candy and fried foods hung in the air, tinged with alcohol and rot. There was a buzz from the neon signs fifty stories tall, flashing reds and yellows and colors Poet couldn't even identify.

Then there were the alleyways, many like this one, where green-skinned creatures would scurry past. Where products of the dreamscape in the form of men and women—*Dreams, living, breathing creatures of their own*—would sometimes tempt a foolish dreamer from the Waking World into an erotic nightmare, the sort they came back for time and again. The sort they liked.

But the Dreamworld was more than an extension of the waking reality. It was its own reality, Dreams and creatures and all, and Poet never forgot that it was real. It was *never* just a dream.

Poet started down the alley toward the orange glow coming from around the corner—a trash fire, most likely. He could hear laughter, some cursing. Poet sent a rush of electricity to his fingertips, letting it snap on his skin with a sharp sting. He enjoyed the pain of it—a reminder of his power.

It'd been a while since Poet had to fight Night Stalkers, and almost a year to the day since he battled REM in the Grecian Woods. The Dream World was serene now in comparison, but Poet never relaxed into this newfound peace. He never quite trusted it.

Last time they'd met on the battlefield, he'd been so close to defeating REM. His brother Alan was with him at the battle, beside him, and he almost came home. But at the last moment, Alan slipped away, back into his coma, his thinning body still laid motionless in a hospital bed in the Waking World.

REM himself had disappeared after that night, absconding into the Dreamscape. Even the Night Stalkers, REM's soldiers, seemed to fall away. Genesis and the rest of the Dream World existed in peace...except for a few raucous poets.

But the former poets served a purpose. They were helping Poet Anderson train, prepare for what was to come next. And this time Poet wouldn't let REM survive. He would make him pay for what he'd done to his brother.

A figure turned the corner of the alleyway in front of him, and Poet's mouth twisted up in surprise. "Sketch?" he called.

Sketch stopped dramatically, ducking down as if he couldn't believe what he was seeing. "Holy shit, Poet. Where you been, man? They didn't tell me you'd be out tonight."

The two guys slapped hands and pulled in for a hug. "It's been a long time," Poet said, happily stunned to see Sketch. Together, they used to explore the Dream World. They found Genesis together. And, of course, they fought REM together. Poet and Sketch had seen each other only a handful of times over the past year, and only once in the Waking World.

After their return from the battle that took their friend Gunner's life (along with the lives of many others), Sketch came to the Eden Hotel for an informal memorial. Alexander Birnham-Wood, leader of the Dream Walkers, put on the entire affair to see who was left. The results were staggering. Whether all of the Dream Walkers were dead, or they just didn't want to show, remained to be seen, but there were only six Dream Walkers at the hotel that day.

And then there was Sketch, a lucid dreamer. Along with Poet, he'd survived REM's worst. Warriors had been torn down that night, but a punk artist with few skills beyond tagging managed to make it. Poet was grateful for that.

In front of him now, Sketch looked the same as he did last year: spiky blond hair, baggy paint-stained jeans, and large gauges in his ears.

"What are you doing here?" Poet asked, stepping back. "I didn't think you liked the other poets."

"I don't," Sketch said. "No offense, but your friends suck." He smiled. "I was running an errand for my girl, and Callum tunneled me in."

"Wait," Poet said with a laugh. "You've got a *girl*? A real one?"

"Hell, yeah, she's real!" Sketch paused. "I mean, well…, it's complicated. She's real enough. Maybe you'll meet her sometime."

"That'd be cool."

"Ay, Poet Anderson," Callum called from the other end of the alley, just out of sight. "Quit wanking off and get over here. And tell Sketch to get in the tunnel before I send him to the middle of a lake instead of his bed."

Poet turned back to see that the tunnel Callum had created for Sketch was spiraling into the brick wall, its edges starting to fray. Poets were the only ones who could make direct tunnels between the Dream and Waking worlds. The rest of the dreamers had to wake up on their own.

"Yes, thank you very much, Callum," Sketch called back to him with an annoyed pleasantness.

"Any time, mate."

Poet looked at Sketch apologetically, but he waved him off. "No worries, man," Sketch said. "I had to wake up anyway. We'll catch up soon. All right?"

They exchanged another quick hand slap, and then Sketch walked over to the brick wall. He looked over the tunnel with a gulp, stepped through, and disappeared. The tunnel sealed up behind him with the scratchy sound of reforming bricks.

A bottle clinked on pavement behind him, and Poet imagined the other poets were on their second bottle of whiskey, but probably more like their third. Callum was British, an egomaniac, and a damn fine poet. He was the first poet to come to Jonas in the Waking World. He then brought Jonas to the others, and together they made a contingency plan to defeat REM.

But REM was gone, and now they just drank a lot of a whiskey together.

Up until a year ago, it was thought that the other poets were extinct, but they were in hiding, waiting until it was safe. They'd been living solely in the Dream World—bodies and all; these poets had the power to cross realities, and that power was a great temptation for REM. In his hands, a poet could have been used to destroy the Waking World. But now that REM was gone, the poets returned. None of them liked to be called Poet anymore, though. They claimed the title was Jonas's alone.

Jonas Anderson was Poet—he was the one who guided dreamers. Who met with the Dream Walkers when needed.

He was the one the Dream World looked to when there was a problem. The former poets offered advice, but rarely help. As they said, it wasn't their job anymore.

Anti-social at best and nearly impossible to find, they were unruly and dangerous. Each had their own brand of power, sometimes hidden, sometimes obvious. Poet didn't quite feel their equal since his power was more unstable, and he was far less experienced.

Since the battle in the Grecian Woods, Poet hadn't been able to manipulate his surroundings—the elements—in the same way. He imagined it had to do with nearly losing his brother. Although all poets could create—make a weapon, for example—Poet had the unique ability to shift landscapes. Bend the Dream World to his will. Destroy it if he wasn't careful.

Poet turned the corner into a bridge-covered back alley, lights flickering all around from the signs of shady establishments that lined the streets. Smoke rose from the grates at the curbs.

Suddenly, Poet was struck with a bolt of white-hot energy, knocking him nearly off his feet. Defensively, electricity shot through his hands and exploded from of his fingertips, wild and out of control. He staggered back a step as sparks faded from the air in front of him.

The other poets laughed, and when Poet recovered, he shook off the electricity on his skin and looked around. "Assholes," he murmured as Callum lowered his arm.

"You should have been expecting it, mate," he said with a chuckle. "What if I were a Night Stalker?"

"Then you'd be a better shot," Maeve Greer called. Maeve grinned and went back to sharpening the end of her knife on a piece of slate.

Maeve was an absolute fascination to Poet. She was well over six feet tall with a shaved head, full lips, and an angular jaw. Beautiful. Deadly. Like a fashion model who decided to slaughter the entire runway instead of walk it. Her eyes were midnight blue, or at least one of them was. The other was permanently white, as if the electricity in her body were always keyed up and ready to explode—which wasn't far from the truth. Maeve was always ready to fight, but never to argue. She'd sooner stick a knife in someone's gut than have an actual conversation. Poet thought it was her most charming quality.

"Where's your girlfriend, Poet?" Maeve asked, and looked sideways at him, the flash of her ghost eye catching his attention. "You know how much I enjoy hanging out with both of you."

"Uh, I know how much you don't even mean that."

"Not true," Maeve said with an exaggerated pout. "I like her better than you." She held out the bottle of whiskey, and Poet took it and sat on the barrel next to her.

The green toxic-looking fluid sloshed around, and Poet took a long swig, the alcohol burning his throat the entire way down. He'd gotten used to the burn, though, and immediately took another sip before handing it back.

It had been strange meeting the other poets at first. They were inherently distrustful, and still hadn't told him where they'd been hiding, or how they had evaded REM all these years. Or how…they hadn't aged. Every one of them was still young, here *and* in the Waking World, although they claimed to have known Jarabec when he was a boy. Then again, Poet wasn't exactly an open book either. Callum was the only one who knew about Alan. Poet didn't want the others to have emotional blackmail to use against him.

Poet darted his eyes around the group, feeling he was being watched. He forced power to his fingertips, and, just as it sparked, Winston Clyde threw an empty bottle in his direction. Before it could hit him, Poet sent a streak of heat, shattering the glass and sending shards of it showering down on the other poets.

Maeve quickly put up her arm to block the glass and cursed. "Watch the face," she growled.

Poet sniffed a laugh, and Winston kicked the glass from where it had fallen around his heavy boots. "Better," Winston told him. Winston Clyde was heavyset, with messy tufts of bleached hair sticking out from under his beanie. He wore that hat every day with a suit and tie, like a real gentleman. He motioned Poet toward the wooden crate next to him so he could talk to him. Poet moved to the other side of the fire and let the electricity fade from his eyes.

Of all the poets, Poet Anderson enjoyed Winston the most. Besides throwing a bottle at his head, he didn't have the ego of the others. Just a regular guy most of the time. He'd been helping Poet with the rain, learning how to start and stop it reliably. Winston was good with control—helpful, considering his power.

Winston Clyde made fire. Anywhere, everywhere. A true pyromaniac. He said that was why he liked Poet so much.

Since Poet could control the rain, Winston thought they were the perfect match. His own personal fire extinguisher.

"What was Sketch doing here?" Poet Anderson asked the group. "I didn't know you guys were friends."

Callum screwed up his face like Poet's comment was completely juvenile. "Friends?" Callum said. "Oh, yes. I have lots of those. I'm very congenial."

Maeve snorted. "Callum has never had a friend in his life," she said, and he winked at her.

"Why was he here?" Poet repeated.

"It's certainly none of your business," Callum said, "but his *girlfriend* owed us."

This time it was Winston who smiled, although he tried to cover his mouth with his palm. "Girlfriend. Right."

Callum picked up a carved wooden box, ornate and delicate. He lifted the lid, and inside was a small knife with a glowing white blade. "It's a beauty, right?" He reached in to touch it, but stopped himself. He looked around at the other poets, and then closed the box. "She stole it years ago, so it was time to get it back."

"Who did she steal it from?" Poet asked.

"Me," Callum replied as he set the box near his feet. Poet was about to ask how exactly he knew Sketch's girlfriend, but he could already guess.

"Sorry about the shot earlier," Winston said, bumping Poet's shoulder. "Just testing you."

"It was fun," Poet replied deadpanned. "No, really. I love when you throw bottles at my head. That's how I know you care."

Winston laughed and patted his leg. "So where were you last night? We waited for you at least five minutes. Maybe four. You missed out," he added.

"Bet he was with his girl," Marcel Beaumont called, grinning in Poet's direction. Marcel was black with long dreads that went halfway down his back; he wore a sleek, tailored gray suit and had a scratchy voice that always sounded like it was on the edge of a jovial laugh.

"Maybe," Poet said. "And where were you last night, Marcel? Heard you got your ass kicked in uptown."

"Psht," Marcel said, waving his hand. "It was a scratch. That's what happens when you stay in the Dream World, Poet Anderson. You experience things."

Poet smiled. "I experienced plenty."

Maeve rolled her eyes. "Good for you. Now where's the whiskey you promised? All I can find here is that green shit." She crossed her long legs at the ankle, and leaned forward, elbows on the knees of her crisp black pants. "Tell me you grabbed the good stuff from that high-class hotel you work for."

Poet reached into the inside pocket of his jacket and pulled out a small bottle of whiskey he'd stolen from the top shelf of the Eden Hotel bar when he first crossed into the Dream World. Hanging with other poets wasn't exactly free.

Maeve smiled and clapped her hands together before holding out her palm. "If you were my type," she said, taking it from him.

"Aw, come on," Winston said. "Poet Anderson is everyone's type."

"Not this time," Maeve said. "Not with that pretty face." She unscrewed the top of the bottle and took a long sip, before licking her lips and passing the bottle to Callum. "Definitely the good stuff," she said.

Poet leaned back on the crate. He'd grown used to watching the other poets get drunk and belligerent. And he enjoyed the escape—the pointlessness of it. The freedom in it.

But still, he felt that familiar twinge of guilt and sadness, that ache of loss that his waking life offered. Poet wished his brother could be here instead. But Alan was resting peacefully in a long-term care facility while Jonas worked as a doorman at the Eden Hotel. Busywork that paid little more than room and board.

But, of course, there was Samantha Birnham-Wood—his dream girl, who was probably dreaming right now, far from here. Maybe he'd find her later.

"Where's your girlfriend tonight, Anderson?" Marcel asked. Poet snapped back to this reality. He reached out his hand, and Maeve tossed the closed bottle to him.

Poet smiled, took a sip, and passed it on. "She's far away from you fuckers, that's for sure."

"Smart man," Callum agreed, and they all laughed.

There was a rattle down at the dark end of the alley, like an empty can being kicked along gravel. All five poets looked in that direction, and Marcel lowered the whiskey bottle from his lips.

Poet felt the electricity in his body kick up. Maeve tilted her head, listening closer, and Marcel stood, staring as if he could see in the dark.

Callum sat perfectly still, and Poet didn't understand his non-reaction until he turned slightly and saw his eyes were glowing white. In his hand, a long-barreled gun was slowly forming from blue lines of electricity—appearing out of his own thoughts.

There was another shuffle. Step, step, drag. Repeat.

Poet's heart began to race, and across from him, Maeve got to her feet and wiped the blade of her knife on the side of her pants before tightening her grip on its handle.

"Who's there?" Marcel called, chin down and eyes up. Winston leaned forward on his crate, facing directly down the alley. But it was too dark to see what was coming.

Poet looked at Callum again, and the other poet nodded, letting him know to be ready. Callum had a sense about things—premonition. Poet and the others broke his balls about it sometimes, mostly because it hadn't been useful in the past year. But they knew it was real, although not always reliable.

Marcel took a step toward the alley. "I said *who's there*, motherfucker?" Marcel called. A figure appeared and Poet fought to keep his power under control. He'd grown wild and careless with the other poets; he didn't want to hurt someone unnecessarily.

A man stepped into the light, his leg dragging limply behind him. His clothes were tattered and filthy, and he kept his scruffy face downturned. Poet noticed sores on his cheeks, cracks in his lips. Maeve was the first to put away her weapon.

The man took another step toward them, and, as he staggered, Marcel reached out to help steady him. Poet watched, still standing, and saw Callum slowly tilt his head as he watched the old man, his eyebrows pulled together. Poet noted that Callum's grip on his gun didn't relax.

"Night Stalkers," the man whispered. "Down on the east side." He choked on his words and started coughing heavily, his shoulders shaking. The man spit on the pavement. He seemed beat up and worn down as he clung to Marcel, even though Poet couldn't see any injuries.

Something about him...felt *off*. Poet remained tense, and Callum watched in silence as the stranger started another round of coughing.

"Take it easy, man," Marcel said. "We've got you." He'd started to walk the man toward a crate so he could sit, when the man moved out of Marcel's grasp.

"Naw, friend," the man said, slowly lifting his head. "We've got you."

The man's eyes were black and soulless—the eyes of a Night Stalker. A lens dropped down over his face, forming a helmet, and black armor raced over his body with a series of metallic clicks. A black orb formed and began floating over his shoulder.

Poet quickly flung out his hand, ready to create a gun, but he didn't get the chance before the Night Stalker lifted his weapon and fired.

CHAPTER TWO

MAEVE YELLED FOR EVERYONE TO TAKE cover, but the blast was out, as well as shots from Callum and Winston. Poet then noticed the red streak hanging in the air, the crisscrossing of lasers, crawling slowly forward. Everyone else was equally still, his own energy frozen while creating a weapon. Time had slowed.

Marcel's eyes were squeezed shut, his teeth gnashed. No one could move, but that was how Marcel's power worked. He could slow time to a near standstill, make a moment feel like it lasted forever, so that those involved had time to plan action, make a better decision when time caught up. Poet had never seen Marcel use his power before—only heard him discuss it once.

Frozen in time, the poets watched as the laser—a small red ball of fire—slowly inched its way from the Night Stalker's weapon toward Winston's chest. And none of them could do anything to stop it.

Poet saw a tear welling up in the corner of Maeve's ghost eye. Callum stared at Winston, his jaw clenched and his finger shaking where it was still pressed on the trigger of his gun. He was trying to break out of time—they all were.

A green light from a neon sign cast down on Winston, making him look sickly pale. His eyes were wide with horror, as if he were already dead. Across from him, the Night Stalker's face was hidden behind the black lens of his helmet; the creature didn't even care about the shots heading towards him. Night Stalkers were soulless. They didn't fear death. They *were* death.

There was a low grunt as Marcel lost his grip on time, and all at once—so fast it could be missed in a blink—the laser hit Winston, knocking him backwards and over the barrel.

One shot struck the Night Stalker, while his Halo—the black orb floating above his shoulder—blocked the second. The laser barely pierced the outside of his armor. The Night Stalker stumbled back a step and then raised his weapon again. There was a deep groan from Winston, but everything was moving so quickly, there wasn't time to check on him. Two more lasers fired, shots ricocheting, and then one caught the Night Stalker and chipped a corner of his helmet, temporarily disorienting him. His Halo shot toward Callum, who fired at it, striking it twice.

Then it was Maeve's turn. She used one foot on the barrel as leverage and leapt over the fire. Her attack was sudden and violent. She jammed her knife under the helmet of the Night Stalker, and there was a sharp hiss as he fell back, tripping over a crate. As he was falling, Maeve's hands worked fast, stabbing him repeatedly, too quickly to count. And when the Night

Stalker hit the ground, she put one foot on his arm, the sound of his crunching bone echoing, leaving him weaponless.

On the other side of the fire, Marcel and Callum were doing what they could to destroy the Halo—what was left of the Night Stalker's soul—before it could come back to protect him.

Maeve bent down and once again stuck her knife under the helmet, sawing at it, prying it from the man's face. Black ooze-like blood began to leak out over the blade, the handle, and her fingers. The Night Stalker tried to fight, but whenever he did, she stabbed him more. She needed to see his face.

There was a loud crack and then the lens of the helmet flipped back. Blood covered half of the Night Stalker's face, flaps of skin hanging from his left cheek where Maeve had been sawing. The creature didn't call out in pain, didn't call for mercy. He smiled.

In that instant, Poet saw the extent of Maeve's insanity as she brought down the knife and stabbed out both of the Night Stalker's eyes. Black blood spurted across her face, and Maeve wiped it away with the back of her hand. The creature writhed underneath her, this brand of pain perhaps too much for him. Maeve stared down, and then, slowly, she drew her blade across his neck and let the life drain from him. She stayed on top of him until the Night Stalker was dead.

Behind her, the creature's Halo exploded into dust. Maeve turned to look back at the other poets, blood smeared over her cheek and eyelid.

"They're coming," Callum said calmly, and Maeve quickly got to her feet, wiping the edge of her knife on the Night Stalker's suit before sheathing it.

Poet stared down at the body of the Night Stalker, reminded of the fight in the Grecian Woods, the battle where they'd lost nearly all the Dream Walkers. The battle where Alan came back and tried to help Poet save the world.

The intensity of that loss—dark and deep—snapped Poet out of his horror. Engines roared in the distance. Night Stalker airbikes—at least ten—were heading in their direction. There were no Dream Walkers to protect them now— not that poets normally needed protecting. Poet glanced over to where Winston was lying, his feet visible on the side of the barrel. One boot rolled to the side, his entire body still.

Poet walked over, and felt sickness bubble up in his gut as he looked down. Winston was dead, his eyes staring straight up at the stars. Blood slipping from the corner of his mouth, a clear hole burned into his chest. Poet's anger sent a flash of power through his limbs, and he felt the need to destroy, to face the returning Night Stalkers. To send them to hell.

Lightening flashed overhead, and as Poet clenched his fist, storm clouds raced in—red and angry.

"Not now," Callum called, and Poet looked over to see he was talking to him. "It's not the time. You won't win."

Poet's lips parted in surprise, but then he puffed up his chest. "We can't let them get away with this," he said.

"We won't," Callum responded as he took a hat from his coat pocket and put it on. "But we need to get out of the Dreamscape for now." He picked up the box with the knife and tucked it under his arm. His gun transformed into a cane, and he began walking toward the bridge where a tunnel was opening.

Poet glanced over to Marcel who was still staring at Winston on the ground. Maeve came over and knelt beside the body. Poet knew this would change everything. The poets were used to being invincible. No consequences. That was why Poet had liked them—they were fearless. But now the illusion was shattered.

The sound of the bikes was growing louder, and Poet knew Callum was right: They had to go. He reached to take Maeve's arm, but she ripped from his grasp. She leaned down and put her palm on Winston's cheek.

"I'll see you again," she murmured to him. Poet could feel her loyalty, her sorrow, her growing vengeance.

"Marcel," Maeve said, not looking back. "Get Poet Anderson out of here."

"No fucking way," Poet said. "We're *all* going. Now."

Maeve straightened up, casting one last longing look at Winston before turning to Poet. Her jaw was clenched, her skin ashen. "Get out of my way," she said. "I have some monsters to kill."

She started forward, bumping his shoulder with hers and knocking him back a step.

"I can't let you do that," he called after her.

Maeve laughed, and Marcel fell in step next to her, both walking down the alley toward the roar of engines, their jackets billowing behind them. Bright lights filled the other end of the alley. The Night Stalkers were here.

Poet gulped down his fear and began to make a weapon, but before he could finish, Marcel turned back to look at him. His eyes were turned down in grief, sadness. Devastation.

Revenge.

"Wake up, Jonas," he whispered. His hand shot out, and from the tips of his fingers, electricity blasted in a zigzag and tore a hole underneath Poet, straight through the concrete—a tunnel into the Waking World. And Poet Anderson fell through.

"Wait!" Jonas yelled, sitting up in bed. He gasped in a sudden gulp of air, his hand stretched out in a desperate attempt to reach the closing tunnel. The sweat on his skin was sticky, and his white sheets were tangled around his legs. He tried to catch his breath as his eyes struggled to adjust to the lack of light in the room.

There was the gentlest touch on his hip.

"What is it?" Samantha asked, her voice gravelly with sleep. She reached over to switch on the lamp on the nightstand, bathing the room with amber light.

Jonas stared at her for a moment, displaced. Here was Samantha Birnham-Wood in his bed, wearing just his white T-shirt, her short hair matted on one side from the pillow, her creamy skin flushed. Her leg brushed against his as she came closer to move his hair out of his eyes. She kissed the side of his mouth, and wrapped her arms around his shoulders.

Jonas leaned against her, the sweet smell of her hair tickling his nose. The heat of her body against his. He felt alone most days—lost while his brother wasted away, trapped in his own body. But when he was with Sam, Jonas was different. She was his only tether to the Waking World he had left. If not for her, he might never wake up again. And in her arms now, Jonas felt the agony of his humanity. The pain of existing, and always losing.

"Another nightmare?" Sam asked. Jonas had had several in the past few months. When he was truly exhausted, he'd have a glitch—a dream that was slightly off, slightly horrifying. Or worse, he'd get caught in a memory loop, reliving some of the worst moments from his past: Jarabec's death, for instance.

"No," Jonas said, and as he blinked, tears ran down his cheeks. He stared blankly across the hotel room, still hearing Winston's dying breaths. His chest heaved as he tried to slow his heartbeat, willing himself to be calm.

Sam pulled back, noticing his tears. "What happened?" she asked. She looked him up and down, running her hands over his skin. "Are you hurt?"

"Not me," Jonas whispered. Miserable, he turned to her, and Samantha's eyes widened.

"Who?" she demanded, her own tears welling up. They'd been through so much together. Death was nothing new.

"Winston," Jonas said, his heart dipping.

"*No*. But…how?"

Jonas untangled himself from the sheets, and got up from the bed. He pulled on his pants, and brushed his hair back from his face. He turned to Sam, and it was as if all the air were sucked out of the room when he whispered, "Night Stalkers."

Samantha's expression fell. "That's not possible," she said after a moment. "They've been gone for a year. They…" She shook her head, fear crawling into her voice. "Does that mean *he's* back too?"

"I don't know yet," Jonas said, sitting on the edge of the bed. He glanced toward the window and saw the beginnings of dawn. "What time is it?" he asked.

"About six. How are the others?" she asked, sliding out of the sheets and getting dressed. "Callum?"

"Fine," Jonas said waving his hand. "I'm going to talk with him now—I think he's upstairs. Maeve and Marcel stayed behind to fight."

"They're still there?" Sam asked, spinning around to face him. "You have to help them."

"Can't," Jonas said. "I don't know where they are. Callum opened the tunnel to bring me in, and Marcel sent me back. I couldn't find them if I tried."

"Damn it." She grabbed her phone and keycard and shoved them in the back pocket of her jeans. She tossed a T-shirt at Jonas. "Well, then let's go find that British fucker and get back to the Dream World to help them," she said.

Jonas sniffed a laugh, pulled the shirt over his head, and followed Sam out of the room.

Jonas was still barefoot as he climbed into the elevator on his way to the eighteenth floor. Sam was next to him, her arms folded over her shirt. Jonas watched her a moment, admired how strong and clear-headed she was in crisis. He grabbed her arm and pulled her to him. They clung together until the elevator signaled the floor.

They wouldn't need Callum's key. Sam's dad owned the hotel. Even if she barely spoke to him anymore, she had a master key for all the rooms, and she took it out now as they approached room 1865, where Callum resided when he came to the Waking World.

Before Jonas and Sam could stop in front of the door, it swung open. "You can tuck away your murderous rage, Birnham-Wood," Callum said, lifting one side of his mouth in a pained smile. "They're already back."

He pushed the door open for Jonas and Sam to enter the room, and then checked the hallway before closing the door behind them and locking it.

CHAPTER THREE

AS THEY WALKED INSIDE, SAM GASPED and looked around. The hotel room had been thoroughly trashed: the table flipped over, mattresses on the floor, paintings askew, and the TV missing altogether.

Perched on the edge of one mattress was Maeve, her filthy boots on top of the sheet while she drank from a small bottle she must have gotten from the now-overturned minibar. Marcel stood at the window, curtain held aside, staring out at the city. Seattle poured down relentless rain.

In any other circumstance, Samantha would have torn into them for destroying the place, but instead of saying anything about it now, she righted a chair and sat down. She looked at Maeve.

"So you're all right?" she asked.

Maeve lifted one shoulder in a shrug. "I wouldn't say that. But I'm alive. We barely got two shots off before another round of Night Stalkers showed up. They snuck right up on us," she said, turning to Callum. "How did they know where to find us?"

"They're stronger than they used to be," Callum said. "They sensed us somehow."

"And REM?" Jonas asked, making Maeve flinch. "Did you see him?"

"No," Marcel answered for her, turning around. "But Callum's right. The Night Stalkers were improved. If REM's back, he's probably upgraded too. We're in trouble."

"What do you mean?" Jonas asked.

Callum sighed, closing his eyes. "It takes time and a lot of energy for REM to exist—he feeds on the nightmares of dreamers. Your society is crumbling, your peace. He's siphoning his power from here." He motioned around. "Not just from dreamers, but from your waking nightmares. Your fears."

"I don't understand," Jonas said. "I beat him. I—"

"You held him off," Marcel corrected. "And he's surely used that time to rebuild. We're out of balance," he said. "There are too many poets here. You know there should always be balance." Marcel looked over at Callum as if this was a longstanding argument between them.

"REM will still bleed," Maeve added viciously. "I'll make sure of it." But Marcel's shoulders stayed slumped and he turned back to the window.

"No," Marcel said simply. The room fell quiet.

Jonas shifted uncomfortably, and lifted his gaze to Maeve. In the Waking World, both of her eyes were blue, but she was blind in one eye—the ghost eye that worked perfectly in the Dream World. He wondered then about her talent, a secret kept by the other poets. He didn't know what she could do; all he knew was that Callum once told him she was the most dangerous person he'd ever met because of it.

"Where's Winston's body?" Jonas asked softly.

"We couldn't very well leave him there with those creatures," Maeve responded. "Marcel and I…" She paused, and nodded to the closed bathroom door. "He's in there."

Samantha immediately got up and crossed the room, but Callum raced over and met her at the bathroom door, holding up his hand to stop her.

"I wouldn't do that, love," he said, staring down.

Samantha scoffed and pushed him out of the way. She opened the door and ducked her head in. There was silence, and Jonas couldn't tell what she was seeing, but her fingers tightened on the doorframe.

Sam quietly closed the bathroom door, and then, without a word, she came back to sit down, her face a sheet of white.

His heart sank, and he looked accusingly at Maeve. She shrugged him off dismissively.

Jonas imagined that the poets hated having to bring Winston back to the Waking World. The blandness of it. Winston had lived in his dreams, like the others. Powerful enough to walk into their dreams, full-bodied, and stay there. Only the dead would return permanently.

If you could live in a world you mostly controlled, why would you come back?

Sam took out her phone and dialed.

"Who are you calling?" Maeve demanded, nearly ready to pounce on Sam and rip the phone from her hand.

Sam held the phone to her ear, ignoring the question. "I need something," she said quietly into the line. Jonas watched her, her calm presence. Aside from school, Sam had taken over many of Molly's duties at the hotel. Molly had been the assistant manager and a powerful Dream Walker, but she died in the Grecian Woods. Now Sam was Marshall's right-hand woman. Marshall—the manager—had been running the place for years. But one day Sam would control the hotel entirely, if she wanted to.

"Deceased," Sam said into the phone. "1865."

Maeve leaned forward on the mattress, staring at Sam; at the window, Jonas heard Marcel sniffle. Jonas had known them all for only a year, but the small band of poets had been together for decades.

"Yes, have him prepared," Sam said. "And bring Mr. Bran in the back entrance. We don't want the guests to notice anything suspicious." She glanced around the room. "Also, we'll need a cleanup crew." She paused and closed her eyes. "I know. Thanks, Dad."

She hung up, and Jonas was stunned that she'd call her father for a favor. Then again, he was the one who had helped remove the Dream Walker bodies after the battle in the Grecian Woods. The Eden Hotel had a system for the deceased.

Sam turned to Maeve and said, "Our friend Mr. Bran runs a funeral home not far from here. He'll let you say goodbye first."

Maeve watched her a long moment before nodding curtly. "That's okay," she said. "Winston and I have already exchanged our farewells. Just...take care of his body for us. You can do that?" There was a flash of vulnerability in Maeve's expression.

In the Waking World, the poets had no money, no jobs. They couldn't have afforded a funeral, or even this hotel room, for that matter. Who knows what they would have done with the body? Winston might have stayed in the hotel bathroom for weeks.

"Of course," Sam said, nodding to her. Jonas reached over to touch Sam's arm, and she smiled sadly at him.

"You sure you're with the right poet, Samantha?" Callum asked, his accent thickened. "Because if not—"

"I'm good," she said, holding up her hand. Callum laughed and went to sit on the bed with Maeve, leaning his shoulder against hers.

"So, what now?" Jonas asked. "I'll gather whomever I can find, but after the battle...I'm not sure who's left of the Dream Walkers."

"Gather them for what?" Marcel asked. He didn't bother to turn away from the window as he spoke.

"To fight," Jonas said, like it was obvious.

"That's cute," Maeve called.

"What do you mean?" he asked.

"REM is back," she said. "We thought we could prepare in time, but that is clearly not the case. We're not ready, Jonas. None of us. We had a good run, but now it's time to hide. It's the most selfless thing we could do."

"How do you figure?" Sam asked, her voice taking on an edge. Marcel turned to face the small group.

Maeve started to speak, but Callum held up his finger to stop her.

"If REM got himself a poet," Callum started, "he would use him or her to tunnel into the Waking World. I'm sure your Dream Walker mates explained that to you already. But did they tell you it happened before?"

Jonas furrowed his brow. "No," he said. "But if it happened before, then how—"

"Balance," Marcel added.

Callum nodded and continued. "During the Dark Ages, REM got himself a poet and entered the Waking World. He would have destroyed this reality entirely, but as he grew powerful, more poets were created. Poets and Dream Walkers dragged him back to the Dream World, tore him from limb to limb. They barely won, and he didn't have Night Stalkers then. Everyone thought it was the end, but REM rebuilt. He got an army. His form is always changing. Adapting."

"Well, then…where are those other poets? Where are the new ones?" Jonas asked.

"Dead," Callum responded. "The old poets became old men. Some didn't make it that long, thanks to some of the Dream Walkers. They will always fear REM entering the Waking World, and the only way he can do that fully is by taking someone over. Taking a poet over. With that power, he would walk right through the veil. He would break down the wall between the Waking and Dream Worlds."

Callum turned to Sam. "Even your father knew that," he said. "He killed the last poet. The universe didn't like that, so it concentrated power into one last Poet." He looked at Jonas. "Poet Anderson."

"Ansel should have disappeared with us," Maeve said, off-handedly. "He belonged with us."

"Indeed," Callum replied, lowering his eyes. Maeve looked at Sam.

"Your father's a monster," she told her. "And we don't trust Dream Walkers to fight for us. If REM gets hold of us, you'll all be dead; the Dream Walkers would sooner kill us now than let that happen."

She turned to Jonas. "So suit up, Poet Anderson," Maeve said. "You are the last true Poet. There's no more help coming, thanks to Alexander Birnham-Wood. So you're, of course, coming with us. We learn from our mistakes."

"Leave?" Jonas asked, incredulous. "*Run and hide?* I would never do that."

"Yes, we know, you're a hero," Maeve said patronizingly. "But now's not the time to risk the fate of the world. Don't worry, your girlfriend's already impressed."

Jonas stood, ready to call them cowards, but Sam slid her hand into his. He looked down at her, surprised, but she gave him a look to drop it for now. She glanced at the time on her phone.

"I have to deal with my father," she said. "And you should go see Alan before your shift starts," she added, nodding at Jonas.

"You're going to work?" Callum asked with a laugh. "Today, you're going to work a shift at a hotel?"

"It's what my brother would do," Jonas said without looking at him. He leaned down and kissed Sam. "I'll call you when I get back," he told her quietly.

Without speaking to the poets—and without a plan— Jonas hurried toward the door.

"We're not done here," Callum called after him.

Jonas held up his hand, acknowledging the threat, and slipped out into the hallway. The visiting hours at the Sleep Center would start soon, and he wouldn't miss a day seeing his brother. That was one compromise Jonas would never make.

JONAS STEPPED THROUGH THE front door of the Center for Sleep Sciences building. The lobby was unchanged from the past year. Clear plastic chairs, a white rug—everything was modern and dreamy. In the corner, hanging over an array of decaf coffee choices, there still hung the plaque that read "Sweet Dreams Are Made of These."

"You're early," the receptionist said, smiling at him. "It'll be about fifteen minutes. Help yourself." She motioned toward the fruit and coffees.

Jonas thanked her and took a seat in one of the clear chairs, staring out the window at the rainy day. When he and Alan had first arrived in Seattle, Jonas had nothing. He had to rely on the kindness of nurses to sneak him crackers in order to eat. Now that he was working at the Eden, he didn't have to worry about food anymore; he had plenty to eat. But he still didn't have his brother.

After what happened in the sleep study, Samantha's dad forked over the money for Alan to have the best possible care—a free ride more expensive than any college scholar-ship. After all, it was *his* facility that had been infiltrated by REM, *his* patients and doctors who had been compromised and taken over by a Dream World psychopath.

Jonas wouldn't forgive Alexander for that. He could spend millions, and it would never be enough for inviting the Anderson boys to Seattle. In a way, Jonas blamed him for Alan's coma. Without the job offer at the Eden Hotel, they never would have driven in the rain, never would have gotten in an accident, never would have discovered Genesis.

Everything would be different.

The rain pattered against the floor-to-ceiling windows by the entrance, the sound rhythmic and lulling. Jonas was tired from a restless night, and he leaned his elbow on the arm of the chair, his chin in his palm.

He began to drift off, pulling himself awake at the last moment. He blinked, trying to fight, but then, helplessly, he rested his chin again and fell asleep.

POET ANDERSON STEPPED OFF the curb, just missing the bumper of a passing car that hovered several feet off the pavement, blue fire coming out of its exhaust. He spun out of the way and darted across the street, slipping into the sea of people on the sidewalks of Genesis.

He glanced up at one of the telescreens, his picture appearing the instant he looked. "Poet Anderson" it read in bold letters as the camera followed him along the street. He tilted his hat to the people, and then hurried along, preferring to stay anonymous.

"Poet!"

Poet turned around, annoyed, but he smiled when he saw it was Sketch. His friend came running up from a vendor, eating what looked (and smelled) like rancid meat on a stick. Poet put his finger under his nose to block the odor.

"Want some?" Sketch asked, holding it out. Poet could see that whatever he was eating was still moving.

"Hell, no," Poet said, waving him off.

A dreamer walked by and bumped his shoulder, but quickly apologized. The guy continued, gazing up at the bright lights and flying vehicles of Genesis. He was probably a first-timer.

"Poet, are you listening to me?" Sketch asked through a mouthful of food.

"No," Poet said.

"See?" Sketch said. "You never listen. Even Sam said so. You've got your head half in the Dream World while awake and the other way around when you're here. Pick a side, dude." Sketch finished off his meat and tossed the stick in the trash.

Up ahead, a couple of dreamers were arguing on the corner, pushing and shoving. Poet glanced to the other side of the street, but traffic had picked up.

He just wanted to relax, escape the Waking World *and* the Dream World, even if just for a few moments. He had thought Genesis would be the break he needed to reset. Instead, it was busier than he'd ever seen it. He turned to Sketch.

"Tell me about your girl," Poet said. "Tell me…anything." He just wanted a distraction. The dreamer up ahead took

a swing at the other, knocking him back into a shop building. A girl yelled and whacked him, and another person—a
Dream—intervened to stop them.

Dreamers came from the Waking World, while Dreams
themselves were the product of the Dreamscape, whole
beings that lived only here.

Ahead of him, Poet could sense that one of those dreamers was lost, but he didn't want to guide him right now. He
just wanted a fucking break.

Poet and Sketch walked around the crowd that had
formed and turned down a street with rows of restaurants
and shops—buildings that were older, original to the Dream
World. They didn't sit quite right, the sense of gravity off in
the Dream World. Some of the buildings floated altogether,
while others tilted severely to the side. The better ones were
draped in lights, their veneer constantly changing.

"And she's not from the Waking World," Sketch said.

Poet stopped abruptly, and turned to him. Next to them,
a shop door opened and a thick-skinned man, covered in
warts and gristly hair, came out to smoke a cigar. He flicked
his yellow eyes in their direction, and Poet grabbed Sketch by
the jacket and pulled him ahead. The man watched them the
entire way down the street. Poet paused at the corner.

"What do you mean she's not from the Waking World?"
he asked. "Are you saying—Sketch, are you dating a Dream
girl?"

Sketch flinched, and pulled out of Poet's grasp. "She's
real," he said. "Just not..." He waved his hand to the sky.
"She's from this reality, okay? Is it that big of a deal?"

It sort of was. It meant Sketch and his girl could be together only when he was asleep. But Poet wasn't about to piss on his parade.

"Naw, man," Poet said, slapping him on the shoulder. "I'm happy somebody wants to be with you. You know, without getting paid."

"You're fucking awful," Sketch said, even as he laughed.

Poet smiled, and out of the corner of his eye, there was a shift—a movement. He turned and saw the man from the shop, still smoking his cigar. Without moving his shoulders, he turned his head to look Poet dead in the eye.

It felt like someone had just walked over his grave—this eerie sense of someone peering into your soul. Knowing too much. Poet bumped Sketch's elbow and started walking again, away from the shops. But it felt like something was following him.

He glanced up at the fast-moving vehicles, trails of smoke behind them. The sky had taken on a purplish glow, and he felt a sick twist in his gut when he noticed the stars were gone entirely.

"We should get back to the main part of the city," Poet said, jogging across the street to head toward the glow of the billboards. He couldn't see the telescreens from here.

"Want to grab something to eat?" Sketch asked, catching up to him.

"You just ate."

"So?" Sketch said. "It's a dream, Poet."

Poet smiled. "Good point." He checked behind them again, but no one was there. The streetlights flickered above, and just before he turned around, one of the bulbs popped and went out, sending glass down onto the pavement.

"Something's wrong," Poet murmured, and quickened his pace. He turned on the next street corner, but instead of returning to the heart of the city, they were further away. He stopped and spun around, trying to get his bearings.

"What's happening?" Sketch asked. "How did we get here?"

"I don't know."

The shops were gone, the lights of the city only a faint glow in the other direction. They were on an empty street with a few dilapidated, vacant-looking buildings. Creatures slithered in the shadows.

Poet had never been to this part of Genesis before.

Sketch wrapped his arms around himself, an illusion of comfort. "Where is everybody?"

"I think I should tunnel us out of here," Poet said, the hairs on his arms standing on end. It was like...dread creeping over the back of his neck. He turned, but again, there was nothing there.

"Oh shit," Sketch said, sounding far away.

Poet turned again and saw Sketch pointing down to the other end of the block at a figure. Mist clung to the pavement, and the person standing there in the middle of the street was obscured.

"Is that...?" But Sketch didn't dare say it.

It wasn't an enemy.

It was Gunner.

"Gunner!" Sketch yelled, and began waving his hand. He turned back to Poet, his face split with a smile, his eyes watery with grateful tears.

They'd lost Gunner in the battle last year, but here he was. He started toward them.

Poet would recognize him anywhere. Broad shoulders, block head—and when Gunner got closer, Poet was sure he'd see the infectious, gap-toothed smile. God, he'd missed him.

Sketch jumped up, yelling about how much he couldn't believe it. He told Poet to come on, and he started racing toward Gunner. Poet laughed, watching as they approached each other. It was still hard for him to see Gunner's face, though.

"Jonas," a voice whispered into the dream.

Poet shook his head, trying to ignore it. He began to jog forward. Sketch was already there, talking to Gunner. He was boisterous and laughing. Gunner stood still, staring down at him.

It was then that Poet noticed the differences, however slight. Gunner's posture was off: too straight. Too rigid.

"Jonas Anderson," the voice said again.

"Not now," Poet murmured, and he balled up his hand into a fist, willing his power there. His blazed white as electricity shot through him.

"That's not Gunner," he said, only to himself at first, trying to make sense of it. "That's not Gunner!" He said it louder this time, and Sketch turned to look back at him.

"Of course it is," Sketch said. "What are you...? Oh," he said with a nod. "Poet, you're fading. I'll see you around, okay?" Sketch smiled, and put his hand on Gunner's shoulder.

But the person with him was not Gunner, and when it turned, its black eyes on Poet, its face went in and out of focus. Poet held out his hand to blast it away.

"Jonas Anderson!"

Jonas sat up in the clear plastic chair, nearly falling out of it. He steadied his shoes on the floor, and quickly darted his eyes around the lobby of the Sleep Center until he found the receptionist staring at him. Sweat had gathered in his hairline, and he swiped at it with the sleeve of his jacket.

"Sorry," the receptionist said, although she sounded a bit hostile. "I've been saying your name for at least five minutes. You can go up and visit your brother now."

Jonas didn't move right away, the dream sticking to his bones. It took a second as he considered it, and decided it was just a nightmare. *Another* nightmare. Gunner wasn't back. He would never be back. REM killed him.

There was a sharp twist of pain in his heart, and Jonas quickly got up from the chair, wanting the privacy of the elevator. He pressed the call button and got in as soon as the doors opened. He had been so happy for a few moments when he thought it was really Gunner.

"Man," Jonas murmured to himself, staring at his reflection in the elevator doors. "Fuck these nightmares."

He would have to talk to Alexander about them, not that he planned to be part of a sleep study. But Jonas couldn't stand the emotional toll his nightmares were taking. He was supposed to be able to control dreams. Lately, some of them had been controlling him.

Jonas pulled himself together as best he could, and when the signal for the floor dinged, he got out.

The air in Alan's hospital room was heavy with the smell of alcohol swabs, something antiseptic. Jonas had grown to hate that smell. It would cling to his clothes long after he left. The place was sparse, with little to inspire. Jonas figured they didn't bother with decoration when their patients were always asleep and unable to see it.

The noise of the heartbeat monitor was muted, and Jonas went to take his usual seat next to the bed. He reached over and knocked his fist against Alan's where it lay on the white bed sheet.

"Hey, brother," he said, and dropped down in the chair. He noted again how thin Alan had become. His limbs were lanky after a year of non-use. His face was slightly swollen from the medication—and gravity, Jonas guessed. But the breathing tube was gone, removed shortly after their return from battle. Alan could breathe on his own at least, so that was a positive sign.

But still, Jonas longed to speak to his brother. He would settle for Alan yelling at him for skipping school, or calling him out for how much he'd been drinking. He didn't care. He just wanted to hear Alan's voice.

Jonas sniffed, sat back in the chair, and put his foot on the metal rung of the hospital bed. He never missed a day here. Not one. Not a weekend or a holiday. Alan was his only family in the world, and he wasn't going to turn his back on him.

Inside, he was sure Alan knew every time he visited. What would he think if Jonas didn't show up one day? How disappointed he would be. How abandoned he'd feel.

Jonas liked to think that Alan would wake up and immediately slap him across the back of the head for not going to college. Scold him mercilessly. Not that Jonas ever planned on going to school beyond high school graduation—that was Alan's deal. Jonas was the fuck-up; his goals never went beyond a job, a girl, and a little healthy destruction.

Instead, his best friend, his only brother, ended up in a coma while he got tasked with saving the damn world through their dreams. It was a messed-up situation.

So, yeah. College didn't rank on his list of responsibilities.

But at least he had Samantha. She was the only real thing left in Jonas's life. He was sure that without her he'd just float away into the Dream World forever. He'd even fantasized about it sometimes. But the thought of losing her always brought him back. He loved her too damn much.

Jonas looked at Alan, struck again with sadness at the sight of his frail form. Jonas swallowed hard. "Sorry to do this, man," he started. "But I have some bad news. Turns out...the Night Stalkers are back."

Jonas lowered his voice.

"The poets I told you about," he said. "One of them, Winston...he was killed. A Night Stalker showed up as a man pretending to be hurt. Before we could even check him over, he fired. Maeve sliced him up like a real lunatic, but it was too late for Winston." Jonas choked up, and he curled his fist and brought it to his lips. "They're back," he murmured.

"And now the poets want to hide again, said I have to go with them." He shook his head. "But I can't do that," he added. "I don't know what to do. I need your help, man."

Jonas waited a moment, as if Alan might respond. When he didn't, he continued. "You need to wake up," Jonas said. "Or better yet, stay asleep and get your ass to Genesis to help me." Jonas stood and went to the edge of the bed where he leaned in to stare at his brother's face. No one had shaved his beard today, and the scruff made him look disheveled. His blond hair lay limply across his forehead, dull. "Where are you?" Jonas whispered desperately.

But Alan wasn't going to respond. He'd been lost somewhere in the Dream World. Poet Anderson had scoured the Dreamscape looking for him without ever finding a trace.

Jonas waited another second, and then he reached over to brush his brother's hair off his forehead, styling it as best he could. Alan would want to look good. He wouldn't want to lie here, looking weak. Jonas blinked back his tears, adjusted the neck of his brother's hospital gown, and then turned and walked out of the room.

On his way out, he stopped by the nurses' desk and asked them to make sure Alan got a shave today.

CHAPTER FOUR

THE BUS WAS LATE.

Jonas wrapped his arms around himself and poked his head out into the street to look down the block. Wind whipped around him, chilling him. But at least the rain had stopped. He wished he could control the rain here the way he could in the Dream World.

Jonas exhaled breath in a white puff and went to sit on the cold metal bench. He took out his phone and checked the time. He had one missed call from Sam, but when he rang her back, she didn't answer.

The other poets didn't have phones; what would be the point? They wouldn't work in the Dream World anyway. Jonas dialed the front desk and asked for Marshall—the hotel manager. As he waited, he got up to check for the bus again.

"Yes, Mr. Anderson," Marshall said in his deep voice. "What can I do for you?"

"Oh, hey," Jonas said, slightly intimidated. "I was…is Samantha around?"

Marshall let out a heavy sigh. "As I'm sure you're aware, I am your supervisor, not your assistant. I do not know where Miss Birnham-Wood is at the moment, but I assume she left with Mr. Bran. Perhaps try back later. Like when you get here for your shift."

Jonas saw the bus turn onto the street. "Yeah," he said. "I'm on my way in."

"Very good." Marshall hung up without a goodbye.

Jonas laughed to himself and put away his phone. Saving the world last year—even if it was temporary—didn't earn him any of Marshall's affection. He continued to run a tight ship at the Eden Hotel, both here and in the Dream World. But Jonas figured Marshall must like him, considering the room upgrade.

The city bus hissed to a stop in front of the overhang, and Jonas grabbed his card out of his wallet and swiped it as he got on board.

The bus was nearly empty, which was how Jonas preferred it. He grabbed a window seat halfway down the aisle, put in his earbuds, and pulled up his hood. He was still exhausted—it wasn't even eight in the morning yet. Jonas leaned his head against the window, lulled by the vibration of the moving bus.

Wind whipped through Poet's hair, and he spun around in the clearing, surrounded by trees. His feet slid in slick grass, and when he looked down, he saw it was soaked in blood. His eyes traveled around the crimson puddle until he found Gunner's body on the ground.

Poet's heart sank, but he couldn't quite grasp where he was. What was happening? Thunder clapped overhead, and another gust made Gunner's jacket billow in the wind.

"Brother?"

Poet turned and found Alan, dressed all in black, blood splattered on his cheek. But it was the blue of his eyes, how earnest and hopeful they were, that for a moment made Poet felt he were looking straight at his father. Alan's kindness was directly inherited from him.

"Alan?" Poet called weakly, stumbling a step toward him. "You're here?"

Poet felt all his anger drain away. All his hurt. He felt only love; that was all there was in this moment. He smiled, and when he blinked, tears rolled from his eyes. "It's about fucking time, Alan," he said.

"Yeah, I know," Alan replied. "And you better have been going to school."

Poet choked out a laugh, clapping his brother on the shoulder as they hugged.

There was a loud rumble in the distance, like thunder, and the ground shook as the trees groaned around the Anderson brothers. From the Grecian Woods, hordes of Night Stalkers emerged.

There seemed to be no end to REM's army. Poet had to focus, concentrate his power to get him and Alan out of the Dream World. Poet could still make everything right.

He closed his eyes, hearing his heart beat in his head, steady and strong. He was becoming one with his surroundings.

Poet lifted his eyes, bright white with energy, and turned to find REM approaching, his pointy teeth bared. Poet reached out his hand, watching as smoke curled down his arm, forming a weapon in his hand.

But then…somewhere, a part of him whispered that things were off. Poet hesitated.

A dream is a dream is a dream, he thought in a moment of déjà vu. A flash of blue lightning streaked past him, stretching from the ground to the stars. Poet absorbed its energy, but the storm continued. Rain started to pelt down, rivers of blue running over his skin.

"Do your worst, boy," REM spat, taking a step toward them. "I can't die. I'm *born* of nightmares. So, as long as there is a Waking World, I will continue on."

But REM's words grew garbled in the storm, and Poet could feel the disconnect. His weapon disappeared, and he held up his hand.

The scene froze. Droplets of rain hung still in the air. REM stood motionless, with hate in his expression, the beginnings of knives on his metal hand. Knives he'd used against Alan.

"I remember," Poet whispered, relieved that he wasn't about to do battle, but then horrified when he spun to find Alan watching him. His heart broke.

"You're not really here, then?" Poet asked. Alan swallowed hard, coming to life among the frozen world. "I can't save you from this," Poet said, choking up. "It's just a memory."

Tears ran down his brother's cheeks, and Poet knew this was only his interpretation of how his brother would act.

Alan wasn't here. This was a memory loop. One that ended with REM nearly killing his brother.

"What are you going to do?" Alan asked him. "He's coming for you."

"I know," Poet said. "I'll have to be ready."

"You can't trust them," Alan added. "The poets aren't your friends."

The comment surprised Poet, but he imagined there must be a part of *himself* that didn't really trust the poets. He turned to look for REM and instead found that everyone was gone. Only Poet and Alan stood in the middle of the Grecian Woods.

Poet thought he might want to stay there forever.

"Nice try," Alan said, smiling through his tears. "But you have to save the world, little brother. No time for naps."

Alan watched Poet with that look of admiration, bravery, that always inspired him.

"Where are you, Alan?" Poet asked, sadness working its way over him. "How can I find you again?" Together, he and Alan could finish this. Side by side, they could defeat the creature of nightmares. REM had taken everything from them: their parents, their well-being. But nothing could destroy the Anderson brothers. Nothing on this plane of existence or another was strong enough. With Alan, Poet was whole again.

But rather than agree with him, Alan took a step backwards, his boot sloshing in a puddle of blood. The tall trees rocked back and forth as the wind began to pick up once again.

"It always ends this way," Alan said miserably. "I'm sorry, Jonas."

"What do you mean?" Poet asked, even though he already felt it coming. The end of this dream. The inevitable end he could never escape. In fact, he'd lived through this memory nearly a hundred times by now. And every time... Alan died.

"Do you know what your mother said before I took her soul?" REM called, and the Anderson brothers turned to find the creature waiting.

Poet's anger exploded, enough to set the trees around the field on fire. The heat was intense and, combined with the wind, sent sparks into the air, illuminating everything. He couldn't stop what would happen next, as if they were all on a doomed train he couldn't derail.

It moved quickly, Alan's normally handsome face twisting in agony. Him rushing at REM.

As before, Poet screamed for his brother to wait.

And then Alan and REM were face to face, but Alan was stiff, REM's hand clutching and squeezing his neck. Blood poured over Alan's pant leg.

REM had Alan on his toes and his metallic hand had extended into knives, buried in Alan's gut. Alan choked on his breath, blood spurting between his lips. He clawed at REM's hand at his throat, and then he reached out and scratched at REM's face, tearing the flesh from his metallic bones and fragments of yellow skull. The skin fell to the ground in large chunks, and then REM tossed Alan aside in a heap on grass.

"Alan?" Poet said quietly. He fell to his knees where he stood. Never able to save him. Only cursed to watch this moment over and over.

Alan tipped his head to look sideways, rain dotting his skin and gathering in the corner of his eye. "You have to let me go," Alan whispered, blood running out of his mouth as he spoke. "You can't keep doing this or you'll go mad." He coughed, but Poet didn't run to him. Not like he did every other time. He knew he was about to wake up.

The storm thundered above them, lightning splashing the sky in blue and red energy.

"Just tell me where to find you," Poet begged, breaking down. "I can't keep losing you."

Poet closed his eyes, and the wind was deafening, ripping trees from the ground and swirling them above him. When Poet looked, he saw that he and Alan were alone again.

The dream changed, no longer the same memory. Alan's eyes rolled back in his head, and the ground began to rumble and split, opening to a bright hell underneath.

"Destroy it," REM whispered from somewhere unseen. "Destroy it all, boy."

Poet felt energy in his hands, and he held them up, seeing that they were glowing red. He tried to stop the storm, tried to keep it from destroying the Dream World, but he was consumed. His skin was cracking—he was breaking apart and, because of that, so was the Dream World.

Huge pieces of the land began to fall away. In horror, Poet looked at Alan and watched the skin and muscle dissolve from his bones.

Poet would kill everyone.

And just before the entire Dreamscape crumbled completely, Poet got to his feet and created a tunnel. As he stepped through, he heard REM's voice whisper:

"Welcome to your destiny."

JONAS WOKE UP WITH a start, and banged his elbow on the wall of the bus. Next to him, an old lady looked over, concerned. Jonas was surprised to see the bus had filled up while he was asleep. His head spun with the power he'd used, the horror of Alan's death, the message from REM. It didn't feel like the other nightmares.

"Excuse me," he said to the lady before working his way out into the aisle. He wasn't sure how long he'd been on the bus, and he ducked his head to peek out the window as he made his way toward the front. He was two stops past the hotel, and, of course, the rain had started again.

"Stop the bus," Jonas said to the driver. The man glanced in the rearview like he was ready to argue, but Jonas had been riding this bus, this route, every day for a year. He and Clyde had spoken a few times before, so the man—although annoyed—pulled over to the curb. Jonas patted his shoulder as he rushed past him and out onto the street.

The bus pulled away, and Jonas adjusted his hood as rain pelted the cotton fabric and started to dampen it until it worked its way through. Jonas ran, his sneakers splashing in puddles, the ankles of his jeans wet. He took out his phone, but it was too wet to use the screen to call anyone. The Eden Hotel was just ahead, so he slipped his phone back into his pocket and crossed the street, dodging a few cars that honked their horns.

Hillenbrand was at the door, and he watched with an amused smile as Jonas ran toward him. He was dressed in the typical doorman uniform—the same one Jonas used in the Dream World, including the bowler hat.

"No need to run," Hillenbrand said. "Your shift isn't for another half hour."

Jonas flashed him a smile and told him he'd see him in a bit. Hillenbrand had no idea what really went on at the Eden Hotel, and certainly not what happened while its guests were sleeping. And Jonas wouldn't want him to know. It seemed whenever someone got close to him, or tried to help him, they were immediately in danger. Most ended up dead. He wouldn't drag poor Hillenbrand into that.

"Mr. Anderson," Marshall announced as Jonas tried to dart toward the elevators. Jonas's sneakers squeaked on the marble floors and one slid out underneath him, causing him to catch his balance on a passing guest.

"Sorry," Jonas said quickly, and the man nodded and hurried out. Jonas turned to Marshall and his boss lifted an eyebrow, asking him what the hell was going on.

Jonas swallowed hard and walked to where Marshall stood with his arms crossed over his impressive stature. He had dark skin with a bald head, a well-groomed beard, and a sharp suit with shiny cufflinks.

"Well?" Marshall asked in his deep voice.

"Something's happening," Jonas said, making sure no one was listening. "I have to talk to the others."

"They're not here," he said easily. "They all left a moment ago."

"Where did they go?" he asked.

"I assume to meet with Mr. Bran. Or at least, that's where Mr. Birnham-Wood and his daughter were going. As for the undesirables you've been hanging out with lately, I haven't seen them. But room 1865 is empty." He narrowed his eyes. "With a very large damage bill."

Marshall knew of course that they were poets, but he didn't hang out in the Dream World. He thought the poets were a liability. But he'd sworn to keep Jonas safe, and to him, that meant keeping him out the center of the bull's-eye. Or so he said.

"Miss Birnham-Wood will be back shortly," Marshall added. "I suggest you change into your uniform." He looked over Jonas's wet clothes with judgment.

"I don't think you understand," Jonas said. "I have to—"

Marshall took a step toward him. "No, Jonas," he said, sur-prising him by using his first name. "*You* don't understand the stakes. I've been asked to keep you here, working as if noth-ing is wrong, until Samantha and Alexander return. But there is…a situation that needs your attention in the restaurant."

Marshall nodded behind him to where the restaurant was buzzing with people. Jonas squinted, trying to see if someone was waiting for him, and his heart skipped a beat when he noticed her. A woman he didn't know, tall with dark wavy hair, a simple black dress. But it was the way she was sitting and watching him—fearless and expectant—that let Jonas know exactly what she was: A Dream Walker.

"Now," Marshall said, clapping his hands together. "Ms. Santiago requests a meeting. So please clean yourself up and honor her wishes."

Marshall turned and walked behind the front desk, where the other employees tried to look busy so he wouldn't reprimand them. Jonas swallowed hard, looking in the restaurant once again, and then dashed for the elevator to get his uniform.

CHAPTER FIVE

JONAS CHANGED INTO HIS DOORMAN
suit and brushed his hair out of his eyes before putting
on his bowler hat. He caught his reflection on the way
out of the room, and paused. For a moment he saw his father,
the same way he'd seen him in Alan in the dream. But Jonas
had only the resemblance, not the easy kindness that Alan had.

Jonas used to visit his father at work, here at the Eden
Hotel, all those years ago. He missed him now. He missed the
way he'd smell lightly of smoke from standing outside, chat-
ting with guests as they had their cigarettes. He'd be damp
with rain and yet always ready with a smile.

It had been years, but the loss was acute, and Jonas lowered his eyes and walked into the hallway, missing his parents for what felt like the millionth time. His life would have
ended up very differently if they'd survived. If REM hadn't
murdered them both.

Jonas probably wouldn't be at the Eden at all.

He pressed the button for the elevator, weighed down
by his grief. But when the door opened, he put that pain

away. It wouldn't help him now. He couldn't change the past.

Jonas smoothed down the front of his jacket and watched the gold shine of the elevator door. He strode out into the lobby and headed directly for the restaurant. He assumed the Dream Walker had found out about REM's return. The question now was whether she planned to help him.

The woman stood up from her stool at the bar as Jonas entered the restaurant. She was tall, but as he got closer, he saw she wasn't as statuesque as she had appeared from a distance. She didn't look like a Dream Walker at all.

"Mr. Anderson," she said formally as she reached out to shake his hand. Her grip was weak, her hands cold. Jonas nodded a hello. Ms. Santiago motioned to the stool next to hers, and they both sat down. "I like the suit," she said, smiling to herself.

"Uh, yeah," Jonas said. "My uniform. I work the door."

The woman lifted her empty glass and the bartender came over and replaced it with a new drink. She took a sip.

"Not to be rude," Jonas said, "but…who are you?"

"My name is Mariana Santiago," she said. "I'm a consultant with the Sleep Institute."

Jonas narrowed his eyes. "You're a doctor?" he asked. "You work for Alexander?"

"No," she said. "I'm a scientist. But…if I can be frank with you, Jonas, I work *against* Alexander." Jonas watched her for a long moment, and she held his gaze until he had to smile.

"Well, then, I guess we're on the same side," he replied. Mariana laughed, and lifted her glass to her lips.

"What do you want?" Jonas asked. "Do you even know what's going on?"

"I'm well-informed," she said. "And no, I'm not a Dream Walker, if that's what you thought. But I *am* a lucid dreamer, and I've made sleep sciences my life's work." She paused. "I know REM's returned, Jonas. He's coming for you. He's coming through your nightmares."

Jonas felt the blood drain from his face, his recent nightmare still close to the surface. "How do you know that?" he asked, shifting uncomfortably.

"A dreamer told me," she said.

"At the institute?" he asked. The last dreamer that knew him at the institute got possessed by REM and nearly killed him.

Mariana turned on her stool, and leaned in, lowering her voice. Jonas was struck by the intensity in her eyes— as if she knew what she was about to say would rock his world.

"Your *brother* told me," she said.

Jonas's elbow slipped off the bar, and he nearly fell from his stool before he righted himself. He took her arm, drawing her closer. "You found my brother?"

She pressed her lips into a sad smile. "He found me," she said. "But he's not in the Dream World, Jonas. Not where you can get to, at least."

"What?" he asked, dropping his hand. "Then...how—?"

"Experimental new treatment," she said.

"You're *experimenting* on my brother?" he said, his voice rising. "They already tried that. So if this is some sick—"

"You don't understand," she said. "*I'm* the experiment. That's what I do, Jonas. My specialty is contacting those in deep sleep. Comas. I've woken several patients. Ones the medical institutions have given up on. I'm usually hired by families. Very private. Very expensive. And while I was looking for someone, your brother came to me instead. He wanted me—no, *begged me*—to warn you. He wouldn't leave until I agreed. He told me where to find you. Luckily, I know Marshall, and he was happy to facilitate this meeting. He would prefer I didn't involve Alexander."

Jonas felt his eyes well up. Alan was still alive somewhere, existing, worrying about him. Alan was still in there. "What did he say?" he asked, absently sliding back onto the stool. His heart was pounding, and he wiped the heels of his palms quickly over his eyes to clear the gathering tears.

"He said that REM has regrouped. That he's gotten stronger." Mariana swallowed hard, concern creasing the skin between her eyebrows. "He told me that REM has found a way to drain the consciousness. Thrive off dreamers. He said you need to stop him."

"What?" Jonas asked, wondering how his brother could have this kind of information. "I have to get to Alan. Where can I find him?"

"You can't," Mariana said.

"Why the hell not?"

"Because, as I said, he's not in the Dream World. He's somewhere in between."

Jonas scoffed. "Between where?" He leaned in. "I'm a poet, remember? I can tunnel."

Mariana looked him over. "I once knew a poet," she said wistfully. "He was as earnest as you. But that boy died years ago, and I'd hate to see you end up with the same fate."

Jonas wondered if she was talking about the poet Alexander had murdered. It could be why she worked against him now. And although he was sorry for her loss, Jonas wasn't going to leave his brother behind.

"Look," Jonas said, his urgency renewed. "Alan can help. Just point me in the right direction."

She shook her head sadly. "He's between realities, in a void. Out of reach. Alan died in the Dream World, but you tunneled him back anyway. He couldn't reconnect with his body—he's been trying. He should have died altogether, but being a strong lucid dreamer, and holding on to his consciousness, has landed him there. Now he wanders between worlds. But I'm not sure there's a way to wake him up."

Jonas felt sick to his stomach. *He* did this? He had trapped his brother in some kind of limbo? "There has to be way," he whispered, despair ravaging him. "How do you wake others?"

Mariana shifted uncomfortably. "I don't talk about it," she said. "It's—"

But Jonas wasn't going to let her get out of the conversation. "Tell me," he said harshly.

Mariana steadied her gaze on him, and he realized her weak handshake wasn't representative of her drive. This woman was fierce, and he felt himself shrink back slightly.

"I flatline to find those in a coma," she said. "I die, Jonas. And then I bring them back with me when I'm resuscitated.

And it's not something everyone can do. Just like not everyone can be a poet. Consciousness is how we ground ourselves in one reality over another. But your brother is now grounded in the void without an exit. He *can't* wake up. I honestly don't even know how he found me to warn you—I assume his lucid dreaming is stronger than most."

Jonas flinched, and Mariana softened her demeanor. She reached to put her hand over his. "Alan doesn't want you to worry about him anymore," she said. "It's holding you back. He wants you to find the Dream Walkers and fight. Fight like hell."

Jonas lowered his eyes, overwhelmed by the horror of this situation. He would fight—he had already agreed to that—but how could he forgive himself for what happened to Alan? Would it have been better to let him die?

He stopped himself, guilty for even having the thought, and ran his hand roughly through his hair. He needed to get out of here. "Is there anything else?" he asked.

The scientist took out her wallet and dropped a few bills near her glass. "Just one more thing," she told him. "You shouldn't trust the other poets. Imagine my surprise when I learned about you," she added. "I thought all of you were dead."

She took the final gulp of her drink and stood up. She plucked out a business card and held it up for Jonas. "I'm sure you'll have more questions."

Jonas took the card, and without looking at it, shoved it in the pocket of his suit jacket. His legs were numb as he stood, unsteady with grief. He left Mariana standing there and walked through the restaurant, bumping chairs and mumbling apologies to the guests.

He was the reason Alan was trapped.

Jonas got out into the lobby and Marshall called his name, but Jonas continued to the elevator. A person inside held the door for him, and he walked in silently and pressed the button for the twelfth floor.

'You have to let me go,' his brother had said. If Mariana was telling the truth—and really, there was no reason to think she wasn't—then Alan was lost. He was no longer with the dreamers; he was in a void.

"This your floor, honey?" an old woman's voice asked.

Stirred out of his thoughts, Jonas glanced out the open elevator doors to the twelfth floor. He murmured a thank-you to the old woman and walked into the hallway, running his hand along the patterned wallpaper to steady himself. He thought he might break apart right there. Shatter into a million pieces.

"It's my fault," he mumbled. "I'm sorry, brother."

Jonas stopped outside his room, steadying himself on the frame. He didn't care about his shift. What did it matter anyway? What did anything matter?

He swiped the key card and opened the hotel room door.

"What's wrong?"

Jonas looked up just as Sam crossed the room, the belt of her jacket still fastened at the waist. "The poets asked about you before they left, and Marshall just called up. He said..." She stopped dead and stared at him. "Oh my God, is it Alan? Is he okay?"

"No," Jonas said. Sam covered her mouth, but rather than explain, Jonas squeezed his eyes shut, trying not to break down. Samantha took him by the arm and tried to lead him to the chair to sit down, but he pulled from her grasp.

"You have to talk to me," Sam said softly. "I can't read your mind, Jonas." She reached out and ran her palm over his cheek, and Jonas leaned into her touch.

He could feel her power, the energy surrounding her. Samantha's dad was a Dream Walker, and if she wanted, she could use that power too. The electricity under her skin was intoxicating.

Jonas pulled her closer, hugging her to him. And he closed his eyes when she threaded her fingers through his hair and got on her tiptoes, her lips grazing his ear lobe as she whispered, "I'm here."

And for a moment, Jonas forgot what it was like to always lose.

CHAPTER SIX

SAMANTHA WAS IN THE SHOWER, AND Jonas stared up at the ceiling of his hotel room. The sound of her singing drifted out of the bathroom, sweet and perfect-pitched. It would have made him peaceful if his guilt hadn't already begun to eat away at him.

Jonas told Sam all about Mariana Santiago. How Alan had found her to give her a message for him, and how pulling Alan out of the Dream World had somehow trapped him.

Mariana claimed that Jonas wouldn't be able to get to Alan, but she was seriously underestimating him. He could manipulate the Dreamscape; surely he would find a way. But he needed help. And that meant...that meant *not* following Alan's advice to let him go.

Jonas got out of bed and dressed quickly, trying to hurry before the shower stopped. He checked the pocket of his suit to make sure Mariana's card was still there.

He'd have to skip out of work, something Marshall wouldn't appreciate, but this was too important. He needed to find Alan.

"Jonas?" Sam called from the bathroom. He paused at the door, ready to walk out anyway, when he heard the squeaking of the shower knobs turning off. "What are you doing?" she asked.

Jonas looked over to the closed door of the bathroom, a cold chill running over his skin. It didn't sound...it didn't sound like Sam was talking to him.

There was a scraping noise of a shower curtain sliding along the bar, followed by a muffled scream. A thud. Jonas bolted for the room, hand out to create a weapon. But this was the Waking World. He had no power here.

"Sam!" he yelled throwing himself against the door and sending it flying into the wall, plaster crumbling to the tiles below.

Samantha stood in her bath robe, hands up defensively. Alone. Blood trickled from the corner of her mouth, and just as she looked wildly at Jonas, the air in the room sparked with a flash of electricity, a concentration of energy.

A figure appeared in front of Sam, and its hand shot out, hitting her shoulder. She swung back, her fist connecting with the side of a helmet, her next swing hitting an arm.

It took a second for Jonas to understand what was happening, and then the figure flashed out of focus again. Gone. A shimmer of sparks left behind in the air.

Samantha reset her stance, fists raised, drops of blood landing on the collar of her white robe. She darted her eyes around the room, and Jonas still had no idea what the hell was going on.

"That was a Night Stalker," he said. "How—?"

Before he could finish the thought, the creature came into focus again. Sam kicked out her leg, grunting as she made contact. The Night Stalker looked different in the Waking World—less agile. More...human. Its body armor flashed in and out of reality, leaving it vulnerable.

Jonas rushed forward, his shoulder connecting with the side of the creature, slamming it against the wall and cracking the tiles there. There was a growl beneath the helmet, and the Night Stalker pushed Jonas back, his feet slipping on the wet floor.

Samantha grunted again, punching the helmet, driving up her knee into the Night Stalker's side. Jonas hit the creature in the head, while Sam brought both fists down on the Night Stalker's back. They took turns attacking it while it swung out wildly—seeming off center in the Waking World gravity. And then the creature blinked out of existence again, and Sam fell forward with the force of her swing. Jonas caught her by the arm, steadying her, and they looked around the empty room, back to back, ready to fight.

The bathroom was quiet, the sound of water still dripping in the shower echoing in the small space. The sound of their heavy breathing.

There was another flash, and the Night Stalker appeared in front of Sam, wrapping both hands around her neck and driving her into the tiled wall. She groaned in pain, hitting the creature's helmet over and over, her blood smearing across the lens. Jonas grabbed the Night Stalker from behind, forearm around its neck, as he began to pummel the helmet, trying to crack the reflective surface.

Sam was gasping for breath, her toes barely grazing the floor of the bathroom. Both she and Jonas punched and kicked, trying to hold off the Night Stalker. Despite its lack of Dream World power, the creature was strong. Jonas grew frantic as Sam dug in her nails, fighting for her life.

Jonas glanced around for a weapon. He found a pair of scissors near the closet and darted over to grab them. Sam's eyes were bloodshot, starting to roll into her head as she clawed at the Night Stalker's glove.

"Go back to your world," Jonas said to the Night Stalker, and then jammed the scissors into its neck, the small space between helmet and suit. Blood spurted out in a high arc across the white room, and the Night Stalker dropped Sam, cupping its hand over its wound, gurgling behind its helmet.

Jonas didn't stop. He quickly punched the Night Stalker in the gut, making it double over. He grabbed it by the helmet and brought it down hard on the corner of the sink, cracking off a corner of the porcelain. The Night Stalker fell to the tile, the helmet shattering and exposing a human face, eyes black and soulless, even in the Waking World.

Jonas stood above the creature, watching its blood form a river flowing through the grout of the white tiles. The Night Stalker fought for air, blood bubbling from between its lips.

"How did you get here?" Jonas demanded. "How did you cross over?"

The Night Stalker stared up at him, saying nothing. The creature grinned, and then its head fell to the side and it disappeared out of existence.

Jonas jumped back, staring down at the empty space. Blood was smeared in a morbid sort of angel wing on the floor, a few sparks of electricity still in the air. The energy unsettled. But the Night Stalker was gone.

Sam moaned, and Jonas quickly turned and found her sitting, her back against the tub. Her white robe had gone bloody, and she had a handprint across her neck.

"Samantha," Jonas said with a heavy ache, and stumbled to the floor to gather her in his arms. Sam rested against him for a moment, her breathing unsteady. The water and blood on the floor were soaking into the knees of Jonas's pants, but he didn't want to let Sam go.

"How the fuck did a Night Stalker get in here?" she asked, her voice raspy.

"I don't know," he said, and pulled her closer. He wrapped himself protectively around her, and they both rested against the tub, staring at the growing stain on the floor.

The fear hit Jonas then—Sam had been attacked. She'd been hurt. He kissed the top of her head, his eyes still searching the room. Unwilling to leave them vulnerable again.

He reached past her to grab a white towel, and helped her press it to her lip. His body was sore from getting punched in the Waking World, the throbbing not fading because of his power. He still had no idea what happened.

The game had changed. If Night Stalkers could cross over, even unreliably, there was no safe place. No escape from nightmares. For a moment, Jonas wondered if REM had gotten to one of the poets, but this wasn't like a possession. This was something new.

He needed to find help. Jonas got Sam to her feet, and led her to the bedroom, where she could get her clothes. While she was getting dressed, Jonas sat on the edge of the bed, racked with guilt for almost walking out earlier. The Night Stalker found her when she was exposed, her guard down.

"Why did it come for you?" Jonas asked. "Why not me?"

Samantha pulled her T-shirt over her head. "Because killing me would hurt you more," she said, looking over at him. She ran her palm over the handprint. "Don't forget," she adds, her voice still strained. "REM wants a poet. He needs one."

Jonas watched her, and then shrugged one shoulder, miserable. "After this, are we sure he still needs one?"

The phone on the sofa table rang loudly, startling them both. The only calls to the room were generally from the management. It was probably Marshall, wondering why Jonas hadn't shown up for his shift. Jonas wasn't going in today, and he felt brave enough to tell him so.

Jonas crossed the room, and got the phone. "Hello," Jonas answered abruptly. For a moment, the line had only static, and Jonas furrowed his brow. "Hello?" he asked again.

"Poet," Sketch called, sounding far away. "Poet, I need you, man!"

Jonas spun to face Sam, and she straightened. "Sketch?" Jonas asked into the phone. "Where are you?"

"I don't know. Somewhere in a dream," Sketch said, his voice cutting in and out. "They're after me. You've got to help me, Poet!"

"What dream? Sketch—"

The line went dead, and Jonas stared down at the receiver. He'd never heard Sketch sound so scared, not even in battle. As he hung up the phone, Sam got to her feet.

"Sketch?" she asked. "What did he say? Did they come for him too?"

Jonas furrowed his brow, trying to make sense of everything. "He was calling for help. He was...he was calling from a dream."

Sam's lips parted. "From a dream?" she asked. "But that's not possible." She looked back toward the bathroom, highlighting the fact that it seemed entirely possible now.

"He called me for help," Jonas said. He didn't have time to weigh the possibilities; Sketch had sounded terrified. If he really did find a way to contact him from the dream, Poet Anderson needed to get in there and save him. And he'd have to be strong.

"These could be connected," Jonas said. "I have to go."

"Then I'm coming with you," Sam said. She crossed to the dresser, but Jonas met her there and took her hand. Her knuckles were bruised, much like his, and her lip was split. He reached up to gingerly touch it, and she winced.

"You can't come with me," he whispered, and before she could argue, he added, "I need you to help me sleep."

Samantha watched him a long moment, her green eyes raging with disagreement. "You've got an hour," she said. "And then I'm waking you up."

SAM CALLED DOWNSTAIRS AND talked with Marshall, warning him of the possibility of Night Stalkers in the building.

Marshall hadn't heard of anything else happening, but thanked her for the heads-up.

Jonas climbed into bed, and stared up at the ceiling, trying to figure out the best way to find Sketch. As a poet, he should be able to tunnel straight into people's dreams, but that didn't always work. And if Sketch was running, moving from place to place in the Dreamscape, he'd be even harder to track.

Samantha came into the room, her hair twisted up with a white towel. She had a small doctor's bag, and she set it on the side table as she sat on the edge of the bed, next to Jonas. She opened the small latch, and drew out a tiny clear bottle and a syringe.

Jonas watched her, hating the bruises on her skin. He instinctively flexed his hand, feeling the stiffness in his knuckles. The cuts that still bled.

Sam flicked the tip of the needle, and Jonas's pulse spiked.

"How much are you giving me?" Jonas asked.

"Low dose. Just enough to let you dream deeply. After that, it's up to you. You sleep, dream, and when it's time, you get back here." She paused. "I don't like this, Jonas. We don't know all the factors anymore. What if REM—?"

"Sketch needs my help," Jonas said, although he agreed with her. But Sketch had been his friend for too long. They'd gone through so much together. He wouldn't abandon him now.

He believed it was possible for Sketch to call him from the Dream World, because a Night Stalker had attacked Jonas and Sam in their bathroom. There was the uptick in nightmares. The Night Stalkers killing Winston. Seriously too much to ignore.

Maybe the veil had grown weak, the two realities colliding. Jonas needed to save his friend, and then he'd find out what the hell was going on.

Samantha ran her fingertip over Jonas's arm, tickling him. She pressed on his vein in the crook of his elbow.

"What if...?" Jonas started, but paused, knowing how Sam would react.

"I'm not killing you, Jonas," she said, curtly. "If that's what you were going to ask."

"I thought you couldn't read my mind," he said, and when she looked down at him, he smiled.

Sam laughed, and poked the tip of the syringe into his vein. Jonas winced, and an ache raced up his arm toward his shoulder. It faded into heat, and he rested his head back against the pillow.

"But what if I can find Alan?" he asked.

"You don't even know if that woman was telling the truth," Sam said, putting the cap on the syringe and putting it back in the black bag to dispose of later. "But even if she was right about Alan, it means she could also be right about other people not having the abilities she does. She flatlines. She's clearly a fucking lunatic who got lucky by not dying. So, no. I won't let you kill yourself. Besides, don't we have enough to worry about right now?"

Jonas gazed up at her, the edges of the world growing fuzzy. Other than his brother, Samantha was the only person he'd ever trusted completely. That kind of trust, the kind you would hinge your life on, didn't come around often. If ever.

"I love you," Jonas said.

Sam pressed her lips into a sad smile, and she lifted her eyes to his. "I love you too, you idiot. Now hurry back."

THERE WAS A LOUD screech along the tracks, and Poet opened his eyes just as the subway train pulled away from the station. The lights inside the car flickered. Poet yawned, disoriented, and when he turned, Sketch was standing on the seat across from him, tagging the ceiling. For a moment, Poet watched him, reminded of the days when he, Sketch, and Gunner would ride around, talking shit and laughing.

It was one of those times when they'd found Genesis.

Now, Gunner was dead, murdered in the Grecian Woods by REM himself. Poet couldn't save him. That guilt held part of him prisoner, occasionally finding him in his nightmares.

"Dude, Poet," Sketch called. "Toss me the red can." Poet looked down and saw the spray paint on the seat next to him. He picked it up and examined it for a moment, struck by the way the red paint had flowed down the side of the can like blood.

Poet swallowed hard and tossed the can in Sketch's direction. The train swayed again, and Poet's back knocked against the seat, setting his hat askew. Just as he reached to fix it, a thought occurred to him.

Why was he here? Poet felt his chest tighten and he slowly ran his eyes over the empty train. It was just him and Sketch.

Why was he on this train? He didn't need to take a train to Genesis—he was a poet. He could open a tunnel. Poet lowered his head, staring at his shiny black shoes. He couldn't remember how he got on this train. He didn't feel in control of this dream.

"Something wrong, Poet Anderson?" Sketch called. Only there was a change in his voice, a slight growl under his normally high-pitched tone. Poet felt electricity over his skin, and he willed the power to his fingertips, ready to use whatever forces he could conjure.

The lights flickered again and suddenly he was plunged into darkness. Poet immediately dove to the ground and, at almost the same time, bright blue fire exploded in the seat he had vacated, the window above shattering and sending shards of glass over his suit.

In that moment of light, Poet looked to where Sketch had been, only now Sketch was no longer there. A creature clung to the roof of the train. It was a shape—a figure made up entirely of shadows, frantic and chaotic. Scribbled lines that constantly moved, but keeping its form. It radiated terror. He'd never seen anything like it before.

The world went dark again, and Poet scrambled to his feet. There was a flash, and he jumped up onto the seat, running up the side of the wall as light exploded. Gravity fell away as Poet drew on all his power. His eyes blazed pure white, and in his hand he created a gun, firing at the same instant the barrel came to be.

The lasers burned holes into the roof, straight through the creature as if it were air. The shadow scurried above him, fast and unnatural in its movements.

The lights in the train car flickered on, and Poet dropped to the grated floor, swinging around a pole, and continuing to fire. But he was no match for the creature's speed. He lowered his weapon. Across the car, the creature dropped to the floor, and spun to face him.

Poet curled his lip, both fascinated and horrified by the thing in front of him. And as he watched, its form began to solidify, taking on some of Sketch's features: the spiky hair, the blue eyes, the paint-stained fingers. But this…*thing* was most certainly not human.

"What are you?" Poet asked. "Besides super fucking creepy."

The creature laughed, and its long tongue lashed out. Poet recoiled, and pointed his gun at it in warning.

"Why won't you die, Poet Anderson?" the creature asked. Its voice was echoing, like it were coming from somewhere else.

Jonas had once said something vaguely like that to REM. He narrowed his eyes. "Did REM send you?" he asked, fear breaking over his chest.

The creature smiled, its tongue licking out again. A fly buzzed around them, and Poet furrowed his brow. He couldn't remember ever seeing a fly in the Dream World before. A second appeared on the window.

"There are more terrifying monsters than REM," the creature said. "And we're coming for your kind. All of you."

Poet tightened his jaw, assuming the creature meant the poets were in danger, their collective power a treasure to plunder. Something REM had sought to control forever.

The shadow was in complete Sketch form now, and Poet lifted one corner of his mouth in a smile. The creature looked confused by his reaction, and tilted its head.

"Go ahead and try," Poet murmured, and the gun in his hand was enveloped in smoke and transformed, extending into a compact rocket launcher. The creature's eyes widened, and then quickly began to deepen, trying to dissolve back into shadows.

Poet fired.

The creature tried to jump out the way, but the entire back half of the train exploded, sending fire, gnarled pieces of metal, and torn limbs in every direction. The bits of flesh began to dissolve to black dust.

Poet Anderson calmly turned around, tore a hole through the Dream World, and tunneled back into his waking reality.

CHAPTER SEVEN

HE HEARD SOMEONE SNORT A LAUGH, and Jonas sat up in bed to find Callum sitting across the hotel room on the couch, his arm over the back of the red sofa. Samantha was next to him, staring at Jonas with wide-eyes. Jonas blinked quickly, disoriented.

"Well, you look bloody awful," Callum said.

Jonas flipped him off, and noticed a bruised dot on the bend of his elbow. The cuts on his knuckles from the fight with the Night Stalker had scabbed. He shifted, his back sore, his neck stiff. What was going on? Why were they staring at him like that? He'd only been sleeping.

Sam crossed the room and sat next to Jonas on the bed. The bruises on her neck had faded. "Where have you been?" she asked, half angry, half worried. "You wouldn't wake up."

"How long was I out for?" Jonas asked.

"Twelve hours," she said. "I got so worried, I had to call this asshole." She hiked her thumb in Callum's direction.

"Your girlfriend is so sweet," Callum sang out good-humoredly. "Of course I came right over."

Jonas furrowed his brow. "Twelve hours? I—" He glanced around the room, and all at once, the dream came back to him. He'd gone into the Dream World to find Sketch...and somehow he'd ended up on the train. He hadn't meant to go there—shouldn't have gone there. Not unless Sketch was dreaming of it.

"I lost control," Jonas said. "I lost control of the dream."

Sam's lips parted, but it was Callum who spoke first. "What does that mean?" he asked. "Who was in control then?"

"I don't know who it was," Jonas said. "What it was. It looked like Sketch at first. But...then it changed. Crawling on walls and shit. It wasn't solid."

"Jesus," Sam said under her breath.

"Not solid?" Callum asked. "Like liquid?"

"No," Jonas replied. "Like...a shadow."

"Interesting. Did you kill it, at least?"

"I think so," Jonas said.

"You should be more sure. We don't want it getting out of the dream."

"But what was it?" Jonas asked.

"Could be anything," Callum said. He crossed his ankle over his knee and rested back on the cushion of the couch. "Samantha said Sketch called you first. Did the creature use Sketch's voice in the dream?" Jonas nodded, and Callum sighed as if that was unfortunate. "Well, then," he continued. "I suppose that means your mate Sketch is dead."

Jonas scrambled to his feet. "What?" he asked. "How do you know?"

"Shadows," Callum said. "If that is indeed what you saw...they're not good. They are, in fact, *very, very bad* creatures. Demons, really." Callum leaned forward, almost delighting in this revelation. "You know that shadow you catch out of the corner of your eye?" he started. "Or the person you're sure is following you on a dark night? The movement just inside your closet? They're not of this world, Jonas. They're not of any world. And they never take a form, unless..." He paused.

"Unless what?" Jonas demanded.

"Unless they absorb a soul. In the Dream World it means they take on their dream life, but that person will not shake this shadow. It comes home with them. So like I said, your mate, Sketch, was dead the moment that shadow ate up his soul. I only hope he died in the Dream World so his whole family isn't slaughtered as well."

"That's not all," Sam said, her breath catching. "A Night Stalker appeared just before Sketch called. It attacked me."

"Appeared?" Callum asked.

"In the Waking World," Jonas clarified. "It cut in and out of existence. It didn't seem to have power—not like in the Dreamscape. It was...human. But it still kicked our asses until I killed it."

"And then what happened? Where is it?"

"It disappeared again."

Callum's jaw tightened, and he didn't speak for a moment. Then he cleared his throat. "That is an interesting development," he said. "If I were to wager a guess, I'd say the veil between worlds has gone threadbare. The good news is that the Night Stalker lacked power. That means REM doesn't have a poet—no true way to cross-over. So let's stay focused. One crisis at a time," he said, although Jonas sensed he was still thinking about the Night Stalker and the bigger implications of its appearance there.

"Now, I don't mean to sound insensitive," Callum continued, "but when that call came through, it was very likely that Sketch was dead already. What Jonas just described was a shadow person. They absorb the souls of dreamers, usually lucid dreamers. They snuff them out in the Dream World and take on their form, at least for a little while. Eventually the skin peels off, and—" He stopped himself. "The Sketch you know is gone, and I hope Poet Anderson killed it before his body woke up."

Sam spun to look at Jonas accusingly. Jonas sat there, horrorstruck. He might get sick. Did he really kill his friend? Did he really have to?

Jonas stood motionless as he absorbed the idea that Sketch was gone. He'd been there with him since the beginning.

He didn't answer Sam's unspoken question. Instead, he grabbed his coat from where it lay over the arm of the sofa and pulled it on.

"Where are you going?" Sam asked.

He stopped, swallowing down his disgust. "I'm going to Sketch's apartment," he said. "I can't let this...*shadow* out."

"Ah," Callum said. "So you weren't sure. Very well," he added, standing up and straightening his hat. "Let's go finish off your friend."

• •

Sketch kept a small apartment in the Waking World about an hour outside of Seattle. He used to live in Arizona or New Mexico or some dusty place like that, but after the battle he decided to relocate closer to Jonas and what was left of the Dream Walkers. Turned out an apartment in Seattle was too expensive, so he moved to a small fishing community. Sketch said he liked the solitude. He also said it was nice to not worry about some smelly old fisherman turning out to be a psycho Dream Walker. He worked from home and barely left his place, living mostly in his dreams. He said he liked himself better when he was asleep.

The Lyft driver stopped in front of the building, and he shifted his dark eyes to Jonas's in the rearview mirror.

"Would you mind waiting?" Callum asked, buttoning his jacket as he paused before climbing out.

"Not a chance, kid," the driver said, and clicked a button making Callum's phone ding.

Callum glanced down at the phone, and smiled. "Ah, yes. I'll be sure to tip you well, Reginald." The driver sniffed a laugh, and Callum got out of the car. Jonas followed quickly behind him.

"Where did you get that phone?" Jonas asked the minute the driver was gone. He shoved his hands in his coat pockets as he and Callum walked toward the building.

"Some poor soul left it on the bar," Callum said. "You'd be amazed the sort of pictures people keep in their albums."

He tossed the phone into the bushes and pulled open the front door to the lobby of the dingy green building. They started up the stairs to the third floor.

"Christ, it smells like fish in here," Callum said, crinkling his nose. "Unless it's Sketch's rotting corpse." He looked at Jonas with a smile, but he quickly straightened his expression when Jonas didn't laugh.

"It's up here on the right," Jonas said, pointing to a door as his heart raced. The best-case scenario was finding his friend dead. How fucked up was that?

He and Callum got to apartment 323, and Jonas blew out a steadying breath before knocking on the door. The knock echoed down the hall, ricocheting off the peeling, yellowed paint.

The seconds ticked by, and there was movement from inside the apartment. Jonas felt sick. Somewhere in the complex, he heard faint yelling, stomping, a baby crying. He knocked again, more impatiently.

"Should I kick it down?" Callum asked, brushing his hair out of his eyes.

"No," Jonas said. "We don't want to draw attention." He tried the handle, and although it turned, it caught on a metal chain when he opened the door. Jonas cursed, and stepped aside.

Callum chuckled lightly, then lifted his leg and kicked in the door. It swung back and hit the wall, the handle lodging in the drywall. Callum looked at Jonas. "That felt good," he said, and walked into Sketch's apartment. Jonas waited a beat, then slipped inside after him.

The place was grimy and dark, even after Callum switched on the lights. Trash was littered throughout, papers and plastic bottles, pizza boxes. There was the unmistakable stench of BO radiating from every corner of the house. And definitely something rotting.

Callum curled his lip and walked over to the fridge, opening it to peer inside. Jonas looked around the apartment while Callum sifted through the refrigerator. He grabbed a quart of milk and checked the date. "Still good," he said with a hopeful smile, and opened the cap to take a sip.

There was a thump upstairs, and Jonas examined the water-stained ceiling. He had no idea Sketch lived this way. In fact, he couldn't believe it. He glanced around again, and picked up one of the papers from the floor.

"It's a money market report," Jonas said, confused.

"What's the date?" Callum asked.

"Last week." He lowered the paper. "Which means up until then, he was still working. This—" He furrowed his brow. "This isn't his mess."

Callum sighed, and put the milk back in the fridge. He closed the door, and rested his elbow against the freezer. "First, mate, you have to understand…these creatures aren't logical. They're psychotic killing machines; they exist only for the sole purpose of making your life…"

Callum trailed off, and Jonas froze in place. They both heard the noise coming from the bedroom at the end of the short hall, to the left of the entrance. There was scraping against the door, the sound of heavy breathing. A metallic click.

But as suddenly as it started, it stopped. The apartment was silent.

Callum took a deep breath and said in a whisper, "I really don't want to check that out."

"Yeah. Me neither," Jonas said.

As if on cue, the bedroom door opened, and Sketch's head poked out. He shifted his dark eyes from one poet to the other, and it was clear from his waxy complexion that it wasn't Sketch at all. Jonas would have been heartbroken if he wasn't terrified.

"This will end well," Callum said under his breath, and came to stand next to Jonas.

"Sketch?" Jonas said, holding up his hands like he was calming a wild beast. There was little response. "Mitch?" Jonas said instead.

The door opened wider, and when he stepped out— wearing wrinkled clothes, his hair matted and filthy—Sketch flinched. There were bubbles under his flesh, and his lips were cracked. Jonas glanced sideways at Callum, and the other poet shrugged as if saying "I told you so."

"Listen, we're just here to—" Jonas started.

But he didn't get to finish the sentence before Sketch growled and sprinted in their direction. Jonas screamed for him to stop, and Callum picked up the nearest glass bottle and chucked it hard, right at Sketch's face. The bottle shattered on impact, and Sketch cried out and fell sideways, smashing onto the cluttered coffee table.

There was barely time for a breath before he was on his feet again, making a break for Callum. The poet widened his eyes, but couldn't move fast enough to avoid the hit. Sketch punched him hard in the side of the face, and Callum was thrown back against the laminate counter before sliding to the filth-covered floor.

Acting quickly, Jonas kicked in the back of Sketch's leg, making him fall to his knees. He drove his elbow hard against his former friend's head, but elbowing Sketch in the head was like doing the same thing to a cement wall.

"Fuck!" Jonas screamed, the pain vibrating up his arm.

Sketch used the opportunity to get to his feet. He grabbed Jonas by the neck, lifting him to his tiptoes to slam him against the refrigerator door.

"Stop," Jonas wheezed, staring into Sketch's black, soulless eyes. He reached out to pull at his forearm, but found that when he did the skin began to peel away. Rather than try to escape, Jonas stopped. He couldn't hurt Sketch like that. Even if this wasn't Sketch, it still kind of looked like him. "Please," he whispered, hoping to see some flash of his old friend.

But Sketch was gone.

Spots started to appear in Jonas's vision, pushing him toward unconsciousness. Just before he passed out, there was a shout, and the pressure loosened on Jonas's neck before the deafening sounds of silverware and plates crashing to the floor.

Callum jumped onto Sketch's back, tearing at the cut skin on his face. Sketch began to flail, and hurled Jonas toward the wall. He hit it hard and broke through, tumbling into the adjacent apartment, shoulder first.

Plumes of dust rose around him, and Jonas moaned on the floor, curling on his side. He could hear them fighting, and he slowly dragged himself up, the wind knocked out of him. He glanced around and saw that at least the apartment was vacant.

There was another loud crash in Sketch's apartment, and Callum yelled to Jonas, "A little help here, yeah?"

Jonas straightened his back and stepped through the hole back into Sketch's apartment. Sketch threw Callum off his back, tossing him to the floor, and spun to face Jonas. Once again, Jonas held up his hands in surrender.

"Sketch," he said. "If you're in there at all..." Sketch stared at him, blood pouring down his face, his features distorted. It occurred to Jonas that he hadn't heard him speak even once. It was true—the shadow was using him as a vessel. Pure destruction. Pure evil.

"Gotcha," Callum yelled, and popped up to grab Sketch in a headlock. Callum grunted heavily, shuffling his feet to maintain balance. He looked at Jonas and yelled, "Don't just stand there. Give me a knife! Now!"

Jonas went to the wooden butcher block on the counter, and pulled out the longest and sharpest knife he could find. He stared at the shiny metal for a moment, contemplating turning around and just walking out.

But it was too late for that.

Jonas swallowed hard, and put the knife in Callum's free hand. The British poet thanked him, and then unceremoniously plunged the knife into the right side of Sketch's skull with a wet thud.

Jonas gasped, falling back a step, as Sketch convulsed a few times. When the shadow person went limp, Callum dropped the lifeless body to the floor.

Both poets stood over Sketch, staring down as blood poured from his corpse. The black in his eyes ran down his cheeks until they were blue again.

Callum sighed deeply. "Well, that was shitty," he said, reaching to touch the cut high up on his cheek where Sketch had hit him. "I forgot how much it hurts to bleed in this world."

When Jonas could form words again, he looked over at Callum. "What do we tell the cops?" he asked.

Callum laughed. "You're adorable," he said.

Callum went over to the sink and washed the blood from his hands, taking his time, and dried them on a dishtowel. Not sure what to do, Jonas followed suit, his body numb with grief and horror.

This kind of shit in the Dream World was one thing... But here? It wasn't normal. It wasn't bearable. Jonas blinked away tears as the cold water ran over his hands, washing Sketch's blood down the drain.

When he was done, he and Callum walked over to the couch in the living room, dusted it off, and took a seat. They stared at the mayhem of the apartment, Jonas's hands trembling in his lap.

Callum looked sideways at him, and Jonas waited, hopeful he'd have a plan. Callum shrugged.

"Do you happen to have a cigarette, mate?"

CHAPTER EIGHT

JONAS CALLED ALEXANDER BIRNHAM-Wood. He was certainly not Jonas's favorite person, and in fact they mostly hated each other. But he'd been cleaning up messes for decades, and most recently a dead poet in a hotel bathroom, so at least Jonas knew he was competent.

Alexander sent a car for him and Callum, warning them not to get blood on his interior, and they drove back to the hotel while a team cleared the apartment. Jonas still hadn't stopped shaking.

Callum, on the other hand, didn't seem fazed. "You should have made sure he was dead in the dream," Callum said, picking blood from under his fingernails. His eye had swelled, but he seemed proud of the bruise.

"I thought I blew him up," Jonas said for the third time. "What else was I supposed to do?"

"You've got to chop off their heads," Callum said, like it was obvious. "Separate the consciousness from the body." He swiped his hand through the air. "Clean sweep."

"How many of these shadows have you killed?" Jonas asked.

Callum laughed. "Oh, this is my first," he said. "But you *always* chop off the head. It's common knowledge."

Frustrated, Jonas turned to look out the window of the town car, the streets passing quickly. They were almost back to the hotel. He wasn't sure how he'd explain this to Samantha. How could he tell her about the carnage that he'd been a part of. What did it make him?

"So…Alexander?" Callum said. "You trust him, then? Even though he killed a poet?"

Jonas looked across the car at him. "No," he said simply. "But we don't have many choices out here. Sometimes you have to rely on the enemy of my enemy and all that."

"Lovely," Callum replied, sounding unconvinced.

The town car pulled up at the hotel, and the two poets waited a moment before Hillenbrand came to open their door. He widened his eyes when he saw it was Jonas.

Jonas nodded politely to him and hurried past, glad he'd spent an extra minute at the apartment cleaning the blood from his face and clothes. Well, for the most part.

"Probably should have used the back door," Jonas said, walking quickly toward the elevator. He could feel the receptionists watching him, and he was ready to break into a run when Callum took his arm.

"Relax, Jonas," he said in a hushed voice, leading him to the elevator. "You're acting like you just murdered someone."

Jonas tried to steady himself, his shoe tapping on the marble floor, until the elevator door opened and he rushed inside.

• •

SAMANTHA WAS WAITING IN the hotel room for them, her hair disheveled, her makeup long worn off. She was frantic when they got inside the door.

"Well?" she asked. "What happened? How is he?"

Jonas wasn't sure how to tell her that their friend was dead. How to tell her he took part in that death. Justified or not, he felt dirty. He felt like a killer.

"Jonas," she said more loudly. "Tell me!"

Miserably, Jonas lifted his eyes to hers and murmured how sorry he was. Samantha watched him for a long moment, fighting back her tears, and then she covered her mouth as she cried. She and Sketch had been friends too. She'd saved his life once.

"I'll be going," Callum said, shoving his hands in his pockets. "And I'm sorry about your friend, but this is only the beginning of awful things. It's no coincidence that the shadow appeared now. The Night Stalker. There must be a strong darkness in the Dream World. Our time here is quickly coming to an end."

Callum opened the door, but paused before he left. "You know that your Waking World is causing this, right?" he asked, glancing back. "Your fear, your nightmares. You're feeding them."

"Goodbye, Callum," Jonas said as he sat on the couch, his head in his hands.

Callum watched him solemnly, and then he walked out, leaving Jonas and Sam to their grief.

• •

Jonas made Samantha a cup of tea, and the two of them sat silently. She didn't ask for details about Sketch's death—or rather, the shadow's death—and Jonas was glad for that. He couldn't have relived it.

It was getting late, and the only light came from the TV, set on mute. It sent a prism of color along the wall, but neither he nor Sam got up to turn it off.

"We have to do something," Jonas said, his voice scratchy.

"I know," Sam responded. She didn't look at him. "But what?"

"I wish I knew. For now, I think I need to talk to Marshall." He closed his eyes, willing himself stronger. "I need to get in contact with some Dream Walkers. See what they know about these shadow people. About how the veil between realities allowed a Night Stalker through."

Sam didn't answer, and when Jonas turned to her, he felt an extra pang of grief. He grabbed the blanket from the back of the couch, and laid it over her shoulders. Sam smiled at him, and he leaned in to rest his forehead against hers, bonded in grief.

"I'll be downstairs if you need me," he whispered. Sam told him she'd make some calls, and then Jonas changed and went downstairs to find Marshall.

Marshall was behind the front desk with one of the other staffers. He glanced up when Jonas walked out the elevator. His expression was unreadable, and Jonas had to wonder if he knew about Sketch—if Alexander had told him. Exactly how much did the owner of the hotel share with his manager?

"Yes?" Marshall said, walking out from behind the desk. "I assume you're not here to work."

Jonas wilted; he couldn't help it. Marshall just didn't take any shit. "I have to talk to you," Jonas said in a hushed voice. Marshall watched him a long moment, and then motioned toward the back offices.

Jonas led the way, and when they were in the hall, he noticed a spot of blood on the sleeve of his white shirt. He quickly tucked his arm, hoping that Marshall hadn't noticed, and when he turned the corner, he folded up his sleeve.

He paused outside the office door and waited for Marshall to unlock it, checking the hall as he did. A sense of paranoia he couldn't quite escape clung to him.

"After you," Marshall said, pushing the door open for Jonas to enter.

The office was a scene of organized chaos—well-decorated but thoroughly cluttered. Stacks of papers sat unsorted while a large desktop computer hummed in the background. Jonas took a seat in one of the boxy chairs in front of the desk. Rather than sit, Marshall stood near the window and rested his elbow on the top of the filing cabinet.

"Are you okay?" he asked. Jonas had to admit the question surprised him, and he fumbled to answer.

"Yeah, I mean...kind of. Actually—" He leaned forward in the chair. "I need your help."

Marshall smiled, and it was as if fresh air washed into the room. "Obviously," Marshall said. "What exactly are we talking about here, Mr. Anderson?"

"I need to find Dream Walkers," Jonas said. Marshall's smile faded, but he made no other indication that he had heard the request. "Have you told them about the Night Stalker?"

"The one in your bathroom?" Marshall replied, making it sound ridiculous.

"It was real," Jonas said, but Marshall held up his hand.

"Yes, I know, Mr. Anderson. We repaired your sink."

Jonas got to his feet, annoyed that Marshall wouldn't get to the point. He took a step toward him.

"I'm serious, Marshall," he pleaded. "You have to help me."

"They won't come," Marshall said with a quick shake of his head. "Not for you. Not again. No matter what you tell them."

"What do you mean? Are you saying…? Do they blame me for last time?"

"Of course they do," Marshall said. "But more than that, they blame you for not finishing it. If you had destroyed REM, the rest would have worked itself out. But when you had the chance, you chose to save your brother instead."

"I was destroying the world," Jonas hissed. "Not just REM. I was dismantling the entire Dream World."

"So?" Marshall asked.

Jonas stared at him. "The balance. Without one—"

"Ah, yes. The balance," Marshall said. "Heard it a dozen times before. But the truth is, the Dream World would have recreated itself. It would have found the balance again."

"And the Dreams that were already there? The Dreams created and living there?"

"Collateral."

Jonas scoffed. "No," he said. "I won't accept that. I'll beat him another way. But I need their help. I need the Dream Walkers."

For an instant, Jonas saw a flash of sympathy in Marshall's eyes. "I'll speak with them, but don't get your hopes up."

"Thank you, Marshall," Jonas said.

Marshall shook off the gratitude and walked to the door, holding it open for Jonas to exit. As he left, Marshall called after him, "And you owe me a shift."

CHAPTER NINE

JONAS WENT UP TO THE ROOM AND found Sam on the laptop, glasses on, while she worked on her college courses. She seemed better, and she told him studying was the best way for her to keep her mind occupied. Jonas called downstairs and ordered dinner.

"I talked to Marshall," Jonas said. "He doesn't think the Dream Walkers will help." Sam looked over. "They won't help because of me," he added, guilt crawling over him.

"I can ask my dad," Sam suggested, removing her glasses and turning to him. "He might still have a few friends. Maybe he can—"

"No offense," Jonas said, "but we've been relying on your dad a lot. You know that the more we do, the more we're indebted."

Sam pursed her lips, seeming to think it over, and slipped her glasses back on. "You're right," she said, and dropped the subject.

Jonas turned on the television, lowering the volume so he didn't disturb Sam. He couldn't focus on anything, though, not even when the food arrived. He set it on the table, and Sam closed the laptop and came to sit next to him on the couch. She grabbed her silverware and shook out a napkin to put on her lap.

"I've been thinking," Jonas said quietly while she picked up her burger. "I—I'm going to see the scientist."

Sam paused mid-bite and turned to him. "The Santiago woman?" she asked.

Jonas nodded, and Sam put down her food and pushed it away. "And do what?" she asked seriously. "What is your plan?"

"I don't know yet," he said. "But I don't know any Dream Walkers. The poets aren't going to help with this. We need to stop those shadows, and we need to stop REM before he tears open the veil altogether. I need help. If Alan can—"

"Jonas," Sam said. "You know I want nothing more than to have your brother wake up. Truly. But not if it means you dying. I can't lose you."

"I'm not going to die," he said, but when he looked over at Sam, they both smiled. "Okay, so yeah, I guess the plan is to die. But I'll wake up!" he added.

They sat quietly for a moment. The news on the television—awful news that had become the norm lately—played quietly in the background. This was the society feeding REM. The chaos, destruction, and lies. The never-ending lies.

"I'm coming with you, then," Sam told Jonas. "I had a Night Stalker interrupt my shower, so perhaps Ms. Santiago can explain how that happened since she knows so much about in-between places."

Jonas took a breath, but he knew arguing was pointless. "Fine," he said.

"Good," Sam said.

"Cool," Jonas responded. They sat quietly for a moment, and then Jonas looked over at Sam, adorable with her hair pulled up, glasses on. She sensed it, and instead of saying anything at all, she pushed him over and kissed him.

MARIANA SANTIAGO DIDN'T WANT to meet at the Sleep Institute. She asked Jonas to come to her rented office on the other side of town. Sam called a car service, and, together, they left first thing in the morning. Sam was missing her biology class.

They pulled up to a small converted office building, surrounded by rundown houses and shopping carts abandoned in the street. Sam looked at Jonas pointedly, but he pretended not to notice. This didn't mean she wasn't legit.

Sam asked the car to wait, and then she and Jonas walked up the leaning porch steps. There was an old black mailbox with no identifying information on it.

"And you said she's a scientist?" Sam asked, looking over at Jonas.

"We can't all own luxury hotels."

Sam swayed like she was hurt by the comment, and Jonas quickly apologized. It wasn't Samantha's fault that her father was rich, but that didn't stop Jonas from lashing out.

It reminded him that she deserved better than what he could give.

Jonas reached to ring the doorbell of the house, and he and Sam stood in awkward silence until there was the clicking of locks—several of them—and the front door opened. Mariana stood behind the screen door.

"You didn't mention you were bringing a guest," Mariana said, glancing from Jonas to Sam.

"I'm Samantha," Sam said with a short wave. Jonas cursed in his head because he hadn't had a chance to tell Sam that Mariana hated her father. And he could see in Mariana's eyes that she knew immediately who Sam was.

"Nice to meet you," Mariana said, her voice terse. "Please, both of you, come in."

Jonas stepped aside to let Sam go in first, and then followed her in. The foyer was surprisingly nice—small-plank wood floors, and old-fashioned yet tasteful wallpaper. There were a couple of chairs set up. Mariana motioned them toward a set of glass doors.

"I'm not sure how much help I can be," she said, leading them into a study. She sat behind a large desk, file cabinets behind her, the shades drawn on the windows. The only light came from a small lamp.

Jonas couldn't figure out why, but the place made him kind of tired. Guess that was the side effect of a person being an expert in sleep. They knew exactly what triggers to present.

"I'm sure you want to talk about Alan," Mariana said. "But I haven't seen him other than that one time."

"Not just Alan," Sam said, taking the lead. "I'll be up front with you, Ms. Santiago," she said. "I don't trust what you do. I've done a little research, and I've only found your name attached to controversial coma patients. Only a brief mention, like it was covered up. So, I'm not sure what you *really* do, but I suspect it's more than helping lost souls."

Mariana smiled, and sat back in her chair as if she admired Sam's directness. "Well," she said. "There is money involved."

"I figured," Sam said. "But we're here because we need to know how you do it. We need Alan. But there's more. Things we can't explain. A Night Stalker came into the Waking World and attacked me. And our friend…" Sam paused, seeming unsure how to phrase what came next.

"Our friend was taken over by a shadow person," Jonas added for her. "Do you know what that is?"

Mariana's eyes snapped to Jonas, and her skin paled considerably. "I do," she responded quietly. "They're creatures of the void. But if *you* know them… Well, I'm surprised you're still alive. You must be as good a poet as they claim. How did the shadow reveal itself?"

"In a dream," Jonas said. "But it pulled me there. It called me on the phone, pretending to be my friend. I think it called me from the Dream World. And it was just after Sam was attacked."

"Interesting."

"And impossible, right?" Jonas asked.

"Not quite. The veil between our realties must be stretched thin. Too much energy—good or bad—on one side.

That can account for the Night Stalker—at least, partly. But about your friend, how strong a lucid dreamer was he?"

"Strong," Sam said. "Loyal."

"The shadow would have sensed that," Mariana said. "And I'm sorry he used it against you." Mariana stared at Sam for a long moment, and then leaned forward in her chair.

"You're a Dream Walker," she said with a touch of awe.

"No," Sam said, shaking her head. "I trained, but didn't complete the process. I—"

"Didn't want to lose your soul," Mariana finished for her, and smiled. Sam swallowed hard, and nodded her response.

"You still have the power," Mariana added. "I can feel it from here. And it's quite unusual." She studied her a moment longer, and then tilted her head. "I know who you are. But I have no idea *what* you are."

Sam and Jonas exchanged a glance, and Sam crossed her arms protectively over her chest. "I don't understand," Sam said.

"You think you get to choose your destiny?" Mariana asked, leaning back in her chair. "No, darling. We all have a path. Yours is waiting to be revealed, I assume. But for now, I think you drew that Night Stalker to you. The bright light within you makes a grand bull's eye for a bullet. You're powerful, exceptional. You have the sort of power that can contact lucid dreamers lost between realities."

Sam said nothing, but Mariana turned to Jonas, color rising high on her cheeks. "Seems she has something you don't, Jonas. As I told you, it's a talent. Just like how not everyone can be a poet. Samantha may be the only one who can go in and get Alan."

Sam scoffed, incredulous, and when Jonas turned to her, she shook her head. "She's saying I'm the one who has to die, isn't she?" she asked.

Jonas furrowed his brow, his stomach upended with worry...and a bit of hope. There wasn't a single person, in any reality, who would understand him the way Sam did. Not a single person who wouldn't have run away by now.

"I would never ask you to do that," Jonas said. "He's my brother. I'm going in. Don't let Ms. Santiago convince you I'm not special."

Sam laughed, but Jonas had a fresh sense of fear. He took Sam's hand and pulled it to his mouth, kissing her fingers. As he did, Marshall's words came back to him.

The Dream Walkers had turned their backs on Poet Anderson because he risked the future to save his brother. And now...he was about to risk his girlfriend. He squeezed his eyes shut, knowing how reckless this was. No guarantees—only a small bit of faith.

He could still walk away from everything. He and Sam could go on with their waking lives, or even run away with the other poets and live in peace.

Jonas let go of Sam's hand, and looked at her. He licked his lips, ready to tell her they'd run away from all of this and be together. But in the end, Jonas couldn't change who he was. He was desperate to find Alan.

Sam seemed to sink into herself a bit before nodding. She turned to Mariana.

"Do you really know how to do this?" she asked her, her voice shaking. "You can tell me how to find Alan and wake him up?"

"I can do the procedure. I can revive you. What happens in the void," Mariana said, "I have no control over. That part is up to you."

"Is it dangerous?" Jonas asked, and immediately felt stupid when both women looked at him.

"Yes," Mariana said condescendingly. "Samantha is going to die for you, Jonas. What have you done to inspire such loyalty?"

The comment was cruel, and Jonas took it like a wallop to the chest.

Samantha was the first to stand, straightening her back and standing tall. "We should get started," she said bravely. "What's the first step?"

Mariana smiled, seeming pleased with this outcome. "We go to the Sleep Center and visit with Alan Anderson."

CHAPTER TEN

SAMANTHA DECIDED NOT TO TELL HER father—or anyone else—about their plan, even though Jonas wanted to at least loop Marshall in. But Sam convinced him that Marshall's first call would be to Alexander, and Jonas knew she was right.

There was no touching or smiling on the way to the Sleep Center. Before leaving, Mariana had given Sam some pills to take in preparation. Now Sam sat close to the door, staring out the window at the passing buildings. And Jonas sat with his guilt.

The car dropped them off in front of the Sleep Center, and Sam told the driver to head back to the hotel so he wouldn't wait for them. It had started to rain again, but when the driver offered her his umbrella she said no.

Sam stood silently on the sidewalk, getting soaked as she watched the car pull away. Concerned, Jonas called her name, and then jogged ahead, his sneakers sloshing in the puddles, to hold the door open for her. Sam thanked him as she passed—again, withdrawn—and they walked inside, where Mariana was already waiting with a large medical bag.

The receptionist eyed them curiously as Mariana led Jonas and Sam to the elevators and pressed the button for Alan's floor. She asked Sam if she was tolerating the pills she'd taken at the house, a sedative that would help her heart rate slow naturally before the procedure to stop it. Sam said she was fine.

Jonas felt left out of this process, dependent on the two of them. He hated feeling helpless. He should be the one looking for Alan. He should be taking the risk.

Alan's floor was quiet, and when Jonas knocked and entered his room, he was once again struck with grief. His brother, though alive, looked more dead each day. Further and further from ever waking up. Ashen skin, limp hair, dissolved muscles... If Jonas hadn't been watching him waste away, he wouldn't have even recognized him.

He turned to see Sam staring at Alan's body. Sympathetic. Brave. Mariana had told them that close proximity to Alan might help with locating him in the void. There was a second bed in the room, and Mariana motioned for Sam to take a seat there while she made preparations. She set her medical bag on a metal tray and began to empty it.

Sam walked to the other bed and climbed in. Her movements were slow, and Jonas wondered how much was reluctance, and how much was the medication. She lay down and put her hands on the bars on the side of the bed. Jonas could see how she trembled, and yet...he still didn't stop her.

He should. He knew he should.

He took one last look at his brother, and went over to sit next to Sam. When she finally met his eyes, she smiled sadly. It nearly ripped his heart out.

Jonas took her hand, folding it in his arm, and laid his head on her hip. This was their only real chance to find his brother. But he didn't want her to do this. He didn't want to lose her.

"I think we're ready," Mariana said, and Jonas heard the wheels of the metal cart moving toward them. He sat up, and Sam moved her hand to hold his cheek—a touch that made Jonas feel vulnerable. Loved.

Mariana moved to the other side of the bed, and Sam shifted so that she could face her. Jonas's heart pounded; his mouth grew dry.

"What's going to happen?" Sam asked, her voice carrying a lilt of sedation.

"You'll feel a burn as this medication enters your system," Mariana said, as she uncapped a syringe and held it up. "It will stop your heart. First I'll give you a round of anesthetics, so you won't feel any pain." She set the syringe aside, and set up an IV, pushing the needle into Sam's hand and taping it on.

Stop her heart, Jonas thought. *She's going to stop her fucking heart.*

"Once I'm d—dead," Sam said unsteadily, "then what?"

"That I can't say," Mariana said. "The void is... It's a reality in a way. You must ground yourself there, but hold on to your consciousness. Every movement must be purposeful. But keep in mind, time moves differently there. It'll be important for you to remember your objective. Find Alan Anderson."

"And when I do?" Samantha asked.

"Look for an exit," Mariana said, as if it were simple. "I'll be monitoring Alan, and when his activity spikes, I'll know you found the way out. I'll resuscitate you. Just be sure Alan comes through whatever door opens." She took out another syringe—the anesthetic—and injected it into the IV.

Jonas furrowed his brow. "Will that work?"

"Alan found me once before. I see no reason why he can't make it out again. He just needs a guide."

"And why can't you do it instead of Sam?" Jonas asked.

Mariana pressed her lips together. "Because I'm not strong enough to get out of the void. She is."

Jonas swallowed hard and looked at Sam, wanting to acknowledge the danger, but her eyes were glazing over from the medication.

He wanted to gather her up, tell her he changed his mind. He looked at Mariana, and she already had the medication to stop Sam's heart poked into the IV line. He felt sick as he watched, and he turned back to Sam, desperate.

"Sam," he said. "Samantha."

Sam looked at him dreamily, her lips tugging into a smile. "I love you, Poet Anderson," she whispered.

"Sam, wait…" Jonas said, starting to tear up. But her eyes closed. He turned to Mariana, wanting to tell her stop this, but she was already disposing of the needle.

The room felt surreal. The entire situation did. The monitor on the other side of the room beeped Alan's steady heart rate. Mariana wheeled over a second monitor, and placed it next to Sam. She attached several wires to Sam's chest, and then turned the machine on.

The sound of Sam's heart began to beat through the machine. Jonas covered his mouth, horrified as he listened to how slow it was, each beat taking longer and longer to come.

He could barely breathe as he listened, and he grabbed Sam's hand, trying to hold on to her. He wanted the medication to fail. It wasn't worth it, he decided. It wasn't worth risking Sam's life.

And then, to his absolute horror, her heart stopped altogether and the sound of her flatlining echoed throughout the room.

JONAS REMEMBERED THE DAY he and Sam graduated from high school. To be honest, Jonas had barely squeaked by with a shining D-plus. Sam had, of course, gotten A's. She earned a scholarship to attend the University of Washington, but opted to take most of her classes virtually. She planned to help more at the hotel, partly to be with Jonas. He didn't think then about what she'd be giving up for him.

They had already walked and gotten their diplomas to little fanfare. Sam's friends didn't understand her relationship with Jonas—a loser transfer student who didn't even own a car. And Sam's father was a no-show. But, oddly enough, Marshall had sent them each a congratulations card.

Afterward, Sam and Jonas had gotten into her car, and were sitting outside the auditorium listening to music with the windows open. Jonas was talking about his shift later that night, about the poets he'd just met. And Sam reached over and took his hand, putting it on her thigh.

Jonas grinned before even looking over.

"I've been thinking," she said.

Jonas tightened his grip on her bare thigh, just under the hem of her skirt. "Yeah, I've lost all ability to think," he said, leaning in to kiss her. Soaking up the smell of her hair, the taste of her lips.

"I'm serious," she said with a little laugh, kissing him back.

"Okay," Jonas said, kissing her cheek, her neck, her shoulder. "About what?"

"Moving in together."

Jonas had a small tug at his heart, but tried to down play how much he actually wanted that to happen. He pulled back and smiled at her. "What are you asking me, Miss Birnham-Wood?" he said teasingly.

"I don't think we should," she said. Jonas's smile faded.

"Oh," he replied, sliding his hand off her leg. "Okay, I understand."

"I'm going to get my own place," she said, studying his reaction. "Unless…"

"Unless what?" Jonas asked. He looked at Sam, helpless in how much he wanted to be with her. His rock. His lifeline.

And in his vulnerable expression, Sam must have seen the answer she wanted. She smiled, licking her lips.

"Unless you beg," she whispered.

A flash of electricity flowed through Jonas's body, and he would have done absolutely anything in that moment. He got up from the seat, climbing over the console, hand up her leg, mouth over hers. And he begged her to move in with him, to live with him. To love him.

And she promised she would.

JONAS WIPED THE TEARS off his cheeks, and gathered his strength. "Wake her up," Jonas said to Mariana, his voice strained.

"Not yet," Mariana replied, staring across the room at Alan's monitor. There were several erratic beats, and Jonas's breath caught. Sam was doing it. She'd found him. She was talking to him.

Jonas reached for Sam, his hand on her upper arm, and the IV line brushed against his skin, cold to the touch. "Wake her up," he told Mariana again. "She's done it."

"She's almost there," Mariana said, more to herself than Jonas. But in her voice, Jonas heard ambition, drive. The kind of eagerness that doesn't care about risk. Doesn't care about others. A thought occurred to him.

"Why are you doing this?" Jonas asked her, glancing up to her determined face. "Why did you agree to help us?"

Mariana was still for a long moment, and then she sighed heavily. She reached out and clicked off Samantha's monitor. Jonas watched her, wondering what she was doing—why she was moving so slowly.

When she turned to him with a steady gaze, Jonas's gut churned. "I'm sorry about your girlfriend," she said. "She seemed very sweet. More than capable. I see very little of Alexander in her."

"What do you mean?" he asked. He stared down at Sam's face, her full lips now tinted blue. "What have you done to her?" he demanded.

"What she asked. I killed her."

Jonas's eyes rounded, and he quickly jumped from the chair, sending it toppling onto the floor. He pulled the IV from Sam's hand, blood spurting out with it.

"That won't help," Mariana said conversationally as Jonas leaned over Sam's body, tapping her cheek.

"Sam," Jonas said, tapping her cheek. "Wake up, Sam."

"She's not asleep, Jonas," Mariana said. "She's dead."

"Fuck you," he said. "Bring her back."

"I…" She pressed her lips together. "I'm not going to do that."

Jonas gasped in a breath, rage building in his chest. "What? Why?"

"You know why," she responded. Jonas was about to tell her he didn't, but it slowly worked itself out in his head.

"Is this about Alexander?" Jonas asked, falling back a step.

"I knew you were smarter than you looked," Mariana said in a teasing voice. She walked over to Alan's bed, keeping an eye on Jonas. "Alexander Birnham-Wood," she said venomously, "is a plague on this world. A monster in human clothing. The Waking World doesn't want him, the Dream World doesn't want him."

Jonas was still trying to figure everything out when Mariana turned to him. "Don't you get it?" she asked. "Sam and I aren't all that different. We both loved poets. She was an easy mark."

And then he understood. "He killed him," Jonas said. "Alexander killed your poet."

"Correct," Mariana said. "And I've spent the years since trying to take everything from him. Not easy for a man without a soul. He has only one treasure in his life." She motioned toward Sam in the bed.

"I had no idea she would willingly volunteer to save your brother," Mariana added. "I thought it would take a bit of convincing on your part, you begging her. I should have known better. Tends to work out that way with poets, I suppose. Every connection more intense."

Time ticked by, and Jonas wasn't sure how long Sam could be dead before she never woke up again. He was growing desperate.

"Alexander's an asshole," he said. "I get it. But please don't take her from me. Please, Mariana."

Mariana tilted her head in a position of faux sympathy. "It's not all hopeless for you, Jonas. Bright side—" She looked down at Alan. "He might wake up. You can still have everything you want. There is a bargain to be made—if you're willing to take it."

Jonas was ready to do anything. "Just tell me what I have to do."

Mariana's lips flinched with a smile. "Samantha is the only link Alexander has to his humanity. The only person in the world he cares about. Without her, he would crumble. I enjoy the idea of his pain, but I hate to settle. I can't get to Alexander. He's too guarded in the Waking World, too strong in the Dream World. He's a Dream Walker, for Christ's sake."

Jonas narrowed his eyes. "So what are you asking?"

"I need you to kill Alexander Birnham-Wood," she said simply. "That is the cost of your girlfriend's life."

CHAPTER ELEVEN

JONAS WAS COMPLETELY CAUGHT OFF guard, and he took a step back from the scientist. He couldn't kill Samantha's father. He couldn't believe Mariana would even ask him. "I can't do that," he said.

"Then our time here is done, Jonas," Mariana responded, and started for the door. Jonas beat her to it, barring her way, his arm across the frame. Mariana looked up at him expectantly.

Jonas's mind raced. He turned toward Sam's body. He couldn't let her die. He'd give up anything—everything—for her. He spun back to face Mariana, anger flooding him.

"This was your plan all along," he said. "It's what you always wanted me to do. Jesus, did you ever even talk to my brother?"

"Of course," she said like she was offended. "I may be vindictive, but I'm not a liar. And no, I wasn't lying about Samantha's light either. I've watched her. I've spoken with Marshall about Molly's assessment. Samantha is a strong young woman—but I'm sure you already sense that about her. Her potential is limitless from what I can tell."

"Let me wake Sam up and then we can—"

"Not a chance," Mariana said. "First, you kill Alexander."

"She's dead," he growled. "How much time do you think there is? I can't do that and get back here in time."

"I'll revive her body," Mariana said. "She's been gone too long to wake on her own, but I can keep her body alive. And when you get back…we can see where we're at."

Mariana pushed past Jonas, and went to stand over Sam's body, staring down at it. "Let me be clear," she said. "Samantha is not in here." She brushed Sam's hair away from her face. "She is between realities with no way to tunnel out— unless your brother figures it out. But as long as her body lives, she has a chance." She turned to Jonas and removed a syringe from her pocket. "So what's your choice?" she asked. "Samantha or Alexander? One of them dies today."

Sam would never forgive him for killing her father; Jonas knew that. She might be angry with him, but he was still her father. Jonas knew she would willingly die in his place.

But Jonas couldn't let her go. He'd rather she lived and hated him forever. He'd give her up to let her live. He swallowed down his guilt, the part of his morality that would be permanently changed by this.

"Save her life," he whispered, and rested back against the door, watching as Mariana smiled and unbuttoned the top of Samantha's shirt, pulling it back to expose her bra.

"A shot of adrenalin to the heart," she said. "Can you please wheel the cart over to me?"

Jonas looked at the cart again, the items laid out. It was clear now that she had no intention of waking Alan. These items were *always* for meant to imprison Sam in the void. Jonas seethed with hatred for the woman, his blood turning to slick, black oil.

He walked over to the metal cart and wheeled it to her side. He could barely contain his anger; even his fingers were shaking.

Mariana kept a careful distance from him. "Thank you," she said. "Now wait over there." She motioned to the chair, and Jonas touched Sam's cheek, his heart breaking.

He sat down, elbows on his knees, head hanging low. He never should have let Sam come here. He never should have brought her into any of this. He needed her to be okay. He really would do anything to make that happen.

Mariana checked the fluid in the syringe and then she carefully aimed and, with a sickening thud, stabbed it into Sam's chest. Jonas flinched, absorbing the shock for himself. He watched, tears beginning to stream down his cheeks.

Mariana depressed the syringe and then withdrew it, immediately checking for a pulse. The room was completely quiet. Jonas looked over at his brother, wishing he were here. But also hoping that somehow...he was with Samantha right now.

She's probably terrified, Jonas thought miserably. *She must know what's happening to her. Must feel that she's trapped.*

Jonas wiped hard at his cheeks to clear the tears, the pain in his chest becoming a throbbing ache. "Come back to me, Sam," he whispered, pressing his palms together.

Mariana picked up the oxygen bag and placed it over Sam's mouth, pumping air into her lungs. Her chest rose and fell, and Jonas waited to see if she'd breathe on her own.

When Mariana removed the bag, nothing happened. Jonas sputtered out a cry, and Mariana put the mask over Sam's mouth again. This time her movements were jerky. Her confidence was waning.

She wouldn't leave this room if Sam died. Jonas wouldn't let her.

"Come on," she murmured, and removed the bag to check Sam's pulse again. The moment seemed to last an eternity. And then Mariana smiled suddenly and looked at Jonas.

"I've got her," she said, like she and Jonas were friends now. As if her killing and then saving his girlfriend had bonded them.

"Now wake her up," he said.

"I told you already that I can't."

"Then tell me how."

Mariana straightened, checking Samantha's pulse again before walking over to place items on the cart. "I'll get a room prepared for Samantha."

"No," Jonas growled.

"We had a deal, Jonas," Mariana snapped. "Alexander for Samantha. I don't care how you do it, or where, but I promise you: if he's not dead by morning, Samantha will never wake up. Understand?"

"You think I'll let you get away with this?" he asked, a fire burning in his chest.

"Considering you need me, yes. I think you will." Mariana picked up the phone and told the nurse she'd need another bed ready.

Jonas wondered how long it would be before Alexander was notified that his daughter was a now a patient at the Sleep Center. Because once he did, Jonas wouldn't have to find Alexander. He would come for him.

JONAS WAS NUMB AS he watched the nurses and Mariana hook up Samantha to the same tubes and instruments his brother had been on for a year. Nothing felt real anymore. Not the way her body hung limply when they moved her. Not the way her head rolled to the side when they placed a pillow underneath it.

But she was alive. She wasn't awake, but she was alive. Jonas followed behind as they wheeled her bed down the hall to a separate room, and he heard one of the nurses whisper that she was Alexander's daughter. Mariana claimed it was an aneurysm, and that she needed to be closely monitored.

Jonas's heart was broken. He kissed Sam's cool skin, and then walked out. He stopped at the nurses' station and asked if he could use the phone.

Alexander answered on the first ring. "How did this happen?" he demanded. Jonas wasn't surprised that he already knew, but his guilt over the situation was hard to keep out of his voice.

"We have to meet," Jonas said. "Alone."

Alexander was quiet for a long moment, and then Jonas thought he heard a low growl in his throat. "Tonight," Alexander said. "In Genesis. I'm on my way to the Sleep Center to see my daughter," he continued. "You'd better be gone when I get there."

Jonas was coated with shame, and part of him wanted to apologize, but he still had more atrocities to commit. He still had to break Sam's heart.

"I'll see you tonight," Jonas replied. Alexander hung up, and Jonas handed the phone back to the receptionist.

He hurried out the front doors and caught a bus back to the Eden so he could dream.

PART 2
WHEN DARKNESS COMES

CHAPTER TWELVE

POET ANDERSON STEPPED OUT OF THE tunnel onto the streets of Genesis, the city teeming with people as far as the eye could see. It reminded Poet of how busy it had been the last time he'd dreamt of Sketch. Maybe that night had been real, and he did, in fact, see Gunner…or, at least, some version of him.

"Watch it," a guy said, pushing past Poet and slipping into the crowd. Poet fell back a step and watched after the man. He realized immediately that he was a Dream; Poet felt no tie to him from the Waking World. In fact, as Poet looked around, he didn't see many dreamers from the Waking World at all. These were all creatures born from the Dream World.

His electricity flared up, and he let it race down his arm and form a gun in his hand.

Something was wrong.

There were a couple of gasps as Dreams saw him with a weapon. Poet began walking purposefully, following the flow of traffic, in search of Alexander. He glanced up at the building and bridges stretching toward the sky. The telescreens flashed his picture, and Poet looked away, hating how the Dream World always sensed his presence.

He walked another block and the crowd began to thin, many going into clubs with thumping bass, orbed lights. Some disappeared down the dark alleys. Why was this place flooded with Dreams, though? And more importantly, where were the dreamers?

There was a flash above him, and Poet looked up to see another image on the telescreen. It was Alexander, standing in the middle of a street. Poet's heart sank when he saw he was in his Dream Walker's armor. He guessed Alexander was there to kill him too.

Poet wanted to turn around and tunnel back into the Waking World. He didn't want to fight—not like this, on someone else's command. But what choice did he have? Sam needed him.

Dreams continued to gape at him; some were scared of him. They all eyed his gun. Poet reached out his hand and turned his gun into an umbrella, and swung it around by the handle. One dream girl smiled at the change. Poet wanted to blend in as he headed toward the street where he'd seen Alexander waiting.

Poet came upon an isolated area, just behind the tallest building. Cars zoomed overhead, and as Poet stepped out into the street, Alexander toughened his stance. His helmet was pulled back, so Poet could see his face. See his hatred.

"You said you wanted to meet," Alexander said, his voice a barely controlled rage. "Here we are, Poet Anderson. After what you've done to my daughter, this won't end well for you."

"I would never hurt Samantha," Poet said, still hoping there was a way out of this.

"And yet she's the one in a hospital bed," Alexander shot back. "Why is it that everyone who cares about you ends up dead or in a coma? Your parents, your brother, your girlfriend. At what point do you accept your role in all of this?"

"Me?" Poet asked. "What about you? You called me and Alan to Seattle. Samantha is trapped because of a vendetta against *you*. So it seems there's enough blame to go around."

There was the sound of glass rolling along gravel behind him, and Poet spun quickly, surprised to find Callum walking toward him.

The poet didn't have a weapon, but his eyes were burning white with power. He pulled up the corner of his mouth when Poet noticed him.

"Hope you don't mind," Callum said casually. "I'm here to watch."

"What?" Poet asked, irritated. "How did you even know—?"

"I called him," Alexander said.

Poet looked back to him, and shook his head. "Why?" he asked.

"Because we're about to upset the Dream World. Either a Dream Walker or a poet dies tonight—there will be repercussions. Callum may have to help me keep order. Temporarily."

"And why would you agree to this?" Poet asked Callum.

He shrugged. "He said we could leave, either way. If you or he dies, the poets have a free pass to get the hell out of here without Dream Walker interference. Sounded like a fair trade to me."

"Fucker," Poet said. He thrust out his arm and sent power to the tip of his umbrella, making it hot with electricity—ready to fire, angry sparks flying off the tip. In response, Alexander's helmet slid up and covered his face, his suit glowing with power of its own. Lights along the trim like a trail of fire, the world reflected in his helmet.

"You should be happy, Poet," Alexander told him. "I had Callum redirect most of the dreamers to protect other innocents from getting caught up in your chaos."

Every time he blamed Poet, it dug a little deeper. Mostly because Poet blamed himself. Alexander was working his insecurities, taking advantage of them.

Above Alexander's shoulder, his Halo rose up and began to circle him.

This was real. They would have to fight.

Alexander was the first to shoot. Poet acted quickly, using his umbrella to absorb the shock of the concentrated energy, and then leapt to the other side of the road to take cover near a metal trash can. He returned fire, but the Halo easily blocked the shots. He would need to be cleverer if he was going to beat a Dream Walker.

"Don't you want to know why I called you?" Poet asked.

"To tell me about my daughter. But didn't you think *my* Sleep Center would call me the minute they discovered what you'd done?" Alexander fired and then grabbed a second weapon where his suit opened at the hip, firing again. This time it was too much for Poet's umbrella; it flew out of his hands, skidding across the street until it faded into smoke. One of the shots hit the trash can in front of him and exploded, knocking him back several feet. He could feel a burn on his cheek and road rash on his hands as he slowly got up.

He was too exposed like this. Poet glanced up at the bridge. There were vehicles, but he'd be able to find cover. He stored up his power, and then in a quick burst, he ran up the wall, jumping at the last second as he began to lose his balance. He caught the edge of the bridge cable, slicing open his hand, but holding on. He pulled himself up, and when he hopped over the guardrail, the vehicles swerved upward to avoid him.

A tunnel opened next to him, and Callum walked out. He didn't even look at Poet as he headed into the middle of the street. He held up his hand for the drivers to stop, and then in a swift movement, brushed his hands aside and all the vehicles began to vibrate with electricity before falling from the sky and crashing onto the bridge, making it rattle.

Poet quickly steadied himself, his eyes wide as he watched how much power Callum wielded. He wondered if all the poets were this strong. He wondered if he was that strong.

There was a sudden wallop of pain and Poet fell forward onto his knees, the back of his head sending stars across his vision. He reached to feel the area, and his hand came back bloody. He turned, groaning, and saw Alexander climb over the guardrail and drop the red metal rod he'd used to hit him.

Alexander's helmet folded back, exposing his face. A deep dimple in his chin and the lines around his eyes were the only signs of his age. He didn't have even a second of remorse as a gun came out of the forearm of his suit, and he aimed it point blank at Poet.

"You're a coward," Poet said, touching again at the sore spot in the back of his head. "If you really wanted a fight, you would have done it bare-handed. No weapons."

Alexander laughed. "You know I'll kill you either way," he said.

"Probably," Poet responded. "But at least this way I can look you in the eyes as you try."

"And your eyes?"

Poet knew this was a terrible idea—forgoing his power, his only defense. But he didn't have much choice. Alexander would kill him. Poet shook his head, blinking as his power faded, and color poured back into his irises. He looked at Alexander and smiled bitterly.

Alexander's Halo retreated back into his suit, and piece by piece the plates of armor clicked away. Alexander stood there in a high-end track suit, as if he was out for a morning jog and not about battle in the Dream World.

Callum laughed, and hopped up onto the hood of one of the crashed cars, watching the two men. The dreamers were all gone, and most of the Dreams had fled back to the city. A few stood around to watch, hidden behind debris.

"It was a bold choice," Alexander said, as he walked towards Poet. "I seem to remember the last time you got in a bare-knuckle fight, you didn't even get a punch in before some kid at school knocked you into the Dream World."

"I was defending your daughter," Poet answered. He and Alexander circled each other, moving to the center of the road.

"Samantha never needed you to defend her. She's the one who saved you."

Poet's heart ached at the thought, and his fists lowered as he thought about Sam in the hospital, lost somewhere in a void. Alexander used this distraction and lunged at him, punching him hard across the cheek, making his teeth rattle in his head.

Poet fell back against a car, but quickly righted himself and put his fists up defensively. He spit out blood and narrowed his eyes on Alexander.

"Now tell me what you did to her," Alexander said. "How did she end up like that?"

"I'm trying to save her," Poet growled, his face already hurting.

Alexander stepped forward, swinging at him again. Poet dodged, but before he could straighten, Alexander spun and slammed both fists down onto Poet's back, sending him hard to the pavement.

Poet struggled to get to his knees, and Alexander stepped away, smiling as he enjoyed Poet's suffering. "Kid," he said. "I've been fighting long enough to know all possible outcomes, every possible move or tactic. You don't have a chance."

To try to prove him wrong, Poet jumped forward, fist curled, and took a shot. Alexander moved out of the way easily, grabbed Poet by the arm, and swung him around to slam him into the door of a car. Poet coughed and slid down, gathering himself on the road before getting to his feet again.

Callum let out a low whistle.

Poet gritted his teeth, seeing that Alexander was getting prideful. This time, as Alexander continued his victory lap,

Poet ran at him to tackle him. But when Alexander turned around, ready to block, Poet dove under his outstretched arm and hopped up to kick him hard in the back, sending him headlong into the road.

While he was down, Poet kicked him in the head. And Alexander rolled quickly to avoid another blow. He got to his feet and bared his teeth; they were red with blood.

"Come on!" he shouted, pounding his own chest before charging Poet.

Poet met him halfway and they collided. Alexander's considerable size was too much, and he quickly grabbed Poet by the hair, and brought his face down to meet his knee, smashing his nose.

Poet fell flat on his back, temporarily stunned, blood gushing over his face. The pain was incredible, and as blood rushed down his throat, he began to choke.

He turned to the side, and glanced over to Callum, who was still sitting on the hood of the car, although now he was leaned forward, fraught-looking. Poet shifted his eyes to Alexander, and his intent was clear.

Alexander was going to kill him.

Poet got to his knees and pulled himself up, using the side of a car. Alexander was a hulking mass, panting and ready to finish him off. Poet might have kept fighting—fight to the death, even—but this wasn't about him.

He spit out blood, and then willed his power to flare up. His eyes went white, and blue snaps of electricity lashed out from his body. Above him, thunder cracked across the sky, chasing a streak of lightning.

"I'm sorry, Alexander," Poet said, his voice thick. "I had to choose between you and Sam. And I chose Sam."

Alexander's head tilted, his eyes wide. "What do you mean?" he demanded.

"Mariana Santiago," Poet said. He rested against the car as he spoke, trying to look casual and not like he was about to fall down. His power was siphoning into the world, creating electricity. Charging him up. "She wanted you dead," he added.

"She can join the club," Alexander said, spitting out a mouthful of blood.

"Mariana came to me at the Eden," Poet said. "She told me she'd spoken to my brother, spoke to him while he was in a coma."

Now he had Alexander's attention. "She did?" he asked. "Why didn't she tell me?"

"You knew what she could do?" Poet asked, caught off guard. "That she could reach coma patients—those who were lucid dreamers?"

"Why do you think I've worked with her all these years?" Alexander said.

Another flash of anger sent electricity through Poet's body, spitting out around him in blue flashes, licks of flames. Alexander took a step back.

"And what else did Mariana say?" Alexander asked, sounding doubtful.

"Samantha came with me to see her. Mariana said Sam was powerful, and that she'd be able to find Alan in the void. She convinced us, and then she killed her."

Alexander's fists curled at his side. "Why would she send her without my knowledge?" he demanded.

"Because Mariana hates you," Poet said, taking a bit of satisfaction in the words. "She tricked us, tricked your daughter to get to you. You killed her poet. And now she wants you dead."

Behind him, Callum let out a long "Oooo..." and Alexander froze.

"You're lying," Alexander said.

"No." Poet shook his head, and the first drops of rain began to fall. "You know I'm right. Mariana's been waiting for a moment to pay you back. She's using your daughter to do it. Once Samantha flatlined, Mariana refused to wake her up. She left her in the void. She wouldn't resuscitate her until I agreed to kill you."

Alexander's expression tightened, the strain on his heart obvious. There was a scrape on his chin, just below the dimple, from when he'd fallen earlier. Poet watched as a small trickle of blood ran down in the rain and dripped onto his shirt.

"And if you kill me?" Alexander asked. "Then what happens?"

"She'll wake her up. If she won't do it herself, I'll make her send me. I'll go get her."

"Oh, Christ," Callum muttered.

Alexander glanced at him, and then steadied his gaze on Poet. "Then what are you waiting for?" he asked.

Poet furrowed his brow. "What?"

"If you have the chance to save my daughter, then what the fuck are you waiting for?" He screamed the last part of his sentence, and Poet flinched back from his ferocity. "I would have killed you in a heartbeat," Alexander said, a little gleefully.

"Sam won't forgive me," Poet said. Thunder clashed.

"I know."

"So what am I supposed to do?" Poet asked.

"You do what's right: you save her, despite your selfishness," Alexander said.

"What if you—?"

Alexander held up his hand to stop him. The rain fell more freely, tinged blue and pooling around their feet.

"It's too late," Alexander said. "Every moment that Samantha is in the void, the harder it will be to bring her back. I've known Mariana for years, and I never put together what she was after...although I should have. That sort of vindictiveness is something I understand. There is no compromise she'd make with me. In fact, if you don't do exactly what she says, you'll likely never find my daughter."

Poet tried to gather his bravery. Instead, he thought of Sketch—or rather, the shadow wearing Sketch. He'd helped kill him too. What was Poet becoming? How many people would he kill? The blue rain turned red, and Callum seemed to notice first, looking around the bridge.

"We don't have time for this, Poet Anderson," Alexander snarled.

"Yes," Callum called out. He hopped down from the hood of the car, adjusting this hat. "The public is waiting." He motioned above them to the telescreen. Poet and Alexander were being broadcast throughout Genesis, bloodied and bruised.

And Poet saw how savage he looked, soaked in red—eyes blazing white. He looked ruthless, even though he was trying to *not* kill Alexander. He turned back to his girl-friend's father.

"We can figure this out," Poet said.

Alexander eyes softened for an instant—maybe with a slight touch of admiration—before whatever part of human-ity he had seemed to slip away. "You were always such a coward," he said. He took a step forward and swung out, punching Poet in the jaw.

Lightning struck the bridge, making it rattle. Poet was nearly spun completely around from the hit, but he quickly recovered, the inside of his mouth bleeding from where it caught on a tooth.

"Please," Poet said. "I don't want to—"

Alexander extended out his arms and his Dream Walker suit slipped over his body, helmet back in place. Poet wouldn't be able to beat him—not as a Dream Walker.

"You know what you have to do," Alexander said, stomp-ing toward him.

Poet dodged his grip, and headed to the side of the bridge, looking over. People were starting to gather, the telescreen broadcasting everything, a soundless battle.

"End this," Alexander said.

Poet could feel Callum just behind him, willing him on. Poet wasn't sure he had the strength, though. And he didn't want Mariana to win like this. The rain poured down harder.

"Your brother would," Alexander said, his voice carrying. "Alan would have been brave enough."

Poet looked up, the mention of his brother a shot of adrenaline.

"I told Samantha," Alexander said, stalking Poet, "that she ended up with the wrong Anderson brother. Alan would have looked out for her."

"Shut up," Poet said.

"Alan was the one who should have saved the Dream World. He wasn't a failure like you. A piece of shit. A useless—"

"Shut the fuck up!" Poet screamed and threw his head back, lightning striking directly into his eyes, filling him with power. His skin felt like fire, the world coming undone around him. The bridge shook, the sky moaned as rain soaked everything.

Alexander stood at his full height in front of Poet, his back to the city of Genesis. "You should be the one in the coma," he said cruelly. "I wish your mother hadn't left the Dream World with your loser father. I shouldn't have let her leave."

"Stop," Poet said, his voice deep. The electricity was about to break him apart, but Alexander could read his rage, and he smiled.

"If I could do it all again," he said. "I would have killed your mother before you were ever born."

And before he even realized what he had created, Poet lifted his arm and fired his gun while the electricity was still forming the edge of the handle. It tore a hole straight through Alexander's forehead, tipping him backward and off the bridge.

CHAPTER THIRTEEN

THERE WERE SEVERAL SCREAMS, AND POET felt the gun fade from his hand. The power drained from him. Large cracks zig-zagged the pavement, and the rain fell away.

Poet didn't want to look, but he leaned over the edge of the bridge and saw what remained of Alexander Birnham-Wood. Several people surrounded the body, checking on Alexander before looking up to point at Poet. To accuse him.

On the telescreen, they replayed the moment backwards and forwards. Alexander being shot again and again. Poet Anderson holding the gun.

"Well, fuck," Callum said, coming up behind Poet to throw an arm over his shoulders. "You just killed your girl-friend's dad."

"Go away, Callum," Poet said weakly. His hands shook, his body swaying in the wind. The battle had taken too much from him. He looked around and felt the disruption. The destruction.

"A Dream Walker," Callum added, and then quickly backed away when he thought Poet might hit him. "I'll tell you what," he said. "I'll give you some time to process. I actually want to talk to you about something, but I can tell now isn't the time."

"No, it's not." Poet glanced down at his hands, bloody knuckles, scraped palms. Hands of a murderer. "I have to get to Sam," he said more to himself than Callum. He began to create a tunnel, the wind blowing over his face. Across the bridge, people were staring at him, Dreams and dreamers both. Some looked entertained, but others were horrified. Scared.

Poet swallowed hard, ashamed, and stepped into the tunnel and out of the Dream World.

JONAS SAT UP ON the couch in his hotel room. His head ached, and when he reached to touch the back of his head, he half expected it to still be bleeding. But it wasn't. That was in the Dream World.

But the guilt he felt was true in both realities. It was breaking him, and all he could do was push it away. Far away.

Dazed, Jonas changed into his uniform—he wasn't even sure why. He'd seen it hanging in his closet, and it made him think of his father, his parents. It made him stronger, so he put it on, and hurried out of the Eden to catch a cab to the Sleep Center.

IT WAS LATE IN the evening, but there was still a glow on the horizon. Jonas raced up the steps and tried the door of the

Sleep Center, only to find it locked. He began to knock on the glass. After a moment he curled his hand into a fist and pounded. He took out his phone, about to call Mariana, but the receptionist appeared from a back room, wearing her coat with her purse looped over her shoulder. Her lips made a perfect O, and she jogged ahead in her heels and unlocked the door.

"Sorry," she said. "I was supposed to look out for you, but it'd gotten so late and—"

Her eyes traveled over him curiously, and Jonas moved past her and headed for the elevator. He didn't have time for small talk.

"She's waiting upstairs," she called after him. "Let her know I went home, okay?"

Jonas waved her off, and took the elevator up. He wasn't sure which room Samantha was in, so he checked each doorway as he made his way down the hallway, running and stopping to peek inside. Some of the lights were turned off and the empty rooms were dark. Jonas didn't even know if the Sleep Center had other patients anymore. It felt haunted, and he shivered as the thought passed over him.

It was near the end of the hall, the room next to Alan's, that Jonas saw a sliver of light under the door. He pushed into the room, and Mariana sat up with a start. She looked at him, eyes wide, as she took in his suit and tie. Samantha lay motionless on the bed, and he was struck with unimaginable grief. She looked awful—her skin sallow and jaundiced, dark bruising under her eyes. Pale lips. She looked unnatural, and Jonas put his hand over his heart. He turned to Mariana.

"It's done," he told her. "Alexander's gone."

Mariana clapped her hands together and smiled, color rushing high on her cheeks. Jonas hated her then—this vengeful woman who bargained Samantha's life for her father's. And she'd won. It burned him up that Mariana had won. And yet, Jonas had to trust her now.

"Your turn," he said. "Wake her up."

Mariana bit on her lip, pretending she was sorry for what she was about to say. "I told you it wouldn't be that easy. But I'm willing to guide you. The question is, are you willing to do this for her?" She motioned to Sam. "Does the loyalty go both ways?"

Jonas swallowed hard. "How do I know you're not just going to kill me?" he asked. "Or use me like you did Sam?"

"You don't," she said. "But I have no interest in killing you, despite how it may look. You've, in fact, freed me from my vengeance. I'm sure you can feel it now—the darkness creeping into your soul. It's yours now. I've carried it with me for too long."

Jonas did feel it—guilt, anger, darkness. He'd taken it from her when he agreed to do her bidding. Now it was his soul that was tainted, growing darker each day, it seemed. But he didn't have another choice. He hoped Sam would believe that when she woke.

"And you won't go in?" Jonas asked her. She laughed.

"I told you, I'm not strong enough for the void. And I still don't know how your brother got to me—perfect storm, I guess. See if he can show you what he did. But this is yours now, Jonas. Your decision."

Jonas's eyes trailed to Samantha. He crossed the room to stop next to her, sitting by her side like he had done with Alan for so many months. He took Sam's hand, dismayed by how cool and dry it felt. It reminded him that this was just a shell—the real Samantha was lost somewhere. Jonas brought her fingers to his lips and closed his eyes.

He couldn't bear it without her. He thought he'd rather be lost in the void if it meant surviving there with her. He took a deep breath.

"What happens next?" he asked Mariana.

"I'll inject you with the same serum I gave Samantha— one to stop your heart."

"Will it hurt?" Jonas asked.

"Yes. I won't be anesthetizing you, Jonas. It would leave you too weak to tunnel back out. You will have to feel it all."

It should scare him, the thought of dying, the thought of feeling pain... But, in a way, he welcomed it. It would be a deserved punishment for what he'd done.

"How do I get back out? I don't want to be trapped in a coma."

"I'll be honest," she said. "That might happen. But you're a poet, tunnel them out. When I revive you, you'll get a shock of electricity. It might transfer into the void. So if you can't find how Alan got through, make your own tunnel. At least, I hope you can."

"I'm ready," Jonas said. He kissed Sam's hand one more time before laying it next to her on the bed. He removed his jacket and rolled up his shirt sleeve.

Mariana wheeled an empty bed next to Sam's. Jonas climbed on, keeping his eyes on Samantha, watching her chest rise and fall with each breath. He'd have to find her. It would be nearly impossible, but their connection... He had to believe it was strong enough. And, although there was a slim chance, he might find Alan too.

Mariana pulled up a chair in front of him, and took Jonas's straightened arm, rubbing an alcohol swab over the inside of his elbow. "It will be a moment before the serum takes effect," she said. "You might feel a fluttering in your chest first, and then a slow tightness that grows. You won't die right away. But the minute you are unconscious, you find Samantha and you tunnel her out of there. I'll have no way to know when to start reviving you." She paused, the needle tip just about to pierce his skin. "And if I can't revive you, you'll stay dead. And if you don't tunnel out in time, you'll end up trapped."

"I'm taking the chance," Jonas said. "Just do your job."

Mariana watched him for a moment, and Jonas saw admiration in her eyes. He didn't want it—he hated it, in fact—but in him she must see some of the poet who died years ago. A broken heart can make a person do terrible things.

"Ready?" she asked.

Jonas sat up slightly, looking at his arm. It was his last chance to back out. He lay back on the pillow. "Do it."

He didn't wince when the needle pierced his skin, and he held back as the medicine made his veins fill with fire. He measured his breathing, but his heart was racing with fear. He guessed it wouldn't be doing that for much longer.

"Keep your mind clear," Mariana said as if she could sense that he was overthinking. "There is nothing but Sam. You must focus, Jonas, or you'll miss her. She is a tiny star in a huge galaxy right now. You have to zero in on her. Find her soul."

But the first image that came to Jonas's mind was that of Alexander—the way the light in his eyes extinguished. His blood spurting out. The smell of burnt flesh.

Jonas squeezed his eyes shut, trying to block it all out. And then there was exactly what Mariana described, a fluttering in his chest. A strange upending, like he was going off a cliff on a rollercoaster. A dull ache started in his right arm, just above the elbow.

He flinched, and reached to rub the muscle.

"Stay calm and focused," Mariana said, although she sounded farther away.

"I'm trying," Jonas said, surprised by his strangled voice. He was beginning to sweat, the perspiration gathering at his temples, above his upper lip. He tried to take a breath, but the result was a sharp pain, and then the sensation of pressure on his chest, like someone was sitting there.

Jonas shifted uncomfortably on the bed, staying focused. But the pain had traveled up his arm and settled into his jaw. He moaned softly, and turned on his side, hoping for relief. Instead he was struck with a wave of sickness like he might throw up. His head spun, and he flipped over to his other side, his heels digging into the bed as he began to writhe in pain.

"It's hard to breathe," he mumbled, and then cried out as he brought his fist to his chest, punching it. The tightness increased, and Jonas felt like his eyes were going to erupt from his head. He moaned again, spit sputtering between his lips. "Fucking hurts!" he yelled, although his words were garbled. He gritted his teeth, setting his jaw ablaze with pain, and clutched his arm to his body. He cried out in pain again, and this time he knew he was going to pass out.

He cursed, and tried to focus his mind on Samantha. His thoughts were interrupted with each new flash of pain. He gripped the metal handle of the bed, and forced his eyes open, only to be immediately disoriented. The room spun around him, but he fought. He got himself to a sitting position, and Mariana yelled for him to stop.

But Jonas leaned over the bed, coughing on air—choking on death, he thought—and reached out to take Sam's hand in the bed next to him. The touch was instantly electric, and then the entire world went black.

CHAPTER FOURTEEN

JONAS DIDN'T TUNNEL IN—THIS WASN'T A dream. That was the first thought he had as he opened his eyes and looked around. Jonas lived half his life in the Dream World—he knew it as well as he did his waking life. This…this was something much different.

In front of him was a long road, stretching for miles at least. Along the road were red-flowering trees, rapidly blooming and dying repeatedly. The petals blew across the road. In the distance, Jonas could see tall buildings, gray and unfinished. A city of some sort.

He turned his head and winced, the scenery shifting too quickly. He took a step, and it echoed so loudly he covered his ears.

This was its own reality, he realized. He reached out his hand, willing power to his fingertips, but nothing happened. He stared down, and he could see every line in his skin, every tiny hair, every cell. His senses were sharper—razor-sharp. He lowered his arm and started toward the city. He wasn't sure how long he would have before Mariana revived him, so he started to run, growing accustomed to the echo of his footsteps.

It could have been hours, or seconds—time worked differently here—but Jonas got to the first building and stopped to stare up at it. A dull ache had started in his arm, reminding him of the situation his body was in back in the Waking World. But at the same time, that reality began to grow fuzzy—as if it had been only a dream.

"You're here for Sam and Alan," he reminded himself, closing his eyes. His objective was waning, though. Mariana had warned that it would be hard to stay focused here. He wondered what that meant for Sam. What it meant for Alan, who had been here for over a year.

Large buildings loomed above him, and he noticed how the road through the city was cracked and filled with potholes. Other, smaller streets branched off it. As he walked, pieces of stone fell from the towering buildings and smashed on the concrete near him, sending out clouds of dust and debris.

Jonas checked ahead, worried because the city seemed to go on forever. He hadn't seen even one person. It all felt abandoned. Hopeless.

"Samantha!" he called, and listened as his voice reverberated between the walls, echoing around him. There was no response, and then, up ahead, he saw what looked like a black cat crossing the street. Only it wasn't a cat.

Jonas took a step back.

The figure continued to grow and change, not made of anything solid. No true form—a sketch of lines, forming and unforming. It was familiar to him, but when Jonas tried to recall when he'd seen something similar, he drew a blank. His past was growing fuzzy.

The creature noticed him and began to creep closer. Jonas knew he didn't want it to touch him. He began to run, continually checking back to make sure it wasn't coming after him. The smoke-like being drifted into one of the abandoned buildings.

Jonas reached the end of the street and turned the corner. His breath caught—it was the same. Not just that it looked the same. It was literally the same street. A continuous loop. He turned to go back the way he came, but he got nowhere, always starting back on the same block. His fear spiked. He tried to run between the buildings, but when he came out of the alley, he was still on the same road. He was lost on one single street. He couldn't even get back to the trees.

"You'll give up after a while," a voice said through the open door of one of the buildings.

Jonas spun around, and as the origin of the voice came out into the light, Jonas fell back a step. Alan Anderson stood, filling the doorway with his footballer frame—the way he used to look before his time in a coma robbed him of his muscle mass.

Here, Alan looked alive and well, his blond hair stylishly askew, his face clean-shaven. It was his perfect self. It was the Alan that Jonas remembered.

"Brother," he murmured and rushed over. Alan was waiting and caught him with a hug, slapping him hard on the back.

"I'm really pissed you're here," Alan said, his voice strained with emotion. "But it's great to see you, man."

Jonas pulled back, staring at his brother. It really was him. The Waking World reality rushed back in, strengthened by Alan's presence. The edges grew clearer, and Jonas was beside himself, grateful to have found his brother. *Finally.*

"I've looked for you…for almost a year. I searched the entire Dreamscape. And you've been here the whole time," Jonas said. "It's my fault, isn't it?"

"No," Alan said, shaking his head. "Of course not. When I died in the dream…that could have been the end. But you tunneled me out. My consciousness couldn't get back to my body. It kept me here." Alan smiled. "I'm still alive, man. And that's because of you."

"But you're trapped," Jonas said.

Alan shrugged. "Well, *we're* trapped."

"We have to find my girlfriend," Jonas said. "And soon. Because there's this scientist who's going to wake me up, and—"

"*We,*" Alan repeated with a chuckle, indicating he wasn't talking about him and Jonas. He turned back to the building waiting. Jonas felt his heart skip.

"Is Sam with you?" he asked. Jonas rushed inside the doorframe, and it took a moment for his eyes to adjust to the low light. But then, over by the distant window, he saw Sam, staring out.

Jonas was flooded with relief and called her name.

"Alan?" she responded, looking over dreamily. Her eyes focused on Jonas, and then—seeming alarmed—she got to her feet, steadying herself on the wall.

"I know you," she said. "You're—"

She paused, and Jonas could see her trying to work it out in her head.

"Aw, come on, Sam," Alan said, walking in, and throwing his arm over Jonas's shoulders. "This is my little brother. You know—the one you told me about when you got here?"

Sam furrowed her brow, hesitating. Unlike Alan, she wasn't acclimated to the new environment. She looked too thin and drawn.

Jonas felt sick to his stomach, and his brother looked sideways at him, sympathetic.

"She's confused," Alan murmured. "We looked for an escape, a door, but it's always moving. She waited for you, man." Alan swallowed hard. "Said you'd come. But it's been a long time, Jonas. Feels like years. I'm not entirely clear on how Samantha got here, but the trauma of it... I think maybe she was dead too long. She doesn't seem to have a clear connection to her body. And I'm worried what'll happen if she stays here any longer."

"Poet?" Sam said from across the room, her green narrowed. "You're Poet Anderson?"

Jonas was unsure why she was calling him by that name in this place, but it at least meant she knew who he was. "Yeah," he said with a quick smile.

Samantha walked toward him, exchanging a look with Alan before pausing in front of Jonas. She ran her eyes over him. "Good," she said finally. "Then you must be here to get us out."

Jonas nodded that he was, and he half-expected her to reach out for him, but he saw she didn't quite remember him anymore. His heart ached, and he could only hope the Waking World would make it all flood back. Sam turned to Alan.

"I saw another one of those shadows from the window," she told Alan. "We have to move higher."

"Shadows?" Jonas interrupted.

"Yeah," Alan said, running his hand through his blond hair. "There are these creatures—you don't want to fuck with them. I've seen them devour at least a dozen people already. Now it's just us. And they—"

"I know what they are," Jonas said, as the memory of Sketch flooded back to him. He swallowed his grief and disgust, trying to stay focused. "We have to get out, but I have no power here." He held out his hand as if to prove it. "Is there anywhere that you've found that's...that's connected to the Dream World in any way?"

"No," Sam said. "And we can't find a door out either. So if you—"

Alan shifted, seeming to realize something. "There's one place," he said. "Hair standing on end, a buzz on the skin. I went there once. I'm not sure how, but I crossed over into the Dreamscape. I couldn't maintain the connection, though."

"You were in the Dream World?" Jonas asked, upset. How had he missed him? He'd searched for so long.

"I ended up in the woods where I died," Alan said, his blue eyes growing heavy with grief. "And he was there, Jonas. REM was there, and I could see him with his army. There were more, and he—he had changed. So much stronger. I could feel it radiate across the land, energy making rocks and sticks hover over the ground. And then, suddenly, I was gone from that place. Pulled somewhere else where I talked to a woman." He furrowed his brow. "Is that who found you? That woman I spoke to?"

"The evil scientist who killed my girlfriend?" Jonas asked. "Yep. She was super helpful."

"I told her to find you. Warned you about REM. And then...I was sucked back into the void."

"Whatever you did worked," Jonas said. "And I think that's our way out."

Alan scrunched up his face. "Yeah," he allowed. "I have no idea how I crossed. And there's a reason I haven't been back there—it's also where the shadows come from."

"Awesome," Jonas muttered. "Well, if there's energy there from the Dream World, I could open a tunnel. Or Mariana reviving me might give me the energy I need if it doesn't." He turned toward the door, and then looked back at Sam. "You said you saw a shadow out there. Is there just one?"

"For now," she replied. "There will be more tonight."

"Alan," he said. When his brother looked at him, Jonas was once again flooded with relief. Made whole. He smiled. "Damn, I've missed you," he said.

"I know," Alan said. "I could hear you next to my bed. Man, you talk a lot."

Jonas laughed. "All right, lead the way. It's time to get the fuck out of here."

Alan went to the door to check to see if there was any movement, and then he motioned them ahead. The three crossed the street and walked down an alley that Jonas hadn't noticed before.

A fog clung to the pavement, seeming to deeper the further they got into the alley. Jonas had a moment of worry that the shadows could creep under the tufts of white, and he checked back on Sam, who staring straight ahead, determined.

He wanted so much to ask if she knew him, but there wasn't time for that. Jonas had to get them out of there. At this point, he no idea how long he'd been dead. He had no idea if he'd ever wake up again, in fact. What was to make Mariana keep her word?

Alan studied the buildings, looking for a particular one. "If you try to walk out," he said, "you'll just end up at the start." He got about halfway down the alley, and motioned to a fire escape ladder that went up at least forty stories, all the way to top of the stone skyscraper. The ladder itself had patches of rust. "Which is why we go up."

Jonas lifted his eyes, but the roofline was nearly too high to see. "What happens if we fall?" he asked. "Can you die here?"

Alan sniffed a laugh. "Yeah, dude," he said. "We're not dead—at least not yet. So don't fall."

Samantha smiled, and touched Jonas's shoulder as she moved past him and jumped to grab the bottom rung of the ladder. Jonas watched her, stunned by her touch. The lingering feel of her energy. It took him a moment to catch his breath.

Samantha began climbing first, and Jonas followed behind Alan. The metal ladder was freezing to the touch, bits of rusted metal flaking off with each step. It certainly wasn't the most sturdy for a life-depending escape.

"This is where you went to contact Mariana?" Jonas asked.

"Not on purpose," Alan replied. "I was trying to get back to the Dream World, and I made it. Sort of. Half there, half here, I guess. I was in our field." Alan paused a moment, looking back at Jonas. "The one with the tree by our house."

Jonas still remembered the tree, and it made him suddenly nostalgic. It was a common place the Anderson brothers would go to in their dreams. A meeting place.

Alan started climbing again. "Anyway," he said. "She appeared, and she looked kind of stunned, to be honest. I guess she was drawn to me."

"Most girls are," Jonas commented, and Alan laughed.

"Yeah, sure. Well, when I felt myself fading from the Dream World, getting pulled back here, I told the woman she had to find you. I was worried you'd end up here with me." He sniffed a laugh. "If we get out of here, then I'm glad I told her. Otherwise, I seriously miscalculated your response. I guess you just have a death wish."

"And if we don't get out?" Jonas asked.

"Let's just say we will."

"Fair enough," Jonas replied. He glanced past his shoes to the ground at least ten stories below. The fog had thickened, reaching the final rung of the ladder. It made Jonas uneasy, and he gulped and began climbing again.

"I could always hear you, you know," Alan said seriously. He paused to glance down at his brother. "Even here, lost in this place. At night, lying in one the buildings, eyes shut, I could hear you on the other side. It was faint, but that's what kept me connected to the waking reality."

His eyes gathered tears, and Alan quickly sniffled and started to climb again. Jonas watched after him, touched that his brother had heard him all this time. That he had never left him.

The higher they climbed, the harder the wind blew, whipping Alan's hair back and forth.

"You doing okay?" Sam asked, glancing down. Jonas was about to answer when he realized she was talking to Alan. When his brother said he was, Sam smiled, and kept going. Her eyes didn't even drift in Jonas's direction.

There was a flash through Jonas's body—a jolt of electricity. He flinched, one hand slipping off the rung before he could grab on. He saw a small spark leave his fingers, and then it was gone. He looked up at Alan, who watched him wide-eyed.

"Your power," Alan said. "You're getting it back. You'll be able to tunnel us out of here."

"Come on," Sam yelled from around the fifteenth floor. Her voice echoed and bounced off the buildings.

But Alan watched Jonas a moment longer, as if he sensed his jealousy. Then he turned and, without a word, began climbing. Dirt from his boot would occasionally slip off the ladder and fall on Jonas's arms.

It was at around the twentieth floor that Jonas started to get dizzy. Like everything else in this reality, things were hyper-realized. The sounds were louder, the cold colder, the heights higher. Jonas knew his senses were heightened here. Did that include emotions? And if so, what did that mean for Alan and Sam?

A gust of wind blew over him, and his hands began to shake in the icy air.

Jonas leaned to the side to check on Sam's progress, how close she was to the top. Her hair was dusted in snow, her skin tinted blue. She seemed tired; each pull-up, each push from her sneaker was an effort. She paused to catch her breath— difficult to do at this height.

"You're doing great," he called up to her, trying to sound encouraging, but realizing he sounded desperate instead. Sam glanced down at him, the tip of her nose red, and laughed.

"Sure," she said. "I'm only half frozen."

Jonas smiled, but it was difficult. His skin was tight from the cold.

"Keep moving," Alan announced, reminding them of the task. Part of Jonas also wondered if the interruption had to do with Sam, but he quickly pushed that thought away. None of that shit mattered right now. The only thing that mattered was getting out of here.

A vibration struck the ladder, and Sam screamed. Alan yelled out as he nearly slipped off. Once he gripped the rung again, he looked down past Jonas and cursed. Jonas followed his line of sight and cursed.

At the bottom of the ladder, convening in the alleyway, was a group of shadows, splitting and combining, writhing. Half a dozen of them, possibly.

They'd been spotted.

"Climb!" Alan shouted, and Sam started moving quickly.

Jonas was still for a moment, staring transfixed into the heart of the creatures. It was like a pile of black scorpions combining, a thousand black holes devouring each other. It was pure evil, Jonas thought, in its truest form.

The ladder vibrated again, and this time, a bolt came loose and a section of ladder below became unattached from the building. Jonas quickly turned and began scrambling up the ladder.

The wind blew harder, and his fingers were going numb. There was another rattle, and Jonas saw that one of the shadows had taken on a form—a human-like form with an entire face of sharp teeth. It clung to the wall, digging its nails into the stone as made its way up.

We'll never make it, Jonas thought. He'd seen what these creatures did to Sketch. And if one of those things got to him…Mariana would be waking up a shadow person instead of him.

Jonas looked up and saw that Sam was only a few floors away. The sky looked different; snow fell freely, and she shivered, her entire upper body jerking with the movement.

"What is this place?" Jonas yelled to Alan, his teeth chattering. "Where are you taking us?"

"I like to imagine it's the edge—the line between realities," Alan said. "I think that's why there's power here."

One of the creatures was getting closer, while another was yanking on the ladder, trying to free it from the building.

Jonas swayed with relief when he saw Sam crest the top and climb onto the roof. She reappeared and began to yell for them to hurry, slapping her hand on the wall.

Jonas's head started to hurt, and his chest tightened. He winced and tried to focus on getting to the roof, but he could feel a pull from the Waking World. His body seized, and he quickly looped his arm around a rung so he wouldn't fall. Electricity shot through his body.

Mariana was trying to revive him.

"Are you okay?" Alan called, concerned. Jonas regained his composure. His skin was hot with electricity, the flakes of ice melting the moment they touched him.

"Keep going," Jonas said, keeping the pain out of his voice. He had to open a tunnel for them. He had to get to the roof.

Alan got to the top, and hopped over, holding out his hand for Jonas, who was still two floors below.

"Come on, brother," Alan called. "You've got to hurry."

Jonas looked up, and Sam came to stand next to Alan, staring down at Jonas with concern. She put her hand on Alan's shoulder.

Jonas flinched, and then suddenly he was struck with another volt of electricity, blacking out for just a moment— and the ladder begin to slip from his fingers. He was going to fall.

"Poet!" Sam screamed.

Jonas gasped, and when he looked up, he saw Sam watching him, her eyes wide with terror. Her lips parted.

Jonas grabbed the ladder to steady himself, and as he did, he saw he was wearing his sleek black suit.

He'd become Poet Anderson.

Poet saw the creatures racing up behind him; they would only have a moment by the time he got to the roof. Poet quickly ascended, no longer cold. The snow didn't touch him. Whatever Mariana was doing in the Waking World was working. The energy surged through him.

Finally near the top, Alan held out his hand again, and Poet took it and let Alan help him over the ledge. Alan's skin was ice cold; frost had formed on his eyelashes.

Sam breathed a sigh of relief and wrapped herself around Poet, burying her face at his neck. Poet closed his eyes, grateful to have made it. There was a snap behind him, and Poet spun to see the ladder shaking, the creatures nearly up to them.

"I don't know what to do!" Alan called. "Last time, there was a door, and—"

Poet Anderson called up all his power—stronger here in this strange space on the roof, stronger because of the electricity jolting him in the Waking World. There was only sky above them; no sun, moon, or stars. There was nothingness. And so Poet let the energy turn his eyes bright white, and a bolt of lightning struck the roof, followed by a heavy rumble. Poet Anderson threw his head back and felt the electricity rush through him like a lightning rod.

He opened a tunnel above them, and just as Alan and Sam were sucked in, Jonas gasped awake in a hospital bed.

HIS BODY JOLTED FORWARD, every muscle tensing at once. He garbled out a scream and collapsed back on the bed. There was a thudding in his chest, and it took Jonas a moment to realize it was his heart beating again. It was a weird sensation, noticing it had been gone until now.

"He's awake," he heard a woman say. Jonas rolled his head to the side and saw the midsection of a person in a white uniform—a nurse. He was too exhausted to speak, though. The woman forced an oxygen mask over his mouth.

His eyes rolled back in his head, and he tried to reach up to pull off the mask, but his coordination was off, and he couldn't quite get his fingers to work. He looked next to him, but Sam's body was gone.

"Oh, my God! He's awake!" the woman shouted, more urgently.

Jonas tried to look at her again, wanting to tell her he would be fine, but she was no longer next to him. The nurse was across the room with a silhouette Jonas guessed was Mariana.

He dipped out of consciousness again, and when he came to, he saw nurses and a doctor at the other bed, working frantically. He couldn't understand what they were doing.

But then a nurse moved aside, and Jonas saw his brother, lying there with his eyes open, staring at the ceiling.

CHAPTER FIFTEEN

ALAN ANDERSON WAS AWAKE. JONAS ached from head to toe, but mostly in his chest, where it felt like he'd been punched repeatedly and then dropped from a cliff. His ribs were bruised; one was cracked. There was nothing he could do but rest.

He shared a room with Alan, but both brothers had been in and out of consciousness for the past few hours.

It seemed dying took a lot out of you.

Jonas had asked about Sam several times, but the nurse told him she'd been moved to the main hospital. He didn't know what that meant—was she in a coma? Was she still stuck on that roof?

Jonas blinked quickly, unsure of how much time had passed since he left the void. He forced himself to sit up, wincing at the sharp pain in his right side. He gripped the bed frame.

"Alan," he called. He was happy to see his brother didn't have any tubes hooked up to him. He looked like shit for sure, but he was doing it all on his own. "Alan," Jonas repeated.

Alan's eyelids fluttered, and then he groaned. Before he looked over at Jonas, he said, "Worst. Year. Ever."

Jonas snorted a laugh, and Alan opened one eye and turned to look at him. He said he was having trouble focusing, and that maybe lack of use had left his eyes weak.

"You probably don't want to think about your dick, then," Jonas said, and Alan laughed so hard he began to cough and had to press the call button for the nurse.

As Alan's fit calmed, the nurse helped Jonas to the bathroom, his muscles cramping and uncramping, perhaps from the adrenaline or the shock. When he returned to the room, his brother was sitting up in his bed, pillows tucked neatly behind him. He sat stiffly, like a Tin Man, and every so often he'd outstretch his arm and turn it.

"It worked," Jonas said, smiling. The nurses had left, and the two brothers could finally talk without interruption. "And Sam, she…she got out okay, right?"

Alan pressed his pale lips together. "Yeah, man. She was first one in."

Jonas sighed his relief and let himself fall back on the pillow, moaning out in pain when he did. He'd done terrible things over the past few days, unforgivable things, but he opted not to think about them. He'd fought so long for this moment right here. He looked over at Alan again.

"I've missed you," Jonas said. "It's been a hell of a year without you."

"I'm sure. But, hey—seems you're doing all right for yourself. To be honest, better than I expected. I mean, I knew you were cool, Jonas, but a fucking poet? What the shit? Here

I thought I was raising a typical slacker. Turns out you're going to save the world."

Jonas smiled, comforted by Alan's brand of optimism, his ability to always find hope in a bad situation. He'd missed that optimism.

"And your girlfriend is pretty awesome," Alan added. "No idea how that worked out for you."

Jonas grinned. "Sure you do."

Alan laughed. "Yes, Jonas. I'm sure you blew her mind. But, seriously, I'm sorry I tried to kill her last year."

"You were possessed. I doubt she holds it against you." Jonas turned to stare up at the ceiling. Something was gnawing at him, but he didn't want to bring it up. It seemed petty. "So...." he said anyway. "How long were you and Sam together in that place? She was only out a few hours here."

"I don't know," Alan said. "Seemed like forever."

"And she forgot all about me?" Jonas asked, trying the hide the insecurity in his voice.

"Not entirely," Alan said. "And...she died, man. It wasn't like you didn't matter to her or something. She was in a perpetual state of death-shock."

Jonas tried to accept that explanation, but it still bothered him. "Did you two...I mean, did you like her? Did she like you?" He felt Alan staring at him, and after a moment he turned to him.

"What are you asking me, Jonas? If I was hooking up with your girl?"

Jonas wavered. "Not exactly. But, I mean...you guys were dead. Then you were in a coma. Regular rules don't apply, right?"

"No," Alan said more seriously than Jonas had asked. "It wasn't like that. I helped her survive and dodge shadows. She helped me keep my sanity. We were a good team."

Jonas nodded like he could believe it was true. He swallowed hard. "Now that you're back, though," he continued, lowering his eyes, "maybe the two of you... It's just—I always thought she was the right girl for you. Like the two of you were meant—"

"Stop," Alan said.

"No, I'm serious," Jonas said. "When I met her, it really pissed me off because, if you were around, she would have picked you. You would have picked her. On paper, the two of you—"

"I said stop," Alan replied dryly.

"But she's exactly your type."

Alan laughed. "She's not my type, Jonas. I don't fall for girls in love with my little brother. Stop trying to sabotage the one good thing you have going for you."

Jonas sat quietly for a moment, and then looked over at Alan. "Hey," he said. "I have a job too."

Alan cracked up. "Okay, one of two things you have going. Now stop being an asshole and get out of that bed to check on Sam. I don't care how many of your ribs are broken."

"What about you?" Jonas asked.

"Well, first I'm going to check on my dick now that you've got me worried, and then I'm going to get some rest and schedule physical therapy. The doctor said I probably won't be able to walk for a while. I have to rebuild my muscles." He held up his arm with effort, and the bones in his shoulder stuck out prominently. "Look how scrawny I am," he said. "When the hell did I turn into Jonas Anderson?"

"Fuck you," Jonas said and pulled himself up by the metal bar on the bed. Everything hurt. He imagined it would for a while. He grabbed the prescribed painkillers off the side table, and went to the closet and found his clothes, carefully buttoning his work shirt but leaving off the jacket. He pulled on his pants, and slipped his sockless feet into his shoes, wincing with every movement. He doubted he was supposed to leave, but he dared anyone to stop him.

"Bring me back some clothes," Alan said. "And none of the shit you'd wear either."

"Yeah, yeah," Jonas said, reaching out to steady himself on the door frame. He needed an aspirin. Maybe the whole bottle. He waited a moment and then looked back at Alan. "I'll see you in a bit?" he asked.

Alan smiled, and for a moment the two brothers stared at each other.

Alan was back.

"Give me a few hours," Alan said. "And bring me a cheeseburger on your way back in."

Jonas promised he would, and although the doctors would probably want him to rest too, he walked out of the room. He stopped at reception, asking about Mariana, but the receptionist said she was gone for the day. Jonas would be sure to see her later, but for now he left the Sleep Center, and hopped the bus to the hospital in hopes of finding Sam.

• •

JONAS STOPPED AT THE nurses' desk in the ICU at the hospital. "Samantha Birnham-Wood," he said. The nurse glanced up at him like she was ready to argue, but she must have seen in his expression how worried he was because she pointed down the hallway.

"Room 367. She's awake now."

He thanked the nurse before jogging toward Sam's room, his shoes skidding on the shiny floors. He almost ran past the door, but doubled back when he heard his name. His heart swelled. He took two steps and looked inside the room.

Samantha sat up in bed, an untouched tray of food next to her. She tried to smile, but she looked drawn and Jonas was reminded of what she'd just gone through for him.

"Well?" she asked, her voice hoarse. "Did it work?"

"Yeah," Jonas said. "It did. Alan's awake."

"Oh, thank God," Sam said, running her hand through her hair. "Last thing I remember was getting a sedative and kissing you goodbye. They told me I've been in a medically induced coma. And my chest is killing me." She rubbed the area over her heart,

"That's because she literally killed you and held your body hostage. But I helped bring you back."

"Am I a zombie?" she joked. "Because you're looking kind of delicious."

Jonas smiled, his face flushing. "Aw, come on, Miss Birnham-Wood. Don't pretend you like me for my brains."

She laughed, and told him to come closer. He did, leaning over her bed and wincing as his ribs protested the movement.

He kissed her softly; her lips were dry, but warm. Unlike the last time he touched her.

Jonas grabbed a chair and slid it over to the bed to sit next to her. Sam rested back against the pillows, looking exhausted.

"So you don't remember anything from the void?" he asked.

She took a moment to think it over, and then shook her head. "No," she said. She studied him. "You're hurt," she said. "How the hell did you end up getting me out?"

"Things didn't go as planned at first," he said. "I had to go in and get you."

"You died for me?" she asked.

"Yeah, well, I was returning the favor."

She smiled. "But we're all good now, right? In the end, it worked out?"

"It did."

"Finally," she said. "Some good news. But hey, have you heard from my father?" she asked. "The nurse said she couldn't reach him. I think my stepmother is on her way in."

Jonas swallowed hard. "Um...yeah," he said. "I, uh...saw him before I went to find you in the void." He felt sick. Telling her what happened would destroy her. It would make what he did real. Jonas lifted his eyes to Sam's and her concern visibly grew.

"Sam..." he started, and he saw her eyes widen, knowing he was about to devastate her. "Sam, your dad is gone."

Sam gripped the metal bars of her bed, and pulled herself up.

"What do you mean?" she demanded. "Out of town?" But the shaking in her voice told him that she knew what he meant.

"I'm so sorry," Jonas said, swallowing hard. "He died last night."

"Oh, my God," she said. "Oh, my God—what?" She put her hand to her throat, her face contorting with pain.

She reached for Jonas, and he wrapped both arms around her, ignoring the screaming in his ribs. Sam cried against his shirt, and Jonas was at once grief- and guilt-stricken. He was a monster for comforting her now. He knew he had to tell her. He just wasn't sure how.

There was a quick rap on the door, and both Jonas and Sam looked up to see Callum leaning against the frame. To him, it must have looked like they were in an embrace.

"Christ, you two," he said. "I've been looking everywhere for you." He smiled. "This is good," he said to Sam. "I'm guessing you're not mad that our Poet killed your father."

CHAPTER SIXTEEN

IT WAS LIKE ALL THE AIR HAD BEEN SUCKED out of the room at once. Sam gasped out a sound, pulling away from Jonas, not looking at him.

"What?" she asked Callum in an unsteady voice. "What did you just say?"

He bit on his lip and looked at Jonas for a little help. "Ay, I'm sorry, mate. I thought…"

"Sam," Jonas said softly, reaching to touch her arm. Sam pulled back violently from him, banging her elbow hard on the bed and crying out in pain before turning her anger on him. "Tell me he's lying," she demanded, "Tell me Callum is a lying asshole right now."

"I'd hardly say I deserve that," Callum replied.

"Get out!" she screamed at him so loudly that her voice cracked. Jonas jumped at the ferocity of it. Callum tipped the brim of his hat in a goodbye, and strode out without another word.

The room was silent. Jonas stared at Sam, just wishing she'd look at him so he could explain. He watched as her eyes filled with tears, and when she blinked, they fell on her cheek and ran down.

"Did you kill my father, Jonas?" she asked.

"Yes," he answered.

She whimpered, and it was like a pile of bricks fell on him. The pain in her face—that loss—was palpable. She may have been angry with her father, even hated him, but he was her *father*. He was the only family she had in the world. She was alone now—an orphan, just like Jonas.

"What did you do?" she asked in a whisper. Jonas was sure she could read his guilt. Even if he did it to save her, he had killed her father. He struck the deal.

"Mariana Santiago," Jonas started. "She wouldn't wake you up. She tricked us, Sam. She never intended to get Alan. Not with you. She planned to leave you stranded there, and in return for your life, I had to kill Alexander. I—"

"No," Sam said, pained. "No, Jonas. What have you done?"

"Please," he said, reaching for her again. But she wouldn't let him touch her. She looked up at him with a betrayed expression. "I did it to save you," he said.

"You could have found another way," she said. "You know that."

He shook his head. "Not this time. I told Alexander. I told him about Mariana, and he called me a coward when I wouldn't kill him. He lashed out. He said you deserved better."

"He hurt your feelings," she said. "So you murdered him?"

"It wasn't like that," Jonas pleaded for her to understand. "Yes, I went there to kill him, but then I couldn't do it. He made me. He knew you didn't have much time. He wanted me to save you."

"He wanted you to be smarter," she said, and then covered her face with both hands, crying quietly. Jonas sat miserably next to the bed, knowing that, in some way, Sam was right. There might have been another way. He had just been too desperate to search for it.

"I'm sorry," Jonas whispered. "I love you and I'm so sorry."

"Just leave me alone for now," she said from behind her hands.

Jonas was about to argue, but Sam curled up on her side, facing away from him. Her shoulders rocked as she mourned her father—a rich socialite prick who willingly gave up his life to save hers.

"I'll, um…" Jonas said, standing and feeling like his heart was on the floor. "I'll check on you later, okay?"

Sam didn't speak, and Jonas wished he could make it better, make it hurt less. But he knew that what he'd done might be unforgivable.

JONAS WENT BACK TO the hotel, and after feeling sorry for himself in his empty room, caught between crying and screaming, he decided to go downstairs to see if he could pick up a shift. Anything to block out his thoughts.

Hillenbrand was working, but he was more than happy to take a few hours off. He'd already covered Jonas's shifts that week, and he told him to enjoy, not even commenting on Jonas's condition.

Jonas Anderson stood in his suit and bowler hat, waiting at the door of the Eden Hotel. The night was crisp and cold, but at least it wasn't raining. He had no control over the weather in the Waking World.

The door opened, and Jonas quickly leapt to attention, wincing once at the tightness in his chest, to grab the handle so the person could walk out. He froze when he saw it was Marshall. His boss eyed him, clearly surprised he was there, but he paused on the sidewalk to speak with him.

"I hear your brother's awake," Marshall said, buttoning his heavy wool overcoat. "Should I expect him here looking for a job soon?"

"Technically, this was his job," Jonas said. "You should fire me and give it to him."

Marshall watched him a long moment, trying to figure out what was going on.

"Look, Mr. Anderson," he started. "I'm not sure where this fatalist attitude has come from, and, believe me, I'm really not here to find out, but you are my employee. And when you show up, you actually do a decent job. Turns out hotel folks love a handsome, brooding boy. If your brother wants a job, he'll have to apply like everyone else. I'm no longer in the business of giving charity to the Anderson family."

He stopped then, a small flash of sympathy in his expression. "I did hear about Alexander," Marshall said, and Jonas lifted his head, alarmed. Did Marshall know what happened to him?

"Oh, uh..."

"Samantha called earlier," Marshall continued. "Said he died of complications from pneumonia. The Dream World is saying something different, but I know better than to take the world of Dreams at face value." Marshall took out a pair of leather gloves and slipped them onto his hands. "I expect an explanation in the morning," he added. "I imagine she'll be taking over control of the hotel?"

"I don't know," Jonas said. He honestly didn't.

"I guess it'll be something to discuss when she returns. She tells me she's been in the hospital, as well. I assume that can account for your absence?"

Jonas nodded, feeling sick, and Marshall started to walk away, but paused.

"If you need to take the night off," he said. "I'll give you a pass. You look awful."

"No, I have to work," Jonas replied. "But thank you."

Marshall smiled as if he respected his choice, but quickly straightened his expression. He slipped his hands into the pockets of his coat and began whistling, as he walked down the dark Seattle street.

THE EVENING AT THE hotel was slow, with only a few guests arriving. Every so often, Jonas would have to go inside and warm up, but ultimately he liked the cold. He liked the numbness of his skin.

After a few hours, Hillenbrand came back, smelling slightly of booze. He'd probably had a drink or two, knowing that Marshall was gone for the night. He thanked Jonas for picking up the shift.

Jonas went inside the hotel, nodding at the receptionist as he got in the elevator and went to his floor. Everything seemed quieter tonight. Or maybe he just felt alone. Painfully alone.

He got in the room and kicked off his shoes, then paused to look around. As he stood in the middle of the suite, the emptiness rolled over him. He sat down on the couch, took out his phone, and called the Sleep Center.

"Alan Anderson," he said, rubbing the inner corners of his eyes. There was a series of clicks, and then the nurse picked up.

"Is this Jonas?" she asked pleasantly.

"Yeah."

"Hi, honey. Alan isn't here right now. He said he'd be back later this evening. His progress has been phenomenal. He's using his cane, and walked right out by himself. We all just about cried." She was being so sweet, but Jonas furrowed his brow and leaned forward on the couch. Why wouldn't Alan call him? Was he on his way here?

"Do you know where he went?" he asked.

"Sorry, I don't. I'll let him know you called."

Jonas thanked her and hung up.

He reached over and grabbed the bottle of pills he'd set aside from the doctor. His pain was inching upward, and, although he'd tried to ignore it earlier, it was too much now. He took two, rested his head back on the sofa, and watched the door.

Would Samantha come back here? Was what he did unforgivable? Alexander wanted him to do it—he'd baited him. And sure, it was Jonas's fault that Sam went in to find Alan in the first place, but again...he loved her. She would see that. She'd see that and forgive him.

Jonas had a small twinge of doubt, and he reached for his phone again and called the hospital. He gave the operator Sam's room number and then closed his eyes, both terrified and longing to hear her voice. The line began to ring.

"Hello?"

Jonas's eyes flew open, and he sat up, wincing at the pain in his ribs when he did. "Alan?" he asked. His brother's voice was unmistakable. "What are you—are you with Sam?"

"No," he said in a deep sigh. "She's meeting with her father's estate attorney and her stepmother. She, uh...she told me what Callum said. What you admitted. I told her there's more to the story, and I'm all fucking ears, brother, if you're ready to spill it now."

Jonas felt a lash of shame, and then anger. He didn't like it that Alan was taking Sam's side, that he was there with her instead of him.

"Why are you there?" Jonas asked, ignoring Alan's earlier comment.

"Because she died," Alan said like the question was stupid. "I called to check on her and she asked me to come by. She told me what happened. And then the attorney showed up, said business needed to be settled immediately, as Alexander's final request. You'd think the lawyer would have some compassion."

"Alexander didn't deal in compassion, so I doubt any of his cohorts would."

"Did the two of you not get along?" Alan asked. "Because, Jonas, if this was really about some sort of payback—"

"He was a Dream Walker," Jonas snapped. "In case Samantha didn't tell you that part. He's the reason we're in Seattle. He called us here to keep an eye on us, manipulating the entire situation. He has no moral compass. He took out his soul to be a Dream Walker. So don't make it out like I spoiled that relationship."

Alan was quiet for a moment, and Jonas immediately regretted snapping at him. Of course Alan had his back—he always did.

"Why would he bring us to Seattle?" Alan asked.

"Because he knew Mom. And he was there when she died." Jonas felt a pit open in his stomach when he talked about his parents' death.

"He was on the plane?" Alan asked.

"No," Jonas said. "Mom didn't die on that plane. Alan... Mom was a Dream Walker too."

"What?" his brother said, his voice echoing off the line. "Are you sure?"

"Yeah. Look," Jonas said, "I have so much to tell you. Obviously, you weren't listening that closely when I was at your bedside. Want to come to the Eden? You can crash with me. I don't think... I doubt Sam's coming here tonight."

"I don't think she is either," Alan agreed sympathetically. The admission stung Jonas, but he didn't want to bring it up over the phone. And the truth was, he'd missed his brother desperately. He just wanted him there.

Alan got the room number from Jonas, and told him the first thing he wanted to do when he got there was take a long shower. He said he was on his way over.

Jonas clicked off the phone, and stood up to stretch, groaning. He undid his white shirt and changed into some sweats. He called downstairs and asked them to send up two cheeseburgers. Extra fries. He also asked for a bucket of beers, but the front desk was on to him and told him no. Jonas sniffed a laugh, and got some Cokes instead.

There was a knock at the door a short time later, and Jonas jumped up. "That was fast," he said, swinging open the door. But instead of Alan, he found Callum. The poet shrugged an apology.

"I hope I didn't ruin things for you," he said. "I just figured that'd be the first thing you told her. Like, 'I'm sorry Samantha, love, but I brutally murdered your father.'"

"You were there," Jonas snapped. "You know it didn't go down like that."

"Maybe," Callum said with a sweet smile. "Can I come in?" he asked, nodding into the room.

Jonas sighed, debating saying no, but ultimately, he was curious about why Callum was there.

"And can you put a shirt on, Anderson?" Callum said, going to the couch. "Your bruises and protruding bones are making me feel weird."

Jonas murmured how much he hated him, and went to grab a soft T-shirt from the drawer. He pulled it roughly over his head, ignoring his body's protests at the movement, and sat in the chair facing Callum.

"What do you want?" Jonas asked. "Haven't you done enough today?"

"Not quite," he said. "I need your help. It's a small task, really."

"Then why would you need my help?"

Callum smiled and leaned in. "Because you're Poet Anderson. Everyone wants to meet you. I just need you to come to the Dream World with me for a moment." He waved his hand. "I need you to get me inside a club to meet with a very hard-to-reach Dream. She'll like you. She'll let us in."

"What are you talking about?" Jonas asked. "Why would I do that? I can't fucking stand you right now."

"Because," Callum said, crossing his ankle over his knee as he sat back confidently, "she knows where I can get my hands on a shadow. I'd like to kill it."

Jonas wanted to destroy the shadows too. They'd killed Sketch. And he saw them again in the void with Alan and Sam. "How many are there?" Jonas asked, looking over at Callum seriously.

"Don't know yet," he said. "But I'd like to kill one first. Get a taste for it, you see. Will you help me? Swear," he crossed his heart, "twenty minutes tops. Back before you know it."

Jonas had so much anger rolling around inside of him— there was no place to safely let it out. He didn't want to yell at his brother, or demand Sam listen to his apologies. So he'd take it out on a shadow. He could work with that.

"Fine," Jonas said. "But we have to be back before my brother arrives."

"Oh, the famed Alan Anderson is alive and well, then? How nice. He's staying here with you and Samantha— third-wheeling it?" Callum looked around the room, and Jonas shook his head.

"Are we going or not?" Jonas asked. Truth was, the pain meds had already started to make him drowsy. He'd gladly slip away for a little while.

"Yes, yes," Callum said easily, getting up from the couch. "I'll meet you there."

And then, as if there was an unseen door, Callum stepped forward and dissolved, disappearing into the Dream World.

CHAPTER SEVENTEEN

POET ANDERSON OPENED HIS EYES AND found himself in a part of Genesis he'd never seen before—something he hadn't thought was possible. As a poet, he could find dreamers—sense them and go to them. He'd done it with Callum, although it was an entirely different feeling, a draw to power.

"Took you long enough," Callum said, walking out from an alley. The streets in this part of town weren't nearly so busy, and Poet walked over to join him as they started toward a bridge. "Meant to tell you," Callum said. "We're not *exactly* staying in this Dream World."

"What?" Poet asked.

"It's okay," Callum said, as if he was overreacting. "We'll still be in dreams." He paused in the middle of the street, and Poet turned to face him. "Just not these ones." Callum waved his hand and a tunnel began to open between them. The wind blew across Poet's face, and he had to hold onto his hat.

"What do you mean *this* Dream World?" he asked, having to speak up over the sound of the wind.

"You didn't think there was just one, did you?" Callum asked with a grin. "Come now, mate. Why only two realities? There are multitudes. More than even I've seen."

Poet opened his mouth to answer, to immediately deny it, but yeah, it kind of made sense. But...he didn't fully understand what it meant. He lifted his hand, about to ask a follow-up question, when Callum stepped into the tunnel and disappeared.

The tunnel still spun, and Poet cursed and looked around. He could leave this dream and wait for Alan in the hotel, but part of him was insatiably curious where this tunnel would lead. He'd never been to another dream reality—he had to see it. So he walked into the tunnel and felt himself get swept away.

The first thing Poet noticed when he could focus on his new surroundings was the light. The softness of it—a hazy, sexy filter that clung to everything. The way the air tickled his skin. The smell of candle wax.

He turned quickly to look around, his eyes everywhere at once. It was nighttime, but little sparks floated around, like fireflies—pure energy in the air. Poet ran his hand through them, and sparks clung to his skin. This place was soaked in power.

"Careful," Callum said, coming up behind him. "This reality can be addicting."

Poet turned to look at him, thinking dreamily that he was handsome for an asshole poet. He laughed to himself, and turned away. "What's happening to me?" he asked.

"Probably a hard-on, but other than that? This is a new dreamscape—one of my personal favorites." Callum paused. "Even if I've been banished from here."

"Why do I feel like this?" Poet asked, running his hand over his cheek, down his own neck. He noticed a group of women crossing the street down by a warehouse building. One looked in his direction and Poet felt his heart beat faster. She smiled, and she was beautiful. She looked just like Samantha.

"That's the thing," Callum said, ducking his head so the girls wouldn't see his face. "It's not real... At least, not the way you're seeing it. Dig down, Poet. Ground yourself in the reality—not just what the sirens want you to see."

"Sirens?" Poet asked. And the girl who was smiling at him began to change. Her brown hair grew silvery and long, and her green eyes became the color of pale smoke, wisps of it reaching out toward him, beckoning him. She smiled again, and licked her lips—her tongue was forked at the end.

Poet blinked quickly, and lowered his head to talk to Callum. "What the hell is going on?" he asked quietly. "Who...*what* is that?"

"I told you," Callum said. "A siren. They populate this reality, alongside dreamers. They tend to take on a look that's most pleasing to you. They're manipulative little things, so be careful. Just make sure you see them how they really are—it's the only way to make sure you don't get sucked in. They can be persuasive."

Poet straightened his jacket, and by the time he looked back, the women were gone. There was an open door and music coming from inside the building. A man walked out, standing guard. He was bulky, and he crossed his huge arms over his chest. Poet gulped and turned to Callum.

"Why are we here?"

"I need to get inside there," Callum said, motioning to the building where the women disappeared. "There's a siren I need to talk to."

"And you can't just walk in?" Poet asked. "Because you're banned?"

"Correct," Callum said with his best boyish smile.

"And this person is…?"

"Angelique. At least that's what I called her." He opened his jacket and, from an inside pocket, drew out the box that Sketch had given him that night in the Dream World. Seeing it hit Poet hard, reminding him that Sketch was gone.

"That was—"

"Yes," Callum interrupted. "Sketch brought it to me. It belonged to his…girlfriend. I'm not sure what he called her, though."

Poet widened his eyes. "It was *this* Angelique?"

Callum shrugged and put the box back into his coat. So Callum and Sketch's girlfriend had a past—he sort of knew that. Poet turned to the building, now more curious than before. He was surprised to see it had changed, the walls swelling and pulsing. Alive. Above him, sparks swirled together in the sky like an elaborate dance. This entire reality was to seduce him, trick him, but he wanted to see if this siren had really been in a relationship with Sketch.

"So the plan is," Callum started, "for us to go in and ask to see her. We'll probably get roughed up. Sirens don't care much for poets. They're dream weavers. Fantasies." He smiled. "They're your wet dreams, Poet Anderson. This is where dreamers come to escape. Not all dreamers get in, of course. Only the ones they like."

"And then what?" Poet asked.

Callum tilted his head. "Then people have fun. They get off. And they leave. Well, most of them leave. Sometimes you'll see find a few lucid dreamers who get attached and stick around. But for the most part, this is sin city, mate. Buckle up."

Callum reached over to adjust Poet's hat, and then he slapped him on the back and pushed him toward the building entrance. Poet still didn't know what exactly he was doing here, but he noticed how Callum would look around, checking for someone.

The man at the door puffed himself up as they approached. Callum hung back, letting Poet take the lead.

"Hey," Poet said, and the man sniffed and looked past him to the empty street. "Uh, I'm here to see Angelique?" he added.

"Good for you. She's not here." The man was gruff, and kind of terrifying. He had a pronounced under-bite with sharpened teeth, flared nostrils. His tattoos glowed, racing around his bulky arms.

Poet glanced back at Callum and the other poet rolled his hand for him to keep trying. Poet cursed under his breath.

"I think she'll want to see me," he said with false confidence. "I'm Poet Anderson."

Whether she'd truly want to see him or not, the man turned to him with interest. He looked Poet up and down, sizing him up. "You're the one who killed that Dream Walker," he said, his voice low.

Poet flinched, and he stumbled over his words as he tried to recover. "It wasn't like that. I—I just need to see Angelique, okay?"

The guy smiled then, and it occurred to Poet that sirens must hate Dream Walkers too. "Come on in, kid," he said, and stepped aside for Poet and Callum to enter.

The warehouse was crowded, and all around them were flashing lights and heavy music that weighed you down and vibrated in your bones. Poet blinked quickly, refocusing, and all the beautiful people dissolved into how they really looked.

As Poet and Callum began to cross the room, a shirtless man with silver hair and smoky eyes walked past Poet, running his hand along his arm and smiling slyly. A woman blew him a kiss from the dance floor. It was hard for him to stay focused, the filter going in and out, the beauty and manipulation intertwining and drawing him in.

"I quite liked him," Callum said, turning to watch the shirtless guy leave. He laughed, and glanced around before pointing to a set of stairs that led to a loft high above the dance floor.

Poet pushed his way through the crowd, feeling half-drunk, and he and Callum went up the stairs, where a woman was guarding the entrance. She flipped her eyes from one poet to the other, the smoke licking out at them.

"Poet Anderson," she said, her voice velvet to his ears. "How very nice it is to meet you finally."

"Told you," Callum said under his breath.

The woman rested back on the heels of her boots, brushing her silver hair over her shoulder. "But why would you come here? There's no bargain to be made."

"I have to speak to Angelique," he said. But honestly, Poet had no idea why he was here. He felt Callum looking around again, as if waiting for something.

The siren smiled at Poet, and took a step closer to him. She smelled like Sam—a soft vanilla mixed with lavender. The siren reached out and ran her finger over Poet's hand. And all at once, Poet was sure she was the most beautiful creature he'd ever seen.

She licked her full lips, and took him by the tie, pulling him up the final stair to stand in front of her. Poet blinked dreamily, as she tugged on his tie to bring him closer still.

"Come here, Dream Boy," she said in a soothing voice. She leaned and kissed him gently, her forked tongue touching his lips. When she pulled back, confident in her seduction, she let his tie run through her fingers. "Now tell me why you're really here, Poet Anderson," she whispered.

And he could feel it: the manipulation, the tingling on his skin, the haze in his mind. The way his body screamed to give her everything she wanted. He almost couldn't bear it.

"It's actually a funny story," Poet said, smiling. The siren nodded for him to go on. And then Poet straightened his expression. "One that I'll only tell to Angelique."

The siren's eyes blazed, and she bared her teeth. "You're immune," she growled. "How is that possible?"

"Cause he's already in love," Callum called from behind him. "Your siren tricks don't work. Sorry, sweetheart. Now let us by."

The siren turned her gaze on Callum, her anger at rejection enough to distort her features. She became devilish. "No one's immune," she growled.

"Yeah, well," Callum adjusted his hat. "Clearly, he is. Please, let her know we're here."

Despite her anger, the siren turned and led them through the upstairs floor of the warehouse. There was another bar up above, and she pointed to it, her finger shaky. "Wait there," she said, and stormed off.

There were several people already sitting at the bar, but it was busier than downstairs. Poet and Callum took a seat, and the last bits of seduction faded from Poet's skin.

"When are you going to tell me why we're here?" he asked.

"Soon," Callum replied and tapped on the bar. A male siren came over, smiling and handsome, and Callum asked for two drinks. The guy poured something green into glasses and set them in front of the poets. Callum thanked him and turned on the stool to face out to the loft area.

Poet picked up his glass, but Callum shook his head. "Don't drink that," he said. "Never drink anything they give you here, especially not if you plan to walk out."

"Then why did you order drinks?"

"I didn't want to be rude, mate."

Poet looked down at the green liquid, and to his horror, he saw it shift and move, as if it were alive. He put the glass back on the bar.

"Angelique is strong among the sirens," Callum said in low voice. "They respect her and follow her lead. This is her place." He motioned around them. "I used to come here, I don't know, years ago now. Her persuasion worked on me, and she asked for my most prized possession. It was a knife that my father had given me. He was a Dream Walker." Callum turned to look at Poet, and the seriousness in his eyes was chilling.

Poet knew next to nothing about Callum, and certainly not that his father had been a Dream Walker, like Poet's mother.

"She used it against me after that," he said. He turned away. "I'll let you in on a little secret: that man was the only person I've ever loved. That's why she asked for it. And without it, I was under her power for decades." He laughed to himself, his eyes trailing something across the room. "But I have it back now. And I'm here to prove a point."

Poet didn't like the sound of that, and leaned forward to ask some questions, but the first siren returned, obviously still pissed.

"You," she said to Poet, and motioned him forward with her finger. He stood, and when Callum got up, the siren turned to him viciously. "Not you," she rebuffed.

Callum laughed and sat back down, smiling as Poet was led away. Poet tried to look confident, but he had no idea why he was here. What was he supposed to say to Angelique?

The siren led him to a round table with several people drinking and playing cards. And there was a woman in the middle of the group, silver-haired, beautiful in an unusual way. She wrapped her forked tongue around the straw of her drink and pulled it to her lips to take a sip.

When she set her glass down, she lifted her smoky eyes to look at Poet Anderson. It was strange, the way she watched him. Her eyes weren't a color—they were smoke, a controlled mist that seemed to draw him closer and call to him. They were haunting.

"Why are you here?" she asked simply, her voice delicate like the high keys of a piano. The people next to her continued to play their game as if there had been no interruption. Occasionally, Angelique would reach over and stroke the hand of the guy next to her, and Poet wondered if she was making them play.

Poet didn't know why he was here, so he used the only information he had. "Sketch," he said. "Sketch is dead."

Angelique's soft features pulled together tightly, her white-gray eyes darkening like storm clouds. "When?" she asked.

"Last week," Poet said.

There was a fierce flash of anger, and Poet thought that, despite who she was, Angelique had cared for Sketch. It made the grief over losing him all the more painful.

"Who hurt him?" Angelique demanded. "Who do we have to kill?"

"It was a—"

"Ay, Poet Anderson," Callum said suddenly, coming up to smack him on the back like he just happened to run into him. "How are—oh," he paused, looking at Angelique. "Well, hello to you, Angie."

The siren growled, and pointed a sharpened fingernail in his direction. "Who the fuck let you in here?" she snapped. The others at the table looked up at him, all of them mimicking her fierceness.

Callum smiled, seemingly unbothered by the hostile welcome. He shifted his eyes to Poet and then away. Something was wrong.

Poet quickly turned and followed Callum's line of vision. His body went cold. Clinging to the brick wall on the lower floor, there was a shape crawling toward them, constantly moving, disappearing and reappearing in an instant. It exuded a feeling of unease and malice.

A shadow.

"Shit," Poet muttered.

"What is this?" Angelique called, and stood up from the table, bumping it, and spilling several drinks. She reached out to touch one of the dreamers next to her. "Kill them," she whispered.

A dreamer from the table immediately leapt up and ran full force, ready to tackle Poet and Callum. Callum reacted quickly, ducking, and then kicking the guy to the floor.

Poet barely had time to react. Just as he forced power to his hands, the shadow jumped from the wall, just missing him. The shadow creature surrounded Angelique, pouring into her eyes and ears, between her parted lips and up her nose. She gasped, her body going rigid before she fell backward, missing the chair, hitting the floor hard. Her body convulsed once and then stilled.

Poet stared, wide-eyed, as several sirens and dreamers ran past him, screaming. Callum took a deep breath, as if he wasn't at all surprised, and he stood up, brushing the back of his pants.

"That's a shame," he said. He took out the box again, and set it on the table, careful to avoid the running liquid from the drinks.

Poet's mouth had gone dry, and he wasn't even sure what to ask, what to do.

Callum took out the knife and gazed at it lovingly, adjusting his grip.

There was a shuffle, and Poet turned to see Angelique climbing up from the floor. Only it was no longer Angelique. Black smoke licked out from her eye sockets, a trail of black fluid leaking from between her lips.

As they stood and watched, another siren ran to her, fists out to fight. But Angelique grabbed him easily by the arm and whipped him around, sending him headfirst into the bar, where he cracked his skull.

Poet quickly created a gun, ready to protect himself, but it was Callum who walked forward, with only the small dagger in hand.

"Wait!" Poet yelled to him. But Callum had already shifted the knife in his hand, smiling broadly.

"Do you know why I'm here?" he asked the shadow creature. "Why this particular siren? This particular blade?" He flashed the knife.

Angelique tilted her head unnaturally. "A poet?" she asked, as if confused by Callum's presence. She quickly turned and focused Poet Anderson, licked her lips, and smeared the black fluid across them.

"Sorry about this, love," Callum said to her, drawing her attention again. "This is going to sting a bit."

Callum kicked a chair, knocking it into the shadow's gut, doubling her over for only a split second. In one slick movement, Callum jumped forward and slashed the blade across the siren's neck, sending her head backwards, tearing her wound further.

There was a horrific scream—one that shook Poet's bones. Blood spurted out in all directions, spraying everywhere. People were running, and bottles crashed to the floor.

Poet took a step back from the carnage, and watched as Callum walked calmly over to the dying siren. He looked down at her, not even an ounce of compassion on his face.

"I wish I could say I didn't enjoy that," he said, crouching down next to her. Black smoke began to leak from her eyes, and Callum watched almost curiously. "Don't ever steal from a poet," he whispered. And then he drove his knife deep into her skull. All the shadow inside of her poured out and evaporated.

The siren's eyes turned gray once again, focusing on Callum for an instant, before they closed and her head fell to the side. She was dead.

The warehouse quieted, the music gone. People were standing and staring. Poet felt sick. He'd brought Callum here, got him in the door. He had just murdered someone, even if she had a shadow inside her.

Callum turned around, and wiped his suit sleeve over the blood that had gotten on his face. He picked up the siren's unspilled drink from the table, plucking out the straw and tossing it aside, before taking a sip.

"You're a complete sociopath!" Poet shouted. Callum smiled and took another sip before dropping the drink on the floor.

"I think you mean psychopath," Callum answered, and started past him toward the exit. "Now we'd better get out of here, Poet Anderson, or we're going to have to fight all these sirens."

Callum stopped short, and Poet looked past him to the doorway. Two male sirens stood there, arms folded over their chests. Once again, their gray eyes were haunting—like looking at ghosts. The kinds that will totally fuck you up.

"Tunnel," Poet whispered, but Callum shrugged it off.

"Where's the fun in that?" he asked, and then he created a gun and began firing.

POET BURST THROUGH THE window, onto the street, and began running for the alley. Callum had just murdered a least a handful of people. Dreams—living beings, even if only in this reality.

Poet cursed, his shiny shoes sliding along the gravel as he ducked down a dark alley. He needed to get out of this reality. He had no idea where Callum had taken him, but when he got to the end of the alley, he paused at the brick wall and immediately sent a rush of electricity to his fingers.

He created a wisp of smoke, and began to swirl it out, making it grow bigger, but when he went to step through it, it was immediately sucked away.

"What the hell?" Poet said, checking his hand. There was a sliding sound behind him, and Poet turned to see Callum standing there. In one hand he still carried the bloody knife, but his gun had faded away.

"You going to kill me now?" Poet demanded. He wouldn't let himself fear Callum. Or at least, he wouldn't let him see it. "Is that why you brought me here?"

Callum laughed and slipped the knife into his inner pocket. "Of course not," Callum said. "Why would I kill the only Poet? And put a target on my back? No, thank you." Callum took a few steps, and flipped over a crate, taking a seat. He motioned for Poet to join him, but Poet shook his head.

"Suit yourself," Callum said. He took out a cigarette, a dream version, lit it with electricity from his hand, and took a long drag. "I told you the truth," Callum said, dark green smoke drifting from his lips as he spoke. "I needed you to get me into that club. Sirens are inherently distrustful, especially of poets."

"Oh, I wonder why!" Poet snapped. "You just killed them!"

"I didn't have a choice."

"Yes, you did. You could have warned them when you saw the shadow. We could have left. We could have never gone. What were you trying to accomplish?"

"To catch a shadow, it has to invade a host. And then you have to kill the host. What happens then, Poet?" Callum asked, taking another drag. "Tell me."

"They die," Poet answered, even though he knew it wasn't the entire truth.

"Yes, the dream self dies. But then the shadow wakes up in the human form. They turn into what was left of your friend Sketch. So could you imagine letting another one of those creatures into the ill-equipped Waking World? Those fools wouldn't know what to do. They'd be destroyed."

"I still don't see what this has to do with now," Poet said.

"They're following you," Callum called loudly. "Don't you see that? They're following *you* because you're the last Poet and they want you. My premonition allowed me to see that. But to destroy them, I needed them to infect a Dream— not a person. Sirens can't wake up, Poet. They *are* awake— this is their only reality. It was the best bet."

"You set them up?" Poet asked, horrified by his role— however unknown—in the murders.

"I did," Callum said with little remorse. "Those creatures—sirens—they don't deserve my compassion. And eventually, you'll have to make the same choices. Who to save and who to sacrifice." He ashed his cigarette. "Why would you think being a leader was anything but misery and sacrifice? Did you think—?"

"This was revenge against that siren," Poet said. "A vendetta. You're no better than a Night Stalker. A soulless monster."

Callum stopped, looking over at Poet before laughing. "Oh, God," he said. "You *did* think you could have it all, didn't you? What did Jarabec teach you?"

"Don't fucking say his name," Poet growled.

"You don't get to keep your pretty girl, your weakened brother, your crummy job," Callum said. "You don't get to have those things, Poet. You have this." He motioned around the alley. "You have murder and mayhem, and occasionally whiskey. So get used to it. It's not going to get any better."

Poet spun around, facing the brick wall again. He steeled himself against a possible attack, but he couldn't stay here any longer. He wanted to go home. He didn't want to be part of this reality—*this* poet's version of reality.

"Don't come to me again," Poet said darkly. "Don't show up at the hotel, don't find me in my dreams. I want nothing to do with you."

"You don't mean that," Callum sang out. "You need us."

Poet looked over his shoulder at Callum, disgusted that he'd ever given him the benefit of the doubt. He was the worst sort of predator: the kind that pretended to be your friend.

"If I see you again, I'll kill you," Poet said.

Callum smiled brightly, and tossed aside his cigarette. "Now that's the spirit," he replied, and then he opened a tunnel and disappeared.

JONAS STIRRED, STILL ON the couch. He felt a shift next to him, and the waking reality flooded in. He shot up. "Sam?" he called.

"It's just me," Alan said. Jonas looked over to see his brother on the other end of the couch, a cheeseburger in his hand and two plates of food set out. "I didn't want to wake you," Alan added before taking a bite. "You looked exhausted."

Jonas sat forward and ran his hand through his hair. He was momentarily confused; like always, the dream he'd had was just slightly out of reach.

"And I'm sorry I'm not Sam," Alan added. "She was released and decided—she decided to go back to her dad's house tonight with her stepmom. I'm sure she'll call you tomorrow."

Alan said the last part like he was he hoping it was true, but Jonas could hear the doubt in his voice. He wouldn't acknowledge it, though.

Jonas looked over at his brother and snorted a laugh. "You're wearing my clothes."

"Yeah," Alan said, looking down at the buttoned shirt, sleeves rolled up to his elbows, dark-colored jeans that were a little too short. "This was honestly the best you had. Sam really needs to help you shop."

"I'm fine," Jonas said, reaching for his tray of food. He couldn't remember the last time he ate, and he was starving. But at his first bite, the nightmare came flooding back, and he choked on his burger.

"You okay?" Alan asked, grabbing a soda and holding it out for him.

Jonas took the Coke, but set it aside. He looked over at Alan, shocked at what had just transpired. "The poets," he said. "Callum just set someone up." He shook his head. "A Dream...a siren."

"Whoa, slow down," Alan said, putting down his food. "How did he set someone up?"

"He killed her," Jonas said. "He killed a bunch of them."

"What the hell are you talking about?" Alan asked. "Jesus, Jonas—how many people have you killed today?"

"Not me," he said. "It was Callum. He said it was to kill a shadow—one of those things from the void. He said it's been following me. He drew it out so that it could go into a siren, and then he killed her. Oh, God..." Jonas put his head in his hands, horrified. "There's something wrong with him, Alan.

And...I think I know how he got so strong—maybe how they all did. Callum doesn't have a conscience. He—he's soulless."

Alan narrowed his eyes as he contemplated the thought. "Sam said poets keep their souls."

"Usually, yes, but these poets are different. Stronger. I don't know, man. I can't be around them anymore, especially not Callum. We have to stay away from them. Find another way to take out those shadows. And then there's REM and the Night Stalkers... Fuck!" Jonas yelled, kicking the coffee table and making the plates rattle. "We can't beat them," he murmured desperately. "I don't know what else to do."

Alan watched him, his jaw tightening. "Jonas," he said evenly. "You're one of the strongest people I know. You survived Mom and Dad's death. You survived my accident. You survived going against REM with impossible odds. I know you think you're always failing, but the truth is, you're always surviving. And you'll survive this too."

His brother was awake, and that realization was heavy with built-up grief. So Jonas let himself fall apart, mourning the past year of being without him, trying hard to make him proud. Alan grabbed him by the shoulder and pulled him into a fierce hug.

Jonas felt like a little brother again, and for a moment, he let Alan hold him up.

IT WAS LATE, AND Jonas rolled over in bed, tired and tangled in the sheets, unable to quite fall asleep. He could hear the TV out in the living room; Alan was catching up on a year's worth of *Real Housewives*, it seemed.

But Jonas wanted to escape. His eyes hurt from crying, his chest from dying. And he missed *her*. Sam should be with him right now; she should be the calming voice at his side. The bed was cold without her.

Yes, he killed her father, but he did it to save her. He just wanted her to understand. He just wanted to talk to her.

Then it occurred to him—he was a poet. He *could* see her. Jonas curled up on his side, not weighing the ethical merits of finding Sam in her sleep. He closed his eyes and imagined her, where she would be, whether in Genesis or a memory. He tried to feel for her.

His mouth flinched with a smile. He knew where she'd be. It was the same place he found her the first time. He let go of the Waking Reality and entered the Dream World.

Poet stepped out of the tunnel and found himself standing in front of a set of iron gates, a child's carousel with tinkling music spinning slowly behind it. Crystal lights danced, shining as they spun. Poet's heart swelled at the familiarity; Sam's special place was now part his too.

He felt her then—her presence. Poet looked sideways and found Sam standing along the gate, her hand on the iron fence as she stared wistfully at the ceramic horses spinning around and around.

This was her dream, and Poet knew she'd come back here to find comfort. After her parents divorced, her father had created this loop for her. An imaginary place built entirely for her in her dreams.

"I knew you'd come," she said calmly, not looking over at him.

Poet swayed at the sound of her voice, hurting for her. Wanting her. No—needing her.

"And you came anyway," he said.

Sam turned to him, her hands still on the railing. "Do you remember the first time you were here?" she asked.

"Of course."

She pressed her lips into a sad smile, and turned back to stare at the carousel, the light reflecting in her glassy eyes. "Back then you couldn't remember your dreams, but you'd been looking for me. And I guess..." She tilted her head. "I guess I was looking for you too."

"Sam," Poet said, his voice pained. "I'm sorry. There—"

"Are your hands glowing?" she asked, closing her eyes instead of looking at him. "Like they did that first time? Your power obvious and wild."

Poet looked down at his fingers, but there was no electricity there. It used to pulse between him and Sam, begging to be shared, bonded. Poet's breath caught in his chest, and he lifted his head accusingly.

"What's going on, Samantha?" he asked.

She sniffled, and then opened the gate to the carousel, walked inside, and latched it behind her. "You still have your power," she said, finally meeting his eyes. "You'll always have it. But...the power we created that night—it's gone."

"It's not gone," Poet said, taking a step toward her. "Samantha." He tried to open the iron gate, but found it locked. He shook it, but it didn't open.

Sam's lips downturned, and Poet thought his heart might rip out of his chest.

"Don't leave me," he whispered.

"Don't you understand?" she said. "I'm already gone."

The carousel lights wavered behind her, a ricochet of lights fading out. Piece by piece, the scene began to dissolve, like overexposed film. Sam watched Poet as he looked from her to the carousel.

"What are you doing?" he asked.

"I'm letting go," she said. "Letting go of my father, of you. Do what you need, Poet Anderson. Save the world."

"I need *you*," he said defiantly. But even as he did, Sam's image flickered out, and she was gone.

CHAPTER EIGHTEEN

IT WAS BARELY SIX IN THE MORNING WHEN Jonas woke, and he stormed out into the living room. He found Alan on the couch, the blanket only half covering him. For a second, Jonas debated waking him, but then his anger flashed, and he called his name, rousing him with a start.

"What's wrong?" Alan said immediately, even though he was still half asleep.

"Where is she?" Jonas demanded. "Where's Sam?"

Alan rubbed his eyes, blinking quickly, and turned to look at Jonas. He didn't ask for clarification, and Jonas was smacked with betrayal.

"Where's my girlfriend?" Jonas asked, louder now.

"First of all," Alan said, "this isn't about you. You're not her only reason for existing."

"You don't even fucking know her," Jonas snapped.

Alan sighed and sat back on the couch, always patient during Jonas's outbursts. Always the level head. Jonas had forgotten that.

"I know her, Jonas," Alan said. "Obviously not like you do, but I am her friend. I know it's hard to understand because the void isn't *this* reality, but it's still *a* reality. When I spoke to her yesterday at the hospital, I saw it. She's broken. Not just her ribs. Her *heart*."

"Stop," Jonas said, the guilt squeezing in on him.

"She said she's going away for a while with her stepmom. They have some business to settle abroad, and she thought the break would be healthy. She's got a therapist. She's..." Alan flinched. "She said she wanted to destroy some of the reminders."

"Of me?" Jonas asked, miserable.

"No," Alan said, shaking his head. "Of pain. A doctor that works for her father gave her a drug that can keep her from dreaming. I told her that would probably be safer for now, especially with REM and the shadows all trying to kill you."

"You let her leave," Jonas said bitterly. "And you didn't tell me."

"It wasn't my secret to tell. Look," Alan said, seeming to grow truly concerned. "I don't know what's happening with you, Jonas, but this isn't the kid I knew before the accident. You're *killing people*. You're changing—"

"It's been a year, Alan," Jonas snapped. "You've been gone for an entire year, and I had to figure it out on my own. Sorry that I'm not your lap dog anymore."

Alan scoffed, and stood up from the couch. Jonas immediately felt ashamed as he took in his brother's thin frame, his skin sallow from lack of sunlight.

"Is that what you think?" Alan asked. "That I treated you as...what? Less than? Jesus, Jonas. I gave up my fucking life to make sure you were okay. And now you're holding it against me?"

Jonas closed his eyes, wanting to be mad at his brother for trying to shame him, but ultimately knowing Alan was right. "I'm sorry," he said, and then looked at Alan. He nodded almost immediately, accepting the apology. "I just..." Jonas shook his head. "I just love her, man."

Alan swallowed hard, and eased himself back onto the couch. "I know you do. Just give her some time. Give yourself some time. Christ, you're what—eighteen?"

"Nineteen. You've been asleep, remember?"

Alan laughed. "I'm getting old."

"Should start losing your hair soon. Can't wait for that shit. I'm ready to be the better-looking brother."

Alan ran his hand through his blond hair. "Sorry, man," he said. "I could be three days dead in the grave, and I would still have you beat."

Jonas glanced around the suite, feeling like it was empty now that he knew Sam wouldn't be coming back. He'd have to ask Marshall for a new room—one he could share with Alan.

"Yeah," Jonas said. "So I'm feeling pretty fucking depressed right now. Want to go get a coffee?"

"Coffee," Alan said. "I can't imagine anything I'd like to do more, to be honest."

As Alan took a shower, Jonas waited on the chair, sitting stiffly, and gazed out the window. Wondering where Sam had gone. Wondering if she was okay. And hoping that part of her, even if it was just a small part, forgave him for his role in her father's death.

And he hoped that, eventually, she would find him again.

JONAS HAD NEVER BEEN a huge coffee drinker, mostly because it was an expensive habit for someone who didn't have a job, but he'd found, after working several early morning shifts at the Eden, that coffee tasted really fucking good.

His favorite place was a small shop a block down that had a garage door they kept open when it was warm out. Today was not one of those days, and Jonas tightened his jacket around himself as they walked, with Alan using his cane as little as he could.

The shop wasn't busy. Only a few people sat at tables with their laptops, and Jonas and Alan were able to quickly get their drinks, and Alan a piece of pie, before grabbing seats by the window. Jonas could feel the cold air clinging to the glass, and he kept his coat zipped. Alan, on the other hand, stripped off Jonas's old sweatshirt to reveal a T-shirt he'd found from their old high school.

"I don't know what kind of drugs they gave me when I was out," Alan said. "But I swear, man, I never get cold. In fact, it's hot as hell in here."

"Yeah, sure," Jonas said, keeping his hands around the steaming mug of coffee. He gazed out the window at the street and sighed heavily.

Jonas was tired. Sleep wasn't restful anymore, and the bags under his eyes were dragging down his face. He turned to examine the coffee shop, from its light brown walls with art on display to the tables and booths made of reclaimed wood. The rich smell of coffee lingered in the air, and soothing acoustic music played through the overhead speakers.

Jonas took a sip of his coffee, which was hot enough to burn his tongue, and looked over at Alan, who was shifting in the seat, trying to get more comfortable. His cane rested against the table, hooked on to the side. They didn't know yet if the damage to his nerves was permanent.

"This is delicious," Alan said, taking another bite of the apple cobbler. "But the coffee is too strong."

"You need to toughen up, brother," Jonas said.

"Sure," Alan said. "What's your blend? Black coffee with the blood of an ox and the tears of orphans?"

Jonas looked down at his cup, pretending to inspect it. "Nope," he said after a moment. "Extra cream, extra sugar."

"Never change," Alan said, laughing.

Jonas smiled, and as he was staring at Alan, he noticed the first sparks in the air. A shimmer of a curtain. And then suddenly, there was a flash of blinding light and Jonas felt a hard hit on his cheekbone that knocked him out of the chair and onto the floor.

A person stood above him, just a silhouette in the light outside the window, and then, impossibly, the person disappeared.

Jonas gasped, sliding along the floor as he looked around the room, wide-eyed. Someone had punched him, and incredibly hard. Jonas got up quickly, his hair now disheveled and his breathing heavy. Alan stood up from the table, his face pale white.

"Did you…?" Jonas started. "Was that *you?*"

"Was what me?" Alan asked. "You okay, man?"

Around the room, people stared. One girl closed her laptop and darted out the door. Jonas wasn't sure how much the others had seen, but he guessed it wasn't as much as he had.

Jonas straightened the chair, so fuzzy he couldn't tell if he was dreaming. It—it felt like a dream, the weight in the air. He held up his hand, trying to form a weapon, twisting his fingers and cursing. But nothing happened. He looked deranged, he realized, and quickly looked up. The owner of the shop was glaring at him, and Jonas nodded an apology and sat at the table, close to Alan.

"I'm not crazy," Jonas whispered, looking sideways at his brother. Alan didn't need to answer because Jonas could read by his expression that he was just as shocked.

There was a noise, like fabric tearing, and then suddenly Jonas was hit again. This time, he was ready and swung out, his fist connecting with a figure. A person fell against Alan, sending him to the floor, his cane toppling next to him. There was a flurry of movement behind Jonas as people rushed from the shop.

The figure straightened, and Jonas realized it was happening again. A Night Stalker had breached the veil. Its face was hidden behind a reflective mask, and it grabbed Jonas by the arm. The touch was deathly cold, inhuman, with a slight tinge of electricity.

Or was that Jonas's electricity?

"Time to die, boy," the creature growled behind its mask. It punched Jonas hard in the face, knocking him out of his head for a moment as he saw stars. The creature wrapped its forearm around Jonas's neck, squeezing.

Jonas quickly grabbed the fork out of Alan's pie and drove it deep into the Night Stalker's arm through its suit. There was a fizzle of electricity, but no power.

The Night Stalker groaned in pain, and pulled out the fork to toss it aside. Jonas punched it in the helmet, hearing a crack. He swung again, but this time he got only air. The Night Stalker had disappeared.

Jonas spun around, nearly stumbling, when the Night Stalker reappeared behind him and kicked him in the back of his knee, launching him forward. Jonas's knee hit pavement, and when he looked around, he was on a darkened street, the lights of Genesis blazing above.

He stumbled back a step, his face away awash in the bright colors of the city lights, cars zooming overhead.

He was in the Dream World. His power flared all at once, and his eyes suddenly blazed white, his suit forming, as he became Poet Anderson.

The Night Stalker didn't hesitate. Its black Halo shot out, hitting Poet so hard in the gut he doubled over. It hit him again, knocking him to the ground. Quickly, Poet swung out his leg, balancing, and held out his arm, a gun forming as it blasted the Halo with several shots, sending it toward its creature.

The Night Stalker rushed Poet, and just as the two collided, they slammed against a wall in the coffee shop.

Jonas was momentarily disoriented by the drain in power, and the Night Stalker brought up its knee, connecting with Jonas's sore ribs. He groaned, and pushed the Night Stalker back, but not before the creature grabbed him by the collar of his shirt, and threw him to the floor.

Next to Jonas was the discarded fork, and he picked it up and stabbed it into the Night Stalker's thigh as it came for him again. The creature cried out, falling forward, and swung out at Jonas on its way to the floor. Jonas took the hit, but ripped out the fork and stabbed it into the Night Stalker's neck.

The Night Stalker writhed, and Jonas got on top of the creature, holding it down as black blood oozed all over the floor. He had to kill it here, stopping it from crossing back over.

Jonas held up the fork to stab it again, when suddenly the Night Stalker disappeared, and Jonas was splayed out on the faux wood flooring of the coffee shop.

The creature was gone—sparks gone from the air. Only a puddle of black blood remained. The café was quiet except for the sound of dripping coffee that had spilled on tables as people fled. Jonas and Alan sat side by side on the floor. Broken chairs, cups, and blood were all around them. Jonas looked sideways, and Alan shook his head.

"What the hell was that?" Alan asked.

"You didn't see it?" Jonas asked.

"Uh, yeah," he replied, out of breath. "But what happened?"

"A Night Stalker just came into the Waking World," Jonas said, rubbing his jaw, cautiously waiting for it to reappear.

"That's not possible," Alan said. He grabbed a nearby table, and used it to pull himself up, hobbling once before grabbing his cane. And where did you go? Jonas, you disappeared, man. Straight-up *disappeared*."

"I know," Jonas replied. "It means the veil is thin. You said you saw REM with his army before, right? This is what I think they've been working on. It was stronger this time too. It pulled me straight into the Dreamscape."

Jonas got to his feet, and took out his wallet, grabbing all the cash he had. He set it on the counter, assuming the owner was in the back, probably on the phone with the police.

Alan quickly pulled Jonas toward the exit, looking longingly at the floor. "Damn," he said. "I wish I could have finished that pie."

CHAPTER NINETEEN

"**R**EM'S GOTTEN MORE POWERFUL,**"**
Jonas said in a hushed voice as he and Alan
walked quickly toward the hotel. The wind
was biting, and Jonas's face ached from where he had gotten
punched. "We knew that," Jonas added. "And Callum said the
veil was thin. But how are the Night Stalkers crossing over?
How did it pull me in?

Alan used his cane, trying to keep up. "I think the bigger
question is how they found you," Alan said. Dots of rain were
turning his blue jacket to navy. "How did they find you, twice,
in the Waking World? They can interact with you on some
level—an unseen connection. And it was messed up, Jonas. I
couldn't see *you*. You were slipping in and out of this reality,
but more than that…" He paused. "It felt like you were gone."

"I was in the Dream World," Jonas said.

Alan shook his head. "No," he said. "You weren't asleep.
You were gone—whole body. It felt…unnatural."

Jonas didn't like the sound of that, but it reminded him
of the other poets, how they walked full-bodied into their

dreams. They didn't have a connection to this reality—no body left behind. It bothered him now that he knew Callum's true character. He didn't want to be like the other poets. But they knew more about this than Callum claimed.

"I have to get in touch with the poets," Jonas said, shoving his hands into the pockets of his coat.

"Oh, for fuck's sake, Jonas," Alan said. "Don't involve the poets. Nothing good will come from it."

"Then what? I just got my ass kicked in *this* reality. It's twice now, and they pulled me in. What if it happens again, but there's an ambush waiting? I'll be a sitting duck."

"I think we need Dream Walkers," Alan said. "Not poets."

"Good luck with that," Jonas said. "Dream Walkers hate me."

"Probably," he replied easily. "But they haven't met me yet."

Jonas laughed, and then winced and touched his aching cheek.

"You should get some ice on that," Alan said. "I'm going to talk to the manager. Marshall, right?"

"Yeah. He's a real charmer."

"Perfect."

They grew quiet, the drizzle continuing and cutting through the cold with its own ice. Jonas turned to his brother, his voice strained when he said, "I need you to call Sam and make sure she's okay. The Night Stalker came for her last time."

Alan didn't look at him, maybe sensing the tension. "I will," he said. "But since she doesn't dream anymore, they shouldn't be able to find her."

Jonas didn't like having to ask his brother to contact his girlfriend. He didn't like being out of their lives. But he loved them both more than anything.

"Thanks," Jonas murmured, lowering his head.

"No problem," Alan responded without missing a beat, and walked ahead of Jonas.

WHILE ALAN TRIED TO get a meeting with Marshall at the front desk of the Eden, Jonas went to his room. He filled his hand with ice from the machine, and immediately pressed it to his face with a wince.

Alan returned to the room a short while later, and Jonas was on the couch, his head resting back against the cushion.

"Good news," Alan said as he walked in. "Marshall likes me."

"Figures," Jonas replied.

"He gave me a phone," Alan said, holding up a cell phone. "And you and I will be having company tonight, so don't look like shit and scare her off."

"Her?" Jonas asked.

"Yeah, but keep your hormones in check. She's a Dream Walker."

Jonas's heart quickened its pace. He wasn't sure if any of the Dream Walkers would meet with him again. Especially now. He still hadn't explained to Marshall what happened with Alexander, but he guessed someone must have.

Jonas smiled, feeling slightly relieved that he wouldn't have to rely only on poets. If he could get the Dream Walkers on his side, on Alan's, they might have a chance.

He needed to stop REM. He needed to seal the veil between realities.

THE DAY PASSED QUICKLY, and for a while it was almost calm—Jonas and Alan sitting around watching TV, just like they used to when they were on their own. One of the girls from the front desk sent up cookies from the kitchen. She'd never really been nice to Jonas, so he suspected she had her eye on his older brother.

Only once during the day did Jonas let himself think about Sam. Let himself miss her. But it wasn't going to change anything. And he couldn't let it distract him. After all, they couldn't get back together if REM destroyed the world first.

There was a sharp knock, and Alan grabbed his cane to help him up, but set it behind the door before he opened it. Jonas knew he wouldn't want to look vulnerable in front of a Dream Walker.

Alan's frame blocked Jonas's view of their guest, but he could sense a change in Alan instantly. He sat up a little straighter.

"Hi," Alan said. There was a silent pause, and Jonas got to his feet so he could see over his brother's shoulder.

"You must be the good one," a woman said. Alan laughed, and stepped aside to motion her in.

"I'm Alan Anderson, and this is my brother, Jonas."

The woman looked confident, and Jonas was immediately reminded of how intimidating Dream Walkers could be, even in the Waking World. She was young and beautiful—dark skin with shoulder-length hair, a crisp white T-shirt and jeans, and high-heeled ankle boots. And she seemed wholly unimpressed by his existence.

"Hey," Jonas said awkwardly, holding up his hand.

The woman smiled, and walked over to sit on the couch. "Huh," she said. "So you're the reckless poet. The murderer." She ran her eyes over him. "I thought you'd be...bigger."

Jonas stared at her, and then turned to Alan. Alan widened his eyes like he didn't have anything planned to say. He shut the hotel room door and shoved his hands into his pockets.

"I'm Imani," the Dream Walker said, saving them the effort. "Marshall told me you wanted to talk, and I happen to be the only one willing to in this reality." She looked around. "The only one willing to without my gun. To start off: yes, I've heard the rumblings in the Dream World. I know REM's back."

Her hand clenched into a fist where it rested on the couch. Jonas didn't think she even knew she was doing it.

"Have you seen him?" she asked.

"Not in person, no," Jonas said.

She scoffed and looked pointedly at Alan. "Why am I here, then?" she asked him. "If the poet doesn't know, then—"

"Earlier today," Alan said, "one of his Night Stalkers attacked us in a coffee shop. Attacked Jonas. And it's the second time it's happened."

"So?" she asked.

"So," Alan said, "we were in the Waking World."

Imani narrowed her eyes, considering Alan's words. "You're saying he crossed over?"

"I don't know what happened," he said. "But the Night Stalker came through, and as they fought, it even pulled him into the Dream World. It trashed the café, and, as you can see, Jonas's face."

Imani glanced at Jonas and smiled. "You should learn to fight, kid," she offered.

"I can fight. Just not here," Jonas answered honestly. She laughed.

"But to prove it..." Alan sat next to her on the couch. He grimaced slightly and Jonas wondered how much pain Alan was actually in. Alan took out his phone, and held it out. Imani took it. "It's a story from today," Alan said. "We weren't the only one who saw the event, even if they didn't understand what was happening. The owner claimed hundreds of dollars in damage. What if this is just the start?"

"Start of what?" she asked, looking up and down the page.

"An invasion."

Imani stilled, and slowly raised her dark eyes to Alan's. "Anyone else know about this?" she asked.

"You're the first Dream Walker I've spoken to," he said smoothly. He put his hand over the back of the sofa, and Imani set the phone on the cushion between them.

"What do you think I can do?" she asked. "Am I supposed to tell my friends? Do you think they'll believe me?"

"Yes," Alan replied.

It must have been something in his voice, or that earnest look in his eyes, but Imani smiled like maybe he was right.

"Would you like to have dinner with me, Alan?" she asked suddenly. Alan smiled.

Jonas shifted uncomfortably, and started toward the room to get changed, when Imani held up her hand.

"You too, Poet," she called out. "Tonight, in Genesis. I'll bring my friends. Let's see if *you* can convince them."

"Thank you," Alan breathed out. Jonas wasn't so sure he liked this deal, meeting with murderous Dream Walkers. But it was settled. It was a start.

Imani stood, and held out her hand to Alan. He shook it, and agreed to meet her later. Maybe there was a little bit of flirting in his voice, but Alan never went overboard like that. He never really needed to.

Jonas mumbled a goodbye, and when Imani was gone, he spun to face his brother. "Why did you agree?" he asked. "You must have missed the part where the Dream Walkers hate me. Like, raging hate. They're probably going to try to kill us later."

Alan smiled. "Naw," he said. "Show up as Poet Anderson—they won't touch you."

"You have way too much faith in me," Jonas said.

Alan glanced over to him as if surprised by the comment. "No, brother. You don't have enough faith in yourself."

It was just after dark, and both Jonas and Alan were anxious. They didn't have a set time to meet with Imani, but they knew she would be there. Jonas could feel it. He just hoped she didn't bring along the type of Dream Walkers who wanted to kill him.

Problem was, that just might be all of them.

"So how does this work?" Alan asked, resting back on the couch with a groan while Jonas stood next to the bedroom door. "How do I find you in Genesis?"

"I'll take you there," Jonas said. "You fall asleep, start to dream, and I'll find you and bring you with me."

"And how did you find Genesis?" Alan asked. "God, we spent years looking."

Jonas smiled. "Remember that subway we used to take?" he asked. "When we'd dream? I would ride it every night, looking for you. Eventually, it got me to Genesis. So if you're on a train, don't worry. I'll be there soon."

Alan laughed, and pulled the blanket over his legs. "Shit, I haven't thought about that train in forever. Wonder if I could still tag it?"

"Doubt we'll have time for that. You ready?" Jonas asked.

"See you in Genesis," Alan replied.

Jonas tapped the door frame, and passed through into the bedroom. He was still sore from the past few days, but getting stronger. After today, he realized, he would have to learn to fight in the Waking World. Maybe he and Alan could train together.

He turned off the light, and pulled back the covers of his bed. He climbed in, heavy with emotion that he was trying to bury.

Sleep came easily, and when he tunneled into the Dream World, Poet found himself stepping out of the elevator at the Eden hotel.

Alan might not be asleep yet, he thought. Poet glanced up at the ceiling, as if he could look up to the rooms. He checked over his suit, straightened his hat, and swung his umbrella by the handle as he strolled toward the door of the hotel.

The Eden had its own presence in the Dream World, and was one of very few places to exist on both planes of reality. It was why Dream Walkers liked to meet there. They had even kept their base there. But now the base was empty, devastated by the loss of lives in the Grecian Woods.

In the Dream World, the colors of the Eden were more vibrant, the glass tinted blue, and the walls fading in and out of existence. There were several people milling about, but many of them didn't even know they were asleep. The front desk clerk who liked Alan smiled at Poet as he passed.

Poet walked out of the hotel and stumbled to a stop just outside the double doors. He widened his eyes when he saw a monocycle parked at the curb.

Jarabec's monocycle.

A wave a grief for his old mentor tore through Poet's chest, and he took several tentative steps toward the bike.

Jarabec's dead, he thought. *This...this can't be his. He's—*

There was a laugh, and Poet quickly spun around. A man walked out from the alley that ran along the side of the building. His movements were jerky. Poet clutched the handle of his umbrella, and energy vibrated up his arm.

"That's a nice bike you've got there, boy," the man said. But what first appeared to be a man was clearly not. His eyes were black orbs, demon-like, and the way the skin stretched over his face was unnatural. Like Frankenstein's monster. He wasn't a Dream, but he was not a dreamer either.

"Who are you?" Poet asked, shoring up his power.

"Don't you recognize me, tiny poet?" the creature asked. "Is this skin really such a disguise to someone with your sight?"

Fear, like slick oil, coated Poet and he stepped back without meaning to. His foot slipped off the curb, and he reached out to steady himself on Jarabec's monocycle. The touch startled him, and he turned around to look at it again, expecting it to disappear. But instead, the motor glowed blue, as if fueled by his touch. By his power.

"Ah..." REM said. "It does work. I was wondering."

Poet looked from REM to the bike. He had assumed he had brought it here. But the way his lips twitched, the bravado of his posture, Poet realized that REM had nothing to do with this monocycle.

Poet felt a small lift in his heart.

Jarabec might be dead, but he hadn't stopped looking out for him.

"So you got new skin," Poet said to REM, gliding his hand over the bike and feeling the engine rev louder. He kept his umbrella close to him, powering it up. "Too bad you're still ugly as fuck."

REM laughed. "Yes, your insults *really* hurt my feelings. I'm trying this one out," he said, motioning to his face. "I think I quite like it. He was a strong dreamer. He was nearly strong enough to be a poet. And now look at me: I get to walk into the Eden Hotel if I please. Oh, speaking of, did you like when I killed one of your poets? I only have four more to go."

Poet flinched, and the monocycle stalled, vibrating with apprehension until Poet slipped his palm onto one of the handles. The bike steadied, the back fins glowing red.

"I beat you once," Poet said casually. "I've gotten stronger too."

"Oh, I know," REM said, taking a step toward him, eying the boy and the bike as if prepping to strike. "I can feel you from here." He licked his lips instinctively.

"Gross," Poet replied. In his hand, he felt the umbrella transforming. "I mean, REM," he said casually, "you're just not my type."

REM smiled, widening his mouth until the skin tore in the corners, lines of blood seeping from the flesh and running over his chin. Poet was horrified, but kept his expression neutral. Not that he thought REM would fall for it.

"Maybe not," REM said. "But your Waking World is in shambles, and dreamers are fleeing to me in droves. Willingly giving me their power. I've already poked holes in your waking reality. Soon, I'll tear it all down. But all isn't lost, Poet. We might have a mutual cause. Of course, if you're not up for a discussion, I can find your brother and—"

A sudden and blinding rage clouded Poet's concentration, and the monocycle rumbled with power. Poet held up his umbrella—now a modified shotgun—and fired directly at REM. But a black Halo shot out, hitting the shell and causing it to explode, spraying REM with gravel-sized pieces of metal instead of blowing his head off.

REM's body flew back, the skin on his face torn open, and he collapsed to the ground. The Halo began to circle around him, and Poet climbed on the monocycle. Just as the fins raised and he was about to blast away, he saw REM's body twitch.

Poet took another look around the street and then leaned close to the monocycle, holding on tight. "Take me to him," he whispered, and the bike blasted down the street and into the rest of the dreamscape.

CHAPTER TWENTY

THE GARDEN WAS GONE. JARABEC'S beautiful garden had been destroyed by explosions and tire treads. The Night Stalkers had invaded it and turned it to rubble.

But even in this destruction, Poet could still feel his mentor—the ghost of him.

There was a hollow feeling in his chest as he climbed off the monocycle and headed toward the remains of the stone fountain, the water long since dried up. He sat down and closed his eyes, willing it to thrive again.

He heard the trickle, and when he looked down, water was rushing up from the ground, the stone of the fountain reforming to hold it in. Koi fish appeared, flapping their tails. It didn't look exactly the way Jarabec had it, but Poet was satisfied. He recreated the garden to the best he could remember. Rebuilt the fence. Regrew the flowers.

And then he opened up the sky and let rain soak everything.

Poet had lost track of time, ignoring his obligation to meet with Alan—lost instead inside this place. The memory of Jarabec. When he heard the wind of a tunnel forming, he lifted his head and saw Maeve step through. At first, he tensed, alarmed that he was so easily found. Annoyed that another person got to this place that was just Jarabec's, and now his. Not to mention, he didn't trust any of the poets. Not after what Callum did.

Poet turned away from where he'd been watching the fish, and met Maeve halfway across the bridge. "How'd you find me?" he asked.

She leaned her elbows on the wood railing, and looked sideways at him. "You forget I knew Jarabec too," she said.

He had forgotten, but it wasn't her words that he noticed. It was her eye—the white one. Although on closer appearance, it wasn't white at all. It was gray, like a storm cloud brewing.

It was the eye of a siren, and Poet realized suddenly that she was like them. Maeve was part siren.

"Why are you here?" Poet asked.

Maeve turned to watch the fish. "Because I need your help," she said. "Marcel and I—we can't handle this alone. The Night Stalkers are advancing. They've claimed part of the Dreamscape."

"Just you and Marcel? What about Callum?"

She looked at him pointedly. "I think you know."

Maeve and Poet were silent for a few moments, and he knew she was judging him, lumping him in with Callum for what had happened with the sirens.

"You could have stopped him," she said. "Those sirens didn't need to die."

"Stop Callum from killing people?" Poet asked. "You know he's more powerful—"

She held up her hand. "You're Poet Anderson. You controlled the entire Dreamscape at one point—nearly destroyed it. So don't tell me you couldn't stop another poet from killing my family."

Poet's body chilled. "Your—"

Maeve pointed to her eye, and smiled bitterly. "Half-siren. Half-poet."

"How is that possible?" he asked.

"You're half Dream-Walker."

"But...I thought sirens only existed in the Dream World."

"My father was a siren, my mother a lucid dreamer. She was strong, though—atypical even among them. There are aspects of our consciousness you don't understand yet." Maeve stopped, and turned away. "But you will."

"I don't need your fucking riddles," Poet said. "Just explain."

"I'd have to show you," she said. "Do you want to be even stronger? Harness all that power you have—control it better? I can teach you how to walk in and out of your dreams."

Poet furrowed his brow, unsure now that he was being presented with the opportunity. "I don't think we have time for this, Maeve," he said unsteadily. "I just saw REM. He'd taken on a form and—"

"His power grows by the day," she agreed. "Every tragedy in the Waking World gives him more power through nightmares. And lately, it has been a flood."

"You have no idea," Poet said. "A Night Stalker came through again, right into the Waking World, and attacked me."

Maeve spun to face him, her expression one of total surprise. "When did this happen?" she asked. "Why didn't you warn us?"

He was surprised. "I told Callum. This is the second time it's happened." Maeve turned away. "It was earlier today," Poet continued. "And afterward, my brother and I got in touch with a Dream Walker. We plan to meet tonight to figure out a plan. Or at least, figure out what's going on."

Maeve's jaw was tight, but she didn't respond. Poet didn't have time to figure out what she was thinking. He was sure he'd been gone a long time already, and he pushed off the railing and motioned toward the monocycle.

"I have to go," he told her. "I have to meet this Dream Walker."

Maeve was still for a moment, and then said, "You have other responsibilities," she said.

"What about REM?" he asked. "What's my responsibility there?"

"To protect the Dreams," she said. "Protect this world. Protect all realities. There is only one way to make sure that happens: we hide."

Poet scoffed. "How could you even suggest that? They're already coming through, Maeve. I'm not going to hide from REM."

"If you think a flash was something, you don't understand how bad it can get. He can only achieve that through a poet. We can't risk you getting used by him. We can't risk that when he already has so much power. It's inevitable. This battle has been repeated over and over throughout history. The Dream Walkers always stop him at the last moment. To win, he needs a poet."

Maeve reached to put her hand on Poet's arm, and suddenly, Poet was struck by how beautiful Maeve was up close. The angle of her jaw, the strength there. Her wispy gray eye, glassy with tears. The warm touch of her hand that soaked through his coat like sunshine.

"Just come with me," she said, her voice drawing him closer. Beckoned him. Loved him. "I'll show you how to be more powerful than you've ever dreamed."

Didn't he want that? Ultimately, being powerful enough to beat REM was the goal. He wouldn't need the Dream Walkers. He wouldn't need anybody—not even the other poets. He'd only need Maeve's help. He would do anything for her, despite the nagging in the back of his mind.

"I shouldn't," Poet said, blinking slowly. "I have to meet with—"

A large gust of wind blew across the garden, knocking over a few of the new plants and blowing flower petals across the grounds. Confused, Jonas looked past Maeve and saw two tunnels opening. Callum and Marcel stepped through. Their eyes were white with power, weapons clutched in their hands. They looked like they were prepared for a battle.

"What is this?" Poet asked, taking a step back from Maeve. Her hand fell away, and all at once, his head cleared.

Maeve made an annoyed noise low in her throat, shooting an angry look at the others before reaching for Poet again.

He didn't let her touch him. Now he knew why she was such a danger—her power was persuasion. And she was stronger than any of the sirens he'd met in that warehouse.

"Come along easily," Maeve said simply.

"Where?" Poet demanded. "Why?"

"I told you why," she responded. "REM can do a lot of things, but the biggest damage can only come through the possession of a poet. We can't let that happen."

"And you're willing to go with *him?*" Poet asked, pointing at Callum. "After what he's done?"

The comment seemed to bother Maeve. "I'll find another way to punish him," she said. "Now, if you'll—"

"Duck, Maeve," Callum said an instant before Poet swung to hit her. He missed, and Maeve quickly brought up her knee and rammed it into Poet's ribs, doubling him over.

Poet coughed, but in his hand he began to create a gun. Then, suddenly, everything stopped. He couldn't move. Marcel was on the other side of the bridge, fingers to his temples. No one could move, but he could feel Maeve's presence bearing down on him.

The instant the time-loop broke, she struck—two quick hits, and a sharp, pain exploded in Poet's lower left side. The world seemed to reverberate, and Poet stumbled back a few steps. Maeve's eyes were wide. Poet followed her line of vision, and found a slit in his white shirt.

Red began to bloom in the fabric around the hole. It came faster and faster until it started to drip on the wooden slats of the bridge. Poet looked at Maeve's hand and saw a small knife.

"You stabbed me," Poet said aloud, more of a realization than an accusation.

"Take him," Maeve said, and turned around. With her back to him, Poet quickly regained his composure, ignoring the burning pain in his side, and was about to pounce, but before he could retaliate, Callum was in front of him, a long-barreled gun pointed at this head.

"Honestly," he said in his thick British accent. "We're trying to help you, mate."

"I'm going to kill you," Poet told him through gritted teeth.

"We're on your side," Marcel said, coming to stand with Callum. "Try and remember that."

"No," Poet said. "You're cowards."

Maeve turned around then, her impatience clear. She shook her head, and glanced out at the garden. "I remember him, you know," she said. "Jarabec. He would agree with me now. There is a time to fight, but that time is not now. Not for your sake, not for your bravado, not for your brother or girlfriend—it's for the good of humanity. Of what's left of it. Come with us now and make a plan."

Poet stared back at Maeve, wondering how he had ever trusted her. It would be a hard lesson to learn, the fact that no one could be trusted. That everyone wanted to use him. Whether REM or poets or Dream Walkers—he had no one he could really count on in the Dream World.

The wind began to pick up, and Poet felt a tunnel opening behind him. There was a chance he could get out of this, fight and probably get stabbed some more, but in the end, he knew he wasn't strong enough to stop the poets. Not right now.

Poet swallowed hard, hating the taste of defeat. He'd go with them now, to become strong—stronger than them. And then he'd march back to this Dream World with or without their help, and finally defeat REM, the shadows, and anything else that dared to stand in his way.

Callum chuckled, maybe reading his thoughts, or perhaps seeing what was next. Poet flipped him off, and walked willingly into the tunnel.

The tunnel wasn't like any he'd gone through before. Instead of pulling him into a reality, the air inside felt devoid of oxygen, Poet gasped, clutching his throat. He eyes burned. And then he was propelled into the air.

The Dream World passed him in a blur. He felt the wound in his side open further, as the tunnel tore through the sky. Higher and higher, straight up to the stars.

Poet gritted his teeth, his skin pulled so taut he was afraid he was going to break apart. Shred. And still he climbed faster, and faster. Poet groaned, pain building behind his eyes. He couldn't understand what was happening, or why the poets would shoot him into space. Maybe they *were* trying to kill him.

He was dizzy, his eyelids fluttered, and just before he thought he might pass out, he saw a shape straight ahead. Poet forced himself to stay conscious, willing the tunnel to stop. But he couldn't break the flow. And straight ahead was what appeared to be a black hole.

"Stop," Poet tried to yell, though his voice drifted away before it left his lips. Poet struggled, trying to turn around—to send the tunnel back toward the ground—but there was no ground, only space as far as he could see. He looked at the black hole again, his heart sinking. Just as he slid over the edge into the abyss, he muttered, "Fuck me."

CHAPTER TWENTY-ONE

"**W**AKE UP, POET ANDERSON," A voice said, followed by a splash of something cold. Poet blinked quickly, smelling beer. He wiped his palm over his face and slowly sat up. His memories were two seconds behind him, and suddenly what had just happened flooded in.

Poet quickly spun to look around. He had passed out from the pressure in the tunnel, but as he took in the world around him, Poet knew he hadn't returned to the Dream or Waking World. This was an entirely different reality.

"Pretty, isn't it?" Maeve asked, standing above him with a bottle of beer in her hand.

Indeed, it was pretty. Poet tried to stand, nursing his side where he'd been stabbed, but as he got to his feet, he lifted his shirt and saw that the wound had healed. Around him, the sky was a mixture of oranges and purples with multiple moons, some closer than others, arched in a rainbow, light reflecting off each one differently. Around him were gorgeous weeping willows, blowing in the soft wind. In the distance, he could see taller buildings—a city.

Marcel was sitting against one of the trees, relaxed as if they kidnapped people on a regular basis. Standing in the shadows was Callum, the brim of his hat pulled low, his hands buried in his pockets.

"What is this place?" Poet asked.

Maeve smiled. "It's our home," she said. "We created it on the other side of a black hole, where REM couldn't find or follow us. Not even you could have come here on your own—you would have never found it. And only a powerful tunnel could survive the journey. One you're far too weak to create."

Poet's face drained of color. "Are you saying I can't leave?"

Maeve rolled her eyes, and took a sip from her beer. "You can never just have fun, can you?" she asked. "Of course you can leave—once you learn how. But for now, enjoy this. This," she motioned around them, "is what real power can create. Our own Pleasure Island of sorts."

"With what?" Poet asked. "Just the three of you?"

Marcel's expression hardened. "Well, there used to be four," he said. "But coming back for you changed that. And no, it's not just us. We have our own Dreams here."

Poet turned toward the city, but he couldn't tell what was happening there. A gust of wind blew past him, and he could smell the alcohol coming off of Maeve.

"Your own Pleasure Island, huh?" Poet asked her. "What does that entail?"

"It changes," she said. "We're poets. We create whatever desire we have at the time."

Callum laughed, and Poet turned to him. "See for yourself." He waved his hand and a tunnel opened, yanking Poet inside and spitting him out in the center of the small city.

Poet stumbled, but regained his balance and looked around. It wasn't like Genesis—it was seedy and well-worn. Dreams walked the street, smiling with empty eyes and walking in and out of the establishments. A few neon signs were lit up. Motorcycles lined the street. A band was set up in a vacant space, playing hard, even though few were stopping to listen. They looked exhausted.

The other poets appeared from the tunnel, and stood on the side of the road near the bikes. Poet was in the middle of the road, and Callum made a slow circle around him as he began to speak.

"Ay, come now, Poet Anderson," he said. "This is a playground. There are bars, and restaurants, and theaters," he said as if checking Poet's interest level for each option. "And there is music. So much music."

But Poet wasn't interested in any of this right then. If anything, it only solidified his worst fears about them. "This is why you abandoned the other realities?" he asked, looking over to Maeve and Marcel.

"We're protecting your worlds," Marcel shot back quickly, defensively.

"No," Poet shook his head. "You were supposed to guide dreamers. Instead you used the power for yourself. The real reason you're here is because you can control this place."

"Damn straight," Maeve said.

"And that's the thing," Poet said. "You *control* it. None of this is real. None of the Dreams. You don't have any actual interaction, only fake shit you create. Don't you see how disturbed this is? You didn't want to be vulnerable, so you surrounded yourself in fantasies. But that's not living," Poet said. "No one here actually cares about you."

"Not true," Marcel said. "You know that Dreams have feelings of their own."

"Because they interact. Here, you use them for your desires. They never develop. They never come to truly exist. And that is sick."

Marcel was the first to betray a sign of regret, and Poet wondered if he'd considered the same thing before.

"We can go to the Dream World," Poet said. "Meet with the Dream Walkers—they're waiting right now. We'll get a force together, and then we'll take out REM. And after him, the shadows. We'll set things right."

"Sorry, mate," Callum said, scrunching up his nose. "That meeting happened a long time ago. Did we forget to mention that time moves differently here?"

Stunned, Poet looked at him. "What do you mean?"

"Depends on the sun, on the rotation of the planets, of course, but in the Dream World, they met days ago." He stroked his chin. "I wonder how that force is going."

"I have to get back," Poet said. He began to make a tunnel, but the gravity was different, and it wouldn't form. He grew frustrated and, instead, he created a gun and pointed it at Callum. His skin buzzed with power, fueled by his anger.

Thunder cracked overhead, and a flash of lightning painted them in silver.

Callum lifted his eyes to the sky, and then turned to Maeve and Marcel. "Impressive."

Marcel nodded. "You can learn to hone those skills, Poet," he said. "Use them when you want, not just when you're out of control. You can do more than control the skies."

"*I'm* out of control?" Poet growled, keeping his gun trained on Callum. "God, what do you even want from me? You can't believe I'll just stay here."

"Only for a while," Maeve said, holding up her hands as she stepped toward him. "This is where we came last time REM took control. We refined our skills, but we had so much to learn. As much as you, probably. But then there is your talent—the way you can break apart the Dream World. We want to develop that skill."

"How long?" Poet asked. "How long did you stay here?"

Maeve's expression fell, and she lowered her eyes.

"Sixteen years," Marcel said for her. "We were here for sixteen years."

"What?" Poet asked, his heart sinking. "Didn't you have a family?"

"Once," Callum said. "But like I told you, things like that are not meant for us. The tethers that hold you to the Waking World are what keep you from your full power. You need to let go of them, Poet. They don't belong to you."

"Fuck off," Poet said, but he felt like he might get sick. He couldn't stay here that long.

Callum laughed at the insult, and began to pace once again. Poet lowered the gun; he was outnumbered anyway.

"The siren taught me that," Callum said. "You asked why I killed Angelique, and why I chose to bring the shadow there. She's the reason I have my power."

Behind him, Maeve went to sit on the curb, staring at her boots instead of participating in the conversation.

"When I was like you, Angelique asked me what I loved. And don't get me wrong," Callum said. "I'd enjoyed *plenty* by then. Yet nothing I had was of any value to her. But she kept at it, using her power on me. She wanted proof of my loyalty.

"She learned about me, Poet," Callum continued. "My fears. My joys. And when she found out my father was a Dream Walker, well—she was elated. She wanted one thing from me. She wanted me to kill him and bring her proof."

Poet swallowed hard, reminded of Alexander's death. But this was so much worse. He couldn't even wrap his mind around the situation Callum had been in.

"But you didn't…" Poet started, but his voice trailed off.

Callum watched him, his chin lowered, his bitterness clear. "She had me," Callum said. "Her touch, her whispers. I was helpless to resist. See, Angelique hated Dream Walkers and Night Stalkers more than she hated poets. She had hoped to break their morale, with one of their strongest dying by his own son's hand. She commanded me. And I did what she asked.

"I found my father in the Waking World," Callum said, "reading in his favorite chair. My mother was long gone. He looked up when I came into the room, and I think he knew instantly. He tried to get up from his chair, but he was an old man in that reality. Before he could defend himself, I grabbed his favorite dagger, and I used it to stab him. I killed him before he could utter even one word. I can still feel the warmth of his blood on my hands."

Callum held out his hands, turning them over as he inspected them. Poet, wide-eyed, looked over at the other poets. They'd obviously heard this story before, because although they seemed sickened by the details, they didn't look surprised.

"It changed me," Callum said, glancing up at Poet. "Right then, I felt it. The knife was iridescent with his blood; I glanced around the study and decided I would never go back to that house. I cleaned the knife and put it in a box. And then I opened a tunnel and left the Waking World. My body came with me."

Poet narrowed his eyes. "I don't understand," he said. "How?"

"That's how the siren helped me, even if it wasn't her purpose. I let go of my ties to the Waking World. Cut the tether. Freed myself."

"You killed the person you loved," Poet said. He looked at other poets, his disgust growing. "Did you all do this?" he demanded.

Marcel shook his head. "No, man," he said. "I didn't have to kill anyone—it's not about that. When I became a poet, Callum found me. He told me how I could leave the Waking World behind. And the truth was, I was ready to. Ready to leave the self-destruction behind. At least in the Dream World, I could make it better. I could control what happened to me."

"What did you have to do then?" Poet asked.

"I had to let go," Marcel said, lifting one shoulder in a shrug. "In your heart, you empty it out. A clear decision to give it all up. And that empty space in your consciousness, the one reserved for love, will be filled with more power. No one has to die."

"You're telling me you can't love anyone?" Poet asked, looking to each of them. "You gave up your ability to care about anything, and in return," he motioned around them, "you get a Dream World. Bad fucking deal."

"We can walk into our Dream World," Maeve corrected. "Why should our bodies stay in one reality over another? We live wherever we ground ourselves. So we had to uproot the connection, and the only way was to let it all go."

"People are fallible," Callum added. "Untrustworthy. They will disappoint you."

"But what's the point if you can't feel anything?" Poet asked.

"We can feel," Marcel said. "It's not just weighed down by consequences, worries. Look at Dream Walkers—they take out their souls to help them deal. What we do is much of the same, except we're not as callous. And, of course, we're more powerful."

"This is about power?" Poet asked.

"It can be," Maeve said, walking toward him, her boots echoing on the street. Several Dreams walking by stopped to watch them. "We want you to be stronger, Poet," Maeve said, her siren eye swirling and reaching out to him. "We want you to be a part of this."

Poet resisted the draw to her, and took a step backwards. "Not going to happen," he said.

She smiled. "I can make you do what I want," she said.

"I guarantee that's not true," he replied, although he didn't know if it was.

Maeve looked like she was about to take him up on the challenge when there was a sudden, blinding pain in the back of Poet's head. The ground raced up to meet him, and he heard Callum utter, "Well, that wasn't going well."

CHAPTER TWENTY-TWO

POET OPENED HIS EYES AND IMMEDIATELY cursed, touching the back of his head. It took him a moment to get his bearings, and he looked around the dark, dank room. He could hear music on the other side of a wall.

He stood up from the hard, wooden chair he had been slumped in, and cracked his neck on the way to the door. He paused a moment, listening, but couldn't hear much over the band. It was a different band from the one on the street—a better one.

Poet found the space free of shackles, so he guessed he wasn't a prisoner. At least, not a prisoner of the room. He opened the door.

The light was bright, and Poet had to put up his hand to shield his eyes. There was laughter, and when he could see, he found Maeve and Marcel at the bar with a couple of Dreams, clapping now that he had finally emerged. Callum was nowhere in sight.

The band stopped, and Poet was grateful because the noise was nearly unbearable. His head was killing him.

Several of the dancing Dreams groaned and looked at Marcel. He waved them away, and they turned and filed out the door along with the band.

Marcel avoided Poet's gaze, as if ashamed that he could so easily command them away.

It was only Poet, Maeve, and Marcel in an empty bar.

"What is this?" Poet asked. "Some sort of intervention?"

"You have a choice, you know," Maeve said. "You can leave right now. You just have to let go of your former self."

"I'm not going to do that. Take me back."

Maeve shook her head. "No. You're too weak to go against REM. He'll kill you, and he'll take you over. Then we'll all be dead."

"Then teach me how to use what I have. You say I'm powerful, but you've never tried to help me control it."

"We're helping you now," Marcel said.

"No," Poet responded. "You guys stabbed and kidnapped me."

"We can still teach you," Maeve said, but the impatience in her posture seemed to grow. "You can be stronger, both here and in the Waking World. You'll have full control of your body and consciousness."

But Poet wasn't going to let her manipulate him again. Without Callum here to warn her, he quickly formed a gun and squeezed off two shots before Marcel could stop him. The first one hit Maeve in the shoulder, the second a clear miss. She was being thrown off her stool when Marcel slowed time.

Poet tried to think of the best way out, tried to push as much power as he could to his hands so he could tunnel. To get back to Alan. But it was no use.

All at once time sped up, and Marcel blasted him with enough electricity to send him through the wall, and out onto the street. Poet lay near the curb, his body convulsing.

He heard Maeve's footsteps and saw her and Marcel standing above him. Tears leaked from the corners of Poet's eyes, and he was unable to do anything but shake. Maeve had her hand pressed to her shoulder, blood running between her fingers.

"I'll let you think about what you've done," Maeve said. "We create this reality, Poet Anderson—not you. Sweet dreams."

There was a whipping sound, and then Poet fell through the ground into a tunnel, his heart leaping into his throat. He hit the ground hard, and the wind was knocked out of him. At first it was dark, but his eyes adjusted to the new light quickly.

"Wake up, Jonas," Alan said, pushing his shoulder. Jonas blinked slowly and turned to him, surprised to find his brother much younger. His hair longer. His muscles bigger. Alan's blue eyes were brimming with tears. "Wake up," he begged.

"I'm awake," Jonas replied, and as he sat up, he recognized where he was: on the porch of his childhood home. Rain poured down in sheets beyond the railing. Alan was soaking wet, clutching his arm. Jonas turned and saw the swirling lights of two police cars, a uniformed officer on the phone near the edge of the steps and another still in his cruiser.

It was raining—of course it was raining—and the thunder clapped again, but this time it didn't seem so loud. Nothing could have been as loud as what Alan said next.

"They're gone, Jonas," he told him. "Mom and Dad are gone."

Jonas stared at him, trying to make sense of the moment, but also feeling the suffocating grief that came with those words. He felt tears gather, but he shook his head.

"This is just a dream," Jonas said, and Alan choked back his own cry.

"No, brother," he said. "This is real. It's everything else that was the dream."

Jonas stared at him, panic bubbling up. He searched around again, and he could feel the chill of the night air on his skin. Taste the sleep still in his mouth. Hear the sounds of rain pouring down. It felt real. Oh, God, what if it was?

Jonas took his brother's arm and let Alan pull him up, noticing immediately that he was younger too—his socked feet smaller, his body shorter. He was just a boy.

"No," Jonas said, shaking his head. He pulled away from Alan. "This is a dream. Some kind of trick that the poets are playing on me."

"Poets?" Alan asked. "What the hell are you talking about? Mom and Dad are dead, Jonas. They're fucking dead."

The comment was a slap in the face, but Jonas knew something was wrong. He couldn't have dreamt about years in the future. No—that wasn't possible. He ran his hand through his hair, finding it shorter. Everything was wrong.

"Is there a problem?" the officer asked, putting one foot up on the stair. "Is there something you two aren't telling me?"

"No," Alan said annoyed, glancing back at him. "My brother's in shock. Just…give us a minute."

But Jonas couldn't let it slide. He refused to let the poets get away with exploiting his memories.

"This isn't real," Jonas called to the officer. "You're not real. None of this."

Alan turned to him, looking hurt. But the officer eyed him suspiciously.

"Are you saying your parents aren't dead, son?" the officer asked.

"Oh, no. They're dead. They died years ago. This is a dream."

"Jonas!" Alan begged.

The officer smiled, and took another step up the stairs, his hand automatically going to the gun on his hip. "That so?" the officer asked.

"I want to wake up," Jonas said, challenging him. He wasn't going to play games. He wanted out of the dream. "Wake me up!" he screamed to the sky.

Alan stepped back from him, overcome by emotion. Jonas remembered him being strong the day they were told their parents had died. But, of course, he was still young. Everything Alan did was strong to him.

"I'm going to have to ask you to come with me, son," the officer said, drawing his weapon. Jonas scoffed, and held out his hand, willing power there to create his own gun.

But nothing happened.

"Stop," Alan said to the officer, trying to come between him and Jonas. "He's just upset."

"Out of the way," the officer told Alan.

"No, leave him out of this," Alan said, frustrated, and pushed the officer back. Enraged, the officer turned the gun on Alan.

This wasn't a memory—it was a nightmare. "No," Jonas said, the feeling of impending doom pressing in on him. "Not Alan," he said.

The officer darted his eyes to Jonas then, the irises pure black. His teeth bared. "It's always been about Alan," he said in REM's voice. And then he squeezed the trigger and blew off the top of Alan's head.

"No!" Jonas screamed, running to his brother's side, watching the blood pour in rivers from his exposed brain. Inside Jonas, the rage faded and was replaced with absolute agony. And even though he was dead, Alan looked at him.

"This is your fault," he whispered. "You never do what you're told, and that's why I always die."

"What?" Jonas asked, wiping his tears with the palms of his hands. "Why are you saying that?" Guilt buried him, and he couldn't stand the pain that came along with it. "Don't say that," he said miserably.

"You kill me," Alan said, and closed his eyes. "You're the one who kills me."

"Stand up," the officer said from behind Jonas. Only it wasn't the officer's voice—it was REM's. "It's your turn."

"You're not here," Jonas said, refusing to look at him. "None of you are." And yet, Alan's skin was warm and real. Jonas had to fight his own senses.

"Oh, tiny poet," REM said. "I'm always here."

The officer pulled the trigger, and Jonas felt an explosion of pain in his head, something so sharp and severe he couldn't make a noise. There was a rush of air, hot liquid, and then Jonas fell face first on the wooden porch and died.

"Wake up, Jonas," Alan said, pushing his shoulder. Jonas blinked slowly and turned to him, finding Alan with his hair longer, his muscles bigger, his face younger. Jonas paused a long moment, and darted his eyes around the porch. "Please, Jonas," his brother begged.

"I'm awake," Jonas said carefully as he sat up. He was on the porch of his childhood home, rain pouring down in sheets. Alan was soaking wet, clutching his arm. Jonas turned and saw the swirling lights of two police cars, a uniformed officer on the phone near the edge of the steps, and another still in his cruiser.

Thunder clapped. "They're gone, Jonas," Alan said. "Mom and Dad are gone."

Jonas stared at him, unmoving. Horrified to find himself in the same exact nightmare.

"This isn't real," Jonas said weakly, the back of his head still aching from when he was shot. He turned to look at the officer, and the man watched him curiously.

"None of you are real," Jonas repeated, using the railing of the porch to pull himself up. "Wake me up!" he shouted at the sky. "Goddammit, wake me up!"

"Is there a problem?" the officer asked, his hand slipping to his side and resting on his gun.

Jonas scoffed, waiting for him to turn into REM. "Yeah," Jonas said. "The problem is *fuck you.*"

Alan quickly jumped out to stand in front of Jonas, telling the officer he didn't mean it. He was in shock. But the officer ended up shooting him, much like before. And Jonas waited until the officer killed him again, and he hit the floorboards.

"JONAS, WAKE UP," ALAN said, pushing his shoulder. Jonas opened his eyes, staring at the roof of the covered porch, watching the reflection of the police swirling. "Mom and Dad are gone," Alan added tearfully.

Jonas swallowed hard, and relived the nightmare. Over and over again.

CHAPTER TWENTY-THREE

THE SHOT RANG OUT AND ECHOED OFF the house. Jonas hit the wood slats on the porch, the breeze of wind cool against his skin wet with blood. He could see Alan lying next to him, half of his head missing. He'd watched his brother die so many times, but the worst part was that each time hurt just as much as the first time. Jonas was sure that if this nightmare was going to kill him, he would die of grief.

His eyes fluttered closed.

"Christ," a female voice said, stirring Poet awake. "You'd think at some point you would just go along and try to survive."

Poet opened his eyes and found himself in the middle of a dirty street, trash lined up along the curb. He sat up, trying to figure out where he was, and saw Maeve standing above him, Marcel next to her with his arms crossed over his chest.

Their Dreams—the people they created—looked on curiously. The moons were an arc in the sky, and the wind blew strongly. Poet had a feeling he might be why. He covertly clenched his fist and felt the breeze react with more force.

"How long have I been in that loop?" Poet asked Marcel, his voice rough. He got to his feet, the pain in his head starting to fade.

"Don't know," Marcel said. "We don't keep time here. A while, I suppose. You could have come back sooner, but you're stubborn."

"We thought you'd get desensitized to it," Maeve said. "If you want to go home, you'll have to learn to let him go. But you can't seem to cut ties."

"He's my brother," Poet said angrily.

"Yeah, but notice that you didn't see Sam?" she said, smiling. "Why do you think that is?"

"Shut up," Poet said, reaching to put his hand to his forehead and closing his eyes.

"It's because you won't even entertain the idea of letting her go," Maeve said. "You can't even bring yourself to think of it. And yet...she left you, Poet. Tell me, will she ever forgive you for killing her father? Because, personally, I would have forgiven you. Alexander was an asshole."

"I said shut up," Poet growled, looking over at her.

It was then that he realized Callum was gone. Maeve and Marcel seemed unprepared to fight. Poet knew he had to get out before they threw him into another mental prison.

"So you're saying," Poet began, getting to this feet, "that if I give up on Alan, I'd gain more power. I could do whatever I want."

Maeve smiled. "It'd be a start."

Poet nodded, and a few of the Dreams walking by stopped to watch him. He adjusted his bowler hat and put his hands in the pockets of his suit jacket. "Who did you give up, Maeve?"

Her expression soured. "That's none of your business, Poet Anderson," she said coolly.

"What if it can help me? I want to know how my sacrifice compares."

Marcel sighed, and turned to look down the street. Maeve chewed on the corner of her lip for a moment and then gave in.

"It was my mother," she said. "Like I said, she was a lucid dreamer and my father was a siren. But as she got older…" Maeve cracked her neck, stalling. "As she got older, my mother lost her ability to get to the Dream World. It wasn't something she was willing to give up, so she tried all sorts of things. All sort of…medication cocktails. She eventually ended up in the hospital, committed. Try telling a doctor you're in love with a Dream being and see how they react."

"What happened to her?" Poet asked, taking some pleasure in Maeve's discomfort, if only because it was lowering her guard.

"I'm sure she's dead by now," Maeve said. "That was a long time ago. Callum told me I could become more powerful if I cut my ties to her and grounded my consciousness in the dream reality." Maeve closed her eyes for a moment, and when she looked at Poet again, she smiled. "I told her goodbye while she was ranting and banging her fists on the fourth-story window, begging me not to leave her in the Waking

World. I told her she was pathetic, and that I couldn't wait to be free of her. I said hurtful, hateful things, until she broke down. And I stood there, watching. As her tears fell, I let my love for her drain away until I felt empty and hollow. And then I closed my eyes, and willed myself into the Dream World, body and all.

"The power filled me up," Maeve continued, tapping her chest. "Took up the space. I'm whole now. It feels great."

"It sounds awful," Poet said, his confidence growing by the second.

"You only say that because you're weakened," she replied, but the story had rattled her, and her voice shook.

Marcel came over and put his hand on Maeve's arm, comforting her or telling her stop talking, Poet wasn't sure which. Marcel turned to Poet and shrugged.

"It was my little sister, Leticia," Marcel said, his throat thick with emotion. "But she wasn't part of this." He motioned around them. "She wasn't part of any Dream World. She was just a kid, but uh…" He stopped then, his lips pressed firmly together, his brow furrowed.

"She died," Maeve said for him.

"Yeah," Marcel said. "My sister died after REM took over my neighbor's body. He'd been looking for me. At the time, I was the only poet still in the open. God, it had to be the fifties, right?"

Maeve told him she couldn't remember, and Marcel continued his story.

"I was in the Dream World, guiding dreamers like an obedient Poet, being pushed around by Dream Walkers. REM came for me. He took over a lucid dreamer in the Waking World. Using my neighbor's body, REM broke into my house while I was asleep and stabbed me fourteen times," Marcel said.

Poet was stunned, and ran his gaze over Marcel to find scars. And then, just like that, they appeared on his skin. A raised slash near his ear, one on his throat. Marcel lifted his arm and pushed back his sleeve, defensive wounds marking his skin.

Marcel stood up straighter and the scars faded; he had control over how he appeared, in any reality.

"My little sister," Marcel continued, "came into the room when she heard the noise. When my neighbor—REM—saw her, he attacked her too. Only difference was I survived my wounds and Leticia didn't.

"That neighbor," Marcel continued, "walked out into traffic after that. I wasn't dead, but I was destroyed. I didn't want to be a poet anymore, although the Dream Walkers were intent on keeping me. If anything, I feared them nearly as much as REM. Both are forces that will do anything to achieve their end."

Marcel took a step back then, his hand on his heart. "I couldn't let go of my anger," he said. "I couldn't let go of Leticia's little body, back there in the Waking World. It haunted me. It weakened me. And as I tried to find where to go, I found the sirens." He looked sideways and Maeve smiled sadly at him. "I found Maeve. And she told me I had to let go of Leticia. She showed me how."

Marcel blew out a heavy breath and turned to Poet. "I'll be honest with you, man. There are days when I wonder what it was like to love something... That's how long it's been for me. I can't remember. But the power—" He held out his hand, and sparks hovered between his fingers, ready to become anything he wished. "It's enough to make it worth it."

Those words sent Poet reeling back to the truth. No power was worth giving up his brother. These poets had lost their humanity.

If he hoped to escape, Poet knew he'd have to incapacitate Marcel before he could stop time. It was the only way. So before he could consider the outcome, Poet formed a gun and fired it, shooting Marcel through his outstretched hand.

Several Dreams cried out, and Marcel groaned and fell to his knees, holding his arm by the wrist. Poet took off, aware that Maeve would be close behind. He didn't know how to get out of this reality; he only knew he had to try.

Poet sprinted towards the buildings, hoping to slip between them and find a place to hide. Several lasers shot past him, and Maeve yelled for him to stop.

He wouldn't be able to out-run her. Not when he didn't know where he was going. He turned the corner and saw a line of motorcycles—the souped-up ones he had spotted when he first arrived.

"Hell, yes," he muttered, and cut in that direction. He hopped on the last motorcycle and brought it roaring to life. Another shot flew past him, and he could feel the beginning of a tunnel opening, probably about to send him back into a nightmare.

He pressed on the accelerator, and blasted out of there before the tunnel could take him, his hat flying off.

The buildings zoomed past as he swerved in and out of the streets. Dreams shouted for him to stop. It felt a bit like him against the world—which he guessed it was.

The motorcycle sped forward, and Poet turned onto what looked like a quiet street. He started to relax, and increased his speed. The moons were bright, and Poet had to squint when he noticed something in the road yards ahead.

"Shit," he whispered when he realized it was Marcel. Poet pressed harder on the accelerator, hoping to take a turn off the road before Marcel stopped time. But with blood dripping from his hand, Marcel didn't use his power like that. Instead, wisps of electricity bound together and created a rocket launcher.

Poet's eyes widened, but before he could get out of the way, Marcel fired. There was a huge explosion in front of the motorcycle, catching the wheel and launching Poet forward.

He flipped over the handlebars, spinning in air as the heat of the explosion burned his jacket. He slammed to the pavement in a heap, and rolled to his side, groaning in pain.

There was the roar of another engine, and when it stopped, he heard Maeve's voice. "Jesus, Marcel," she said. "You didn't have to kill him."

"He shot my hand," Marcel said. "Besides, he's not dead. I can see him breathing."

"Get him up," Maeve said. "Before Callum gets back. Where is that bastard?"

"Don't know," Marcel called back, uninterested.

Poet could hear his approaching footsteps, and covertly, Poet reached for a shard of glass next to him on the street from the broken mirror on his bike. He wasn't going back into that nightmare.

"Come on now, Poet Anderson," Marcel said. "Let's call it even."

But just as he paused next to him, Poet swung out and sliced Marcel's shin. Marcel yelled, and fell back a step. Poet used the moment to pounce, and quickly grabbed him, pressing the glass to the artery in his neck, hard enough to let him know he was serious.

Maeve stopped dead in the middle of the street staring at them. She held up her hands to let Poet know she wasn't going to shoot him. "What are you doing?" she asked, her rage barely controlled.

"I'm going home," Poet said to her. He looked at the side of Marcel's face. "Tunnel me out," he said. Marcel turned to Maeve, and Poet saw her eyes had gone smoky gray. An angry storm cloud.

Dreams had begun to arrive and watch from the sidewalks, but now they all looked to Maeve. She gritted her teeth, and waved her hand toward Poet. "Take him down," she hissed, although the sound of her voice was like a song one would remember from childhood, haunting and nostalgic.

All at once, the entire crowd raced toward Poet, fresh with anger, lost in their desire to complete Maeve's bidding. They ran in his direction, and Poet put his mouth next to Marcel's ear, the glass cutting his skin.

"Do you want to die?" he asked him. "Tunnel me out!"

"No," Marcel said, wincing at the pain Poet was causing. And it was that wince that gave Poet pause. He didn't want to hurt him. He just wanted to go home.

"You more than anyone should understand," Poet told him, lowering the glass. "I won't give up my brother. Tell me, Marcel—if you had the chance to save your little sister, would you?"

Marcel turned to him. The Dreams still ran for Poet, ready to take him down as Maeve had commanded. Poet expected Marcel to hit him, but there was something else there—a hint of the humanity that Poet thought they'd lost.

The instant before the Dreams could tackle Poet, Marcel looped his arms in giant circles and tore open a tunnel.

CHAPTER TWENTY-FOUR

HE WAS FLYING THEN. POET COULD barely keep his eyes open as the feeling of dropping out of sky flooded him, along with immense pressure in his head and the sensation that his skin was pulling away. He and Marcel were in a tunnel, and as they crested the top of the black hole, they momentarily slowed. Poet looked at Marcel and saw him fighting with everything he had to get them through it. Poet wasn't sure it was enough, but then, like falling down a hill, they began to pick up speed again, and the tunnel fell through space, stars flying past them, until the Dream World came into focus and spit them out in the center of Genesis.

It wasn't a graceful landing. Poet hit first, and hard, landing on the pavement and having to dodge several flying cars as he somersaulted toward the curb.

Marcel landed with a roll and onto one knee, like he'd done it a million times before. He still had to jump out of the way as cars flew quickly above them, blowing their horns.

Once at the curb, Marcel brushed off his pants, and held out his hand to Poet, offering him help getting up. Poet took it, and when he was standing face to face to Marcel, he was filled with regret. Marcel must have read it because he held up his hand; the hole that was there was almost healed.

"Don't fucking shoot me again," Marcel said.

"I won't. I—" Poet looked around the city, overcome with relief to be back. He glanced up at the telescreen, half-expecting to see his face broadcast there in the darkness. But instead the screen was blank. Poet looked to another screen—same result. The screens were never off in the dreamscape. Something was wrong.

"How long have we—?" Poet started, but then he heard the roar of engines.

He and Marcel spun quickly and looked down the street. But it was too late. Night Stalkers surrounded them. Poet forced energy into his body, his eyes going white with electricity. He stood next to Marcel while the Night Stalkers idled on the sides of the road. No weapons in sight.

And then he appeared. Only this time, he wasn't inhabiting another body. It was REM, in the flesh.

He was changed since the last time he'd been seen. REM's face had been reconstructed, although his eyes were entirely robotic. He was wearing black armor, red in some places. His hands no longer had flesh on them, and on one hand, his fingertips ended in sharp metal points. Connected were vials of some unknown, and most likely unsavory, concoction that would probably melt you from the inside out, or make you put the gun to your own head and pull the trigger. Either way, Poet knew he and Marcel were in trouble.

"We have to go," Poet said under his breath.

But the other poet smiled ruefully. "Naw," Marcel replied. "I'm done running."

As REM walked toward them, his Halo making circles around him, Marcel waved his hand and conjured a sniper rifle. And still the Night Stalkers along the street didn't react.

In a slick movement, Marcel dropped to one knee and fired several lasers in REM's direction, the aim dead-on. But REM smiled, and held up his arm. A gun extended from his suit, and he sent out a barrage of lasers, destroying the shots that Marcel had fired. Sparks spit out over the road.

Marcel cursed under his breath, about to take another shot, when REM began to run. He wasn't human; he wasn't even just a Dream anymore. The way his muscles moved was unnaturally fast, and Poet knew they wouldn't be able to out run him. He was wholly upgraded.

Poet held out his hand to create a tunnel and get them out of there, but REM had reached him just as the wind began to pick up. REM swung a sharp blade, and Poet ducked just in time, only to be pummeled by the Halo. Poet was knocked back toward the building. He crashed against a stone wall, and fell to the pavement with a thud.

Poet was in agony for a few seconds, then got to his hands and knees and looked to where REM and Marcel had already begun to fight. It was strangely beautiful, the two moving shapes in the darkness with occasional blue light conjured from Marcel's hands.

Sometimes, it illuminated both their faces, one with a sinister smile, the other with a fearful grimace. Poet groaned out his pain, and then shot forward, running as he created a razor-sharp spear.

Just as REM turned, his Halo engaged in battle with Marcel, Poet threw the spear. REM didn't have time to react, and the blade slammed directly into his left robotic eye, sticking into his skull.

REM roared, and extended one of the blades from his hand, slashing the air wildly. Marcel used his weapon to hit the Halo, and the orb went back to REM, guarding him from further attack. The creature finally pulled out the spear and tossed it aside, now blinded in one eye.

Poet, breathing hard, went to Marcel's side. The Night Stalkers still hung back, watching everything unfold. REM stared over at them, his eye-hole a gaping wound where black blood dripped from the metal socket.

Before Poet could try to start another tunnel, REM extended a sword, and leapt toward them. He was so unnaturally fast, unnaturally strong, that it caught the poets off guard.

Poet fell backwards from the surprise of REM's attack. But sound and light froze, and Poet realized that Marcel was slowing time. REM was in the air, about to come down on them, but they would have the advantage of seeing where he'd land. Poet would smile if he could move his face.

But as they readied to end this, Poet noticed something, and he could feel that Marcel noticed it too. While they were frozen, they could see REM's body vibrating, even in this bended timeframe. Marcel groaned, gnashing his teeth as he tried to hold on, but REM was too strong.

Poet saw the realization in Marcel's eyes as the world suddenly fast-forwarded back into focus. REM broke from time, faster than the poets. And before he could even shout, REM's sword drove through Marcel's chest, impaling him.

Marcel gasped, and looked down at the long blade sticking into his chest. He reached down and grabbed at REM's hands, trying to fight back in some way. REM laughed, and withdrew the blade, and Marcel fell to the ground.

"What have you done?" Poet asked, horrified. He stared down at Marcel's body. The poet's eyes were closed, his breathing shallow.

"You're right," REM replied with false sympathy. "I just wasted a perfectly good poet. Guess you'll have to do."

Poet felt the anger building up inside of him. Marcel was going to die, and he felt responsible.

No matter what, death was always chasing him.

It was then that Poet noticed the creature, the shadow creeping along the roadway, swerving around Night Stalkers as if evaluating its prey. While they were focused on him, a shadow was about to take one of them over.

Poet gently cast one last look at Marcel, and Marcel gasped in a breath and opened his eyes to look at Poet Anderson. "Don't let him in the Waking World," he murmured, blood spurting between his lips. "Don't..." His eyelids fluttered, and Poet's expression broke.

"Marcel," Poet murmured.

But it was too late. There was a quiet rattle, a garbled breath, and then Marcel was gone.

Poet growled, and steeled himself for battle. He swung out his hand and his umbrella appeared, charged up with energy. Above him, the sky rumbled with anger.

From the corner of his eye, Poet watched the shadow pause at the tallest of the Night Stalkers. And then, like a star being consumed by a black hole, the shadow consumed the Night Stalker's Halo until it was gone. The Night Stalker shook its head and then convulsed once before stiffening.

Night Stalkers don't have souls, but there must be power in their Halos that the shadow could consume and control, and Poet imagined it could do the same to Dream Walkers.

"Well, are you going to use that?" REM asked Poet with a laugh, motioning to the umbrella. REM retracted his weapons, and then stretched his metallic fingers on one of his hands as if they were about to have a bare-knuckle brawl.

Poet wasn't sure how much time he'd have before the shadow made its way to him. He hoped he'd be able to tunnel out in time. But if not, Poet would fight to the death. He would never let himself get taken over by REM or a shadow.

In a sudden movement, Poet yelled and swung around, sending a bright flash of electricity out of his umbrella and hitting REM square in the chest. It was unexpected, and the shot knocked him back. His Halo quickly looped around him and headed for Poet.

REM bared his teeth, and Poet hit the Halo with the umbrella like it was a baseball. There was a shattering noise, and Poet saw his umbrella spark, shorting out.

REM laughed. "My sensors can pick up the chemical traces of adrenaline in your body. You're terrified."

Poet narrowed his eyes. REM was right, he was terrified, but Poet began to replace that fear with anger. He lunged for REM, and the creature quickly grabbed him the collar of this jacket and threw him.

The Night Stalkers watched as Poet got to his feet, stumbling. Before he could even recover, REM grabbed him and, with incredible speed, ran him straight into the wall. He pinned him there, and Poet cried out in pain as REM's fingers extended into long needles, puncturing him. Before the vials could distill any poison, Poet gathered his energy and blasted it out his hands, sending REM flying backward.

Poet shook off the pain in his arm and charged forward again. The Halo smacked him hard in the chest, knocking him off balance, and REM quickly followed it up with a punch to his gut.

As Poet was gasping for breath, REM kicked him in the face, sending him spinning. Poet coughed, unable to get to his feet before REM kicked him hard in the back. There was a sharp crack, and Poet felt his ribs come dislodged.

He screamed out in pain, and this time, when he rolled, he created a machine gun and fired at REM and his Halo. The lasers connected, knocking the Halo aside, but as it hit REM he continued forward as if he couldn't feel a thing, the holes torn into his suit sparking with electricity.

REM got to Poet, grabbed him by the throat, and lifted him off his feet. Poet gasped for breath before a fistful of metal punched him the jaw. REM punched him again, and

Poet felt his nose break. He fought to get free, but when he did, REM smashed him to the pavement again.

He was no match for this rebuilt creature.

Poet's eye began to swell closed, but he tried to get up. He wouldn't just die. REM smiled, watching Poet crawl along the road.

Poet choked on the blood in his throat, thick and metallic as it poured in from his nose. Each cough sent a spurt of blood over his face, dotting it with crimson. He turned on his side, and REM hailed down another series of kicks. Poet's head ricocheted between the end of REM's boot and the pavement. Another kick to his gut and Poet spit out a mouthful of blood.

His vision blurred, and he took in a gasp of breath, only to be met with a painful, crushing ache that assured him his ribs were broken, his lungs possibly pierced. Poet wiped his eyes and realized his head was bleeding too.

Poet wheezed. He was dying, and it was a bit surreal. He could actually feel his life draining away. There was a sharp snap, and he groaned. REM laughed as he lifted his boot from Poet's broken leg.

"Toughen up," REM said. "Or you might die before I break every bone." He grabbed Poet by the collar and pulled him up so he could punch him in the face with his metallic hand. The sound was wet, and it rang in Poet's ears as he was dropped back on the ground. He couldn't feel his lips anymore. His face was swollen, one eye closed completely.

"I don't need your body," REM said, stepping on Poet's wrist to hold his arm down. "Just your soul." Poet cried out as his bone was crushed, and REM laughed. "This brings me actual joy," he added. "Let's see you create anything now, boy."

Poet lifted his head, his body too broken to stand. He looked at REM soaked in his blood. Across the road, he saw Marcel's lifeless body.

Hate poured in.

"Go to hell," Poet managed to say, although his words were slurred because of the swelling in his mouth.

"Yes, indeed," REM said smugly. He grabbed Poet by his injured arm and hauled him up. Poet couldn't stand; his broken leg hung limply and at an odd angle.

"Now," REM said, looking down at him, "we're going to take a trip to the Waking World."

Poet's head rolled back, but he forced himself to stay, to see every terrible moment. He wasn't a coward. Even in death, he wouldn't be a coward. Poet hung on to life as he bled out, and then REM's hand was over his heart.

There was a pull—an unseen tug—and Poet's mouth opened as he gasped out in pain. The gasp turned into screams—his soul was being devoured.

There was a shift of movement, and then suddenly, a flash of light. Poet was weightless, and then he hit the pavement hard. He clutched at his chest with his good hand, his eyes trying to focus on what was going on around him.

The Night Stalker, the one that had been taken over by a shadow, had its electricity-charged sword raised. REM stared up at him from the ground, a burn scorched across his face and neck. The Night Stalker had attacked him.

"What are you doing?" REM demanded, quickly getting to his feet. He produced his own sword, and without so much as an instant of hesitance, lobbed off the Night Stalker's head.

The monster of nightmares was caught off guard, and Poet used that temporary distraction to try to save himself. He closed his eyes, ignoring the pain all over his body. With the absence of kicks and hits, he could concentrate.

Poet felt his energy swim through his body, catching on his injuries, wanting to heal him, but there wasn't time for that. He opened his good eye, blazing with white-hot electricity. He stared at the sky, and a slash of lightning cut it in two. Thunder boomed so loudly, the street shook. It began to rain.

Dots of blue liquid dotted his skin, cooling it where the swelling had grown hot. Around him, Poet could feel the Dream World curving in, protecting him. The road began to split, cracking, separating, widening a rift between Poet and the others.

REM fell back a step, nearly falling into the crevice that had opened. He stared, wide-eyed as Poet took control of the Dream World. Slowly, Poet lifted his head and turned to his side, the blood running off his clothes in rivers with the rain.

Even with a broken leg, Poet got to his feet, swaying as he tried to balance. He stared across the torn earth at REM. "It was a shadow," Poet said to him, his voice garbled. "They've been after me. Thanks for taking one for the team."

REM shook his head. "You don't understand," he said, retracting his weapons as the rain fell over him. "The shadows aren't just after you."

Poet was stunned by this. "What do you mean?"

"They're trying to consume the Dream World. And then it'll be on to the Waking World. And so on through all of the realities."

"That will never happen."

"Then we must work together," REM said. "I wanted your power so that I could take on the shadows myself."

"You're a liar," Poet said, not believing him for even an instant. The rain began to pour down harder, and REM had to shout his words to be heard. "I've been rebuilt to battle them," he said. "Don't you see?"

Pain rocketed through Poet's body as he continued to manipulate the Dream World. He fell to his knees, but didn't let up the storm that began sending gusts of wind that knocked down Night Stalkers from their airbikes.

"You killed my family, REM. My friends." Poet looked at him, trying to conjure enough power to tunnel out. But his right hand was useless, and his left was weakened. "We will never work together. I'll die first."

REM growled, animalistic even though he was covered in metal. "That can be arranged." He pulled out a staff, banged it on the ground, and made it explode with red-hot power. "I will carve you up," he said, and crouched down like he was about to jump over the split Poet had created.

Poet leaned back on his left hand, still on the pavement. "Do your worst," he murmured, and prepared for the next attack.

Beyond the sound of wind and pelting rain, Poet heard a familiar rhythm. He turned and saw a tunnel appear. Maeve stepped through onto Poet's small island of concrete.

The horror on her face when she saw Marcel's body was devastating.

Blue rain ran down her cheeks, mixing with shocked tears. There was a howl, and Maeve looked over to see REM, ready to attack. Her movements were slow but decisive. She opened another tunnel, grabbed Poet by his injured arm, and then pulled him and Marcel into the Waking World.

CHAPTER TWENTY-FIVE

JONAS SPIT OUT BLOOD THE MINUTE HE sat up in bed. He reached up to touch his face, and then gasped when he held up his arms. No bones protruded. The swelling was gone, but his leg ached, and his ribs were tight. It was hard to breathe.

He should be dead. That he knew. Jonas groaned as he got out of bed. He glanced around the room, and realized that it had been changed. This wasn't his room at all. This wasn't his bed. He looked down. These weren't his clothes.

"Alan," he called, and his voice was hoarse and thick. He cleared his throat and tried again, but it was barely a whisper. He didn't understand where he was. He was unsteady on his feet, and he had to hold the rail of the bed before he felt okay enough to make it to the door.

He heard voices on the other side, and he paused to listen, but they were too muffled to understand. Jonas opened the door and, gripping the frame, passed through into the living room of a hotel suite.

The TV was on. Jonas stared at it for a moment, not recognizing the show, and looked around the room. He didn't see anyone, and he hobbled over on his stiff leg to ease himself onto the couch. He was definitely at the Eden Hotel—at least he thought so—but where was everyone?

On the table, he noticed a couple of soda cans, and two still had wet rings seeping underneath them. He glanced toward the efficiency kitchen, and there were plates. Obviously, someone lived here. It must—

There was a beep as someone outside swiped their key card. Jonas stared at the door as it opened. He heard the sound of a woman's laugh and the murmur of his brother's voice. Jonas's heart filled as Alan was first in, holding a cup of coffee in his hands.

"And then Marshall—" He stopped short when he saw Jonas, his face registering his shock.

"Marshall what?" Samantha asked, walking in behind him. "He's such a—" But she stopped too. Tears immediately welled up in her eyes, and her coffee slipped from her hands and exploded out of the cup when it hit the carpet. "You're back," she gasped.

It hurt to see her: *that* Jonas could say. Her hair was longer, her cheeks flushed. She was painfully beautiful, but she felt like a stranger. "*You're* back," he responded.

Sam furrowed her brow, and she and Alan exchanged a look that irritated Jonas. Like they were in on a secret he wasn't.

"Brother," Jonas said in greeting, a little more hostile than he intended. Alan closed the door, and both he and Sam stepped over the spilled coffee that had now filled the room with its aroma.

Alan stopped in front of Jonas, and then he laughed and ran his hand through his blond hair. Jonas noted how much stronger his brother looked, the way his redefined muscles flexed. The clarity in his blue eyes.

"I've fucking missed you," Alan said, breaking out in a wide smile. But Jonas could only stare at him, confused. He looked at Sam.

"What's going on?" he asked, going to sit on the couch.

Sam studied him a moment, and then she came over to him. She reached to run her fingers along his sore cheek. Gentle and loving.

Jonas closed his eyes at her touch, and found himself leaning against her, his face resting on her hip. Sam's fingers traced down the back of his neck. Jonas was so sorry for what happened to her father. He was so sorry that he'd hurt her.

"Jonas," she whispered. He looked up at her, and saw she had started to cry. "You...you've been gone," she said.

"I've been asleep," he said. She smiled, and Alan laughed again. Jonas reluctantly pulled back from Sam, and she sat on the couch next to him, her hands constantly touching him, like she was trying to make sure he was real.

"Okay, I get it," Jonas said cautiously. "How long have I been asleep?" Alan's smile faded, and Jonas felt a surge of panic.

"That's the thing," Alan said. "We couldn't wake you up. You've been—Sam hired a nurse to care for you here because we didn't think you'd want to be in the Sleep Center."

"How long?" Jonas demanded.

Alan frowned and said, "Six months."

JONAS HAD BEEN ASLEEP for half a year. In that time, he'd lost some muscle mass, but other than that, the hired nurse who would come to check on him said he was remarkably stable.

"How did I survive?" Jonas asked, taking monster bites of the sandwich Alan had ordered him. His stomach rumbled with hunger, but the pain in his ribs had subsided the further he got from his dream. Not to mention that the pain meds Sam gave him had taken the edge off.

"Oh, speaking of surviving," Sam said, crossing the room to get her phone out of her purse. She hadn't left Jonas's side since he'd woken up. "I have to cancel the nurse."

"The nurse would come three times a day with a feeding tube," Alan said. "And to empty your...uh, bladder."

"Jesus," Jonas said, putting down his sandwich. "Never mind. I don't want to know how I survived. What else is going on? Things are different, even in the Dream World. What's been happening in these past months?"

"I've been training," Alan said. "Getting stronger with the help of Imani." He paused. "Do you remember Imani?"

"Yeah," Jonas said. "But you're not a Dream Walker, right?"

"No," Alan replied sounding disappointed. "I'm just regular lucid dreamer. And while you've been gone," he added, "REM has been tearing up the Dream World looking for you. At least he hasn't gotten through into this world. No more

Night Stalkers either. But people here," he motioned around to indicate the Waking World, "have been losing their minds. Murders are up. Crime. Fucking espionage. Everything is falling apart, and I'd bet anything the shadows are stealing dreamers and coming through."

Jonas closed his eyes. "And there was no one to stop them," he said.

"Well," Alan said. "I wouldn't say no one." Alan nodded to Sam.

Jonas looked over at her. "You've been fighting?" he asked.

Sam had the phone to her ear, but he could see the wave of emotion pass over her. She hung up with the nurse and turned to him.

"I was looking for you," she said quietly. "And that turned into me hunting Night Stalkers where I could. I thought they had you. Hell, I even went with Callum to—"

"Callum?" Jonas said, nearly dropping his food. He slapped his sandwich down on the plate, his anger picking up. "Where did Callum take you?"

"Nowhere," she said. "He came here to check on your body. He—" She shook her head. "He said he wanted to make sure you were really here."

"Stay away from him," Jonas warned. "The poets are the ones who had me." The reminder made his ribs hurt again, and he rubbed his side.

Alan and Sam stared at him, waiting for an explanation. "They...had you?" Alan asked. "Like, saved you or held you prisoner?"

"At this point?" Jonas said. "Both."

Alan blew out an angry breath, and came to sit across from Jonas in the chair. "And the blood you coughed up on your sheets? Who did that?"

"That came courtesy of REM."

Jonas went on to tell them about the poets tunneling him through the black hole, and how time was different in their created reality. He told them about the nightmare he had to live repeatedly. And he hated how tears dripped over Sam's cheeks as he described REM nearly killing him. He told them how Marcel was dead, but it was Maeve who saved Poet from REM's final blow. He had no idea what happened after that.

"He told me that he wanted to work together," Jonas added with a bitter laugh. "REM said the shadows are going to take over all realities if we didn't stop them."

"Work together with REM?" Alan asked. "He's a madman."

"Yeah, I told him I'd rather die," Jonas said. "He seemed okay with that choice too."

"Then we kill them all," Sam said. "The shadows, REM, the Night Stalkers. And hell," she said, "even the poets if they come after you again."

"We've got two dozen Dream Walkers. Strong ones," Alan said. "It's not an army, but it's something. But we'll need more. Is there anyone else we can recruit? We're severely outnumbered."

Jonas sat back on the couch, ready to say no, when a thought occurred to him. "I might know a place," he said. "But I'll tell you one thing, they hate poets."

"So do I," Alan said. "I mean, except for you, of course."

"Of course," Jonas replied. He stood up, glancing around the hotel room, wishing he had more time to enjoy the Waking World. But if it was falling apart the way Alan said, then this was one of their last chances. At the counter, Sam took off her jacket and rolled up her sleeves.

"What are you doing?" Jonas asked her.

She scoffed. "Coming with you, obviously."

"I don't think you'll like this place," Jonas responded. "For the first time in your life, you won't be the prettiest person in the room."

"Shut up," Sam said, a smile tugging at her lips. She looked at Alan. "You coming?" she asked.

"Hell, yeah," he said. He walked over to the couch, and put out his hand to help Jonas up. "You," he said, "have a bed. Couch is mine."

"Oh," Jonas replied, and looked awkwardly at Sam. "Where will you...uh...?"

"Do you mind if I lie next to you?" she asked him.

Jonas's heart swelled. He had to fight any false hope it would give him. He nodded that it would be fine, and he walked into the bedroom.

Sam followed behind him, and waited as Jonas climbed on top of the covers, moving aside. Sam was silent as she got in next to him, her hair grazing his forearm. She turned so that she faced him, and they lay like that, staring at each other, but not saying anything at all.

And it wasn't until Sam drifted asleep that Jonas closed his eyes.

CHAPTER TWENTY-SIX

POET ANDERSON FELT STRONGER. HE realized it as he opened a tunnel into the siren's reality, a task he wasn't sure he could even complete. But he had more power now. He could feel it under his skin.

"What is this place?" Alan asked as the three of them stepped out of the tunnel. His voice was dreamy as he looked around at the sirens walking by. He spun, taken in, but Poet reached out and put his hand on Alan's shoulder.

"Take a closer look, brother," he said. Alan laughed questioningly, and then shifted his eyes from siren to siren until his mouth formed a perfect O.

"Well," Alan said. "That's...unusual."

"What is it?" Sam asked, moving to stand closer and look over Alan's shoulder. "What do you see? Because I see a bunch of elfin creatures with silver hair."

Poet turned to her. "You do?"

Sam smiled. "Yeah. Do you see something different?"

"No," he said. "But these are sirens. They can make you do things. Tempt or convince you. Callum had said something about how it doesn't work if you're in love—"

Poet stopped short, heat rising to his cheeks. Sam looked away, as an awkward silence fell between him. He wasn't sure if she was in love with him anymore. Maybe she was in love with—

"Follow me," Poet said, cutting his thoughts short, and stomping toward the bar where Angelique and the others sirens had died. "And for Christ's sake, Alan—don't let anyone touch you."

"That…is going to be a problem."

Poet swung around and felt his heart sink as he saw Maeve standing next to his brother. She held a knife to his throat, her hand on his shoulder.

"Maeve," Poet said cautiously. But he could see she had come unhinged. Dark purple and red circles rimmed her eyes, and slashes and bruises covered her arms. Her fingernails had blood embedded underneath them, and her shirt had been ripped at the collar. He knew Maeve could lash out with the kind of insanity that would easily kill his brother. "Please," Poet added.

Maeve smiled ruefully, and pressed the knife harder against Alan's neck. "You got him killed," she said. "Marcel—he's dead, and it's because of you."

"I'm sorry," Poet responded. This time he didn't try to blame his actions on anyone else. Sure, REM was the one who killed Marcel, but Poet had made Marcel take him back to the Dream World. He had put him in that situation.

Maeve leaned in, her lips next to Alan's ear, grazing his skin. "Tell your brother you don't forgive him," Maeve whispered. "Tell him you wish he were dead."

Alan blinked slowly, and then he whispered, "I don't forgive you, Jonas. I wish you were dead."

Even though Poet knew Alan couldn't resist Maeve's control, the words still hurt, and he flinched from them. Maeve laughed, but suddenly Sam appeared next to Poet.

"I'm sorry about Marcel," she told Maeve. "You know I am. But this isn't right either. We're here for help. REM is strong, and between him and the shadows, I'm not sure—"

Maeve turned her face away from Sam, not willing to show her the same cruelty she did Jonas. Poet noted that the knife seemed to press a little more lightly against his brother's skin. "The sirens won't help you," Maeve said. "I've already asked. Callum and Poet did too much damage last time. Sirens are nothing if not vindictive."

Poet looked toward the bar, surprised to find dozens of sirens lining the street, watching their argument. Their stares were intense, and they looked ready to attack. He could feel their anger.

He tilted his head, confused by this new wave of power— the connection he felt. He glanced around at the surroundings, and as Sam continued to try to reason with Maeve, Poet reached up his hand toward the sky. Clouds quickly gathered, hazes of purple and orange. He flexed his fingers and lightning cracked above them. The sirens all looked up.

"What's changed, Maeve?" Poet asked, not looking at her. "Why am I stronger?"

"Balance," she said. "You've absorbed some of Marcel's power. We all have."

The universe had a way of balancing—and with Marcel gone, his power had been redistributed to the other poets. It was all so they could battle REM. But Poet knew that even that wouldn't be enough.

"If you help us," Poet said, "you'll be free of REM forever. Isn't that worth it?" He looked at Maeve and her siren eye was twisting and turning gray clouds. "We can end this, Maeve," he said pleading. "Finally."

Her mouth tightened, and she lowered the knife from Alan's neck. "He was my friend," she said simply. "I'll kill REM because Marcel was my friend, and without him I have nothing to go back for anyway."

Maeve slipped her knife into her pocket, and pushed Alan away from her. Sam caught him by the arms and Alan turned slowly, still seeming out of it.

Poet should have figured. Of course, Alan with his big heart would be easy prey here. Hell, he was a siren's wet dream. Poet looked at Sam.

"Take him back to the Dream World," Poet told her, motioning to his brother. "See if you can gather those Dream Walkers, and we'll all meet in Genesis."

"And then?" Sam asked, pointing out that it was only part of a plan.

"And then REM will find us," Poet said. "Maeve," he said, turning to her. "Shall we?" He nodded his head toward the sirens. Maeve took a moment, then agreed and walked in their direction. Poet went over to clap Alan on the shoulder.

"When you get out of here," he said, "find Imani. Find all the Dream Walkers you can. We'll end it tonight, Alan. We'll free the world."

Alan smiled as if he thought that was a great idea, and Poet looked past him to Sam. "You going to be okay?" he asked her. Sam laughed.

"You forget," Sam said. "I'm the daughter of a Dream Walker."

Poet smiled, longing to reach for her, tell her he still loved her, but it was clear things had changed between them. How much remained to be seen. "Be careful," he whispered, and then Poet began to move the air until a tunnel formed.

Alan and Sam stepped through and disappeared.

Once they were gone, Poet turned and saw Maeve standing with the sirens, waiting for him. They looked pissed, and it was clear that Poet was in danger here, but he'd have to trust Maeve now. He really didn't have a choice. A woman dressed all in white came out of the bar, and he guessed she was the person in charge now that Angelique was gone. She crooked her finger, beckoning him. Poet took a steadying breath and then walked to meet her.

POET WAS LED INTO the bar. Stains of red were still on the floor near the entrance where Callum had murdered several sirens. Maeve was next to him, although she wasn't in the same predicament that he was.

As he passed, sirens stood along the walls, glaring at him. Some hissing. Their eyes weren't smoky and gray, they were angry and violent, swirling tornados. Poet gulped and followed the woman dressed in white up the stairs to where Angelique had been taken over by a shadow and killed by Callum. Unlike Angelique, this woman didn't look like a warrior. But Poet didn't let that convince him she wasn't dangerous.

A siren pulled out a chair for Poet at a table, and pushed him down roughly into the seat. Maeve sat next to him. The woman rounded the table, and took a seat facing them.

Although her hair was silver, the woman was more human-looking. Her eyes didn't shift like the eyes of the other sirens, though they were the color of solid marble. Her lips were stained dark red, her skin porcelain-smooth. Despite what he thought about her power, Poet leaned toward her, transfixed by her presence.

"Tell me," she said, her silky voice inspiring relaxation. "Why have you come here, Poet Anderson? Of all places. You couldn't have thought we would help you."

"But I did," he said, his voice not unlike Alan's—dreamy and lost. And although he could sense what was happening, he couldn't stop himself from telling the truth. "I thought you'd want revenge on the shadows because they possessed Angelique. And I thought then I could convince you to help us to defeat REM."

Maeve sniffed a laugh, and crossed her ankle over her knee. She sat back in the chair, seeming to enjoy the show.

"Ah, the shadows," the woman said. "And what of the poets? The Dream Walkers? You know they are all our enemies, and yet we're supposed to...work together?" She smiled as if this was a silly thought.

"Yes," Poet said. "And then you could come back and live in peace. It could all be over."

"Is that what you think will happen?" she asked, leaning forward in her seat, elbows on the table. "Don't you understand, Poet? Once REM is gone, you're obsolete. All of you." She glanced at Maeve. "There will be no need for poets. Your power will be gone."

"That's fine," Poet said, but Maeve looked away as if she didn't like the idea of being defenseless. "I just want—"

"No," the siren interrupted. "No, it won't be fine. You have a destiny, Jonas Anderson." And as she spoke his name it was as if a rush of air filled his lungs—a harsh, painful blast of cold air—and he gasped. "You're going to destroy the Dream World. You're going to destroy all of us."

Maeve turned fiercely to him, and Poet clutched his chest, trying to breathe. The sirens around him seemed to be closing in, and he jumped up from the chair and took a step back.

"No," he tried to say, but choked on the word.

"In the end," the woman continued as if he weren't suffocating, "the only way to beat REM will be to destroy our world. And you'll do it, under the guise of saving yours. So, no, Poet Anderson. We won't help you."

Poet clutched his throat, and as the siren stood, he was sure she was going to kill him. He gritted his teeth, and in one swift movement, he tore open a tunnel and jumped through.

CHAPTER TWENTY-SEVEN

POET STUMBLED ONTO THE STREET AND fell to his knees, gasping in a breath. He shifted his eyes around and found he was in Genesis. He immediately outstretched his arm and willed power there, his umbrella forming and his eyes going white with power. He knew from last time with Marcel that REM could appear at any moment. He wouldn't get caught off guard again.

"Poet!" Sam yelled, and Poet spun to find her running toward him. She had changed clothes, now in a sleek bodysuit with armor, much like what a Dream Walker would wear. When she got to him, she checked him over and asked if he was okay.

"I am now," he said, fully aware it sounded cheesy. But he meant it. He caught Sam's hand, and squeezed it. Part of him expected her to come closer, to kiss him, but she didn't. Sam smiled and took a step back. As her hand fell from his, Poet felt a burn in his chest, and he swallowed hard and searched for his brother.

He found Alan across the road, talking with Dream Walkers, and watched for a moment. Although Alan was tall, the Dream Walkers still seemed to tower over him, including Imani. Maybe it was their suits of armor. Alan seemed at ease, though, using his hands as he told a story or made a plan, Poet couldn't tell which.

But then Poet noticed a man among the Dream Walkers; someone who stood out not because of his size, but because he wasn't suited up. He wore a brown leather coat, which was fraying at the elbows. His hair was long, but he kept it slicked to the side, stubble on his chin and jaw. But most notably, the man had shiny revolver on his hip.

Poet opened his mouth to ask about him, but Sam stepped forward and called to Alan.

When Alan turned and saw Poet, he smiled broadly. "Oh, thank God," Poet saw him murmur, and Alan came toward him as the Dream Walkers watched. None of them acknowledged Poet.

"Christ, what was that place?" Alan asked, slapping Poet's hand when he got to him. "I wasn't sure if you were heading inside for…" Next to him, Sam shifted uncomfortably, and Alan quickly stopped talking.

"They planned to kill me," Poet said with a nod. "But I tunneled out. Guess the sirens won't help. We're on our own."

"Not quite our own," Alan said. He turned and motioned for the Dream Walkers to come over.

There were six of them, including the guy with the revolver. It was hardly an army, but it was what they had. Poet stood taller as they approached, but he felt small in comparison. The Dream Walkers seemed to revel in the imbalance.

Imani smiled at him, but didn't say anything, leaving him to stand awkwardly as the soldiers stared Poet down. Of course, Alan tried to fill the silence.

"So this is him," he said, putting his hand on Poet's arm. "My brother. In case—in case you didn't know, I guess." Alan smiled. Poet thought the Dream Walkers were more congenial than usual—no one had pulled a gun yet—and he attributed that to his brother's good nature.

The guy with the revolver smiled, hiking up one corner of his mouth. "Holy shit," he said, as if it was an observation for the others. "This scrawny kid is Poet Anderson? Well, we're fucked." The Dream Walkers laughed, and Poet clenched his fist, sending out sparks of electricity.

"Who is this person?" Poet asked calmly. "I hate him. Get him out of here."

"Not a chance, sparky," the guy said with a wink. "I was promised murder and mayhem today. So how about you go wait over in the corner while the adults take care of this."

"This is Merrick," Imani told Poet, hiking her thumb toward the guy. "And Poet's not going anywhere. We need him. He has to open the tunnel."

Poet turned to her. "Tunnel to where?"

"The void," she responded. "Your brother told me about it. We want to send REM there. Trap him along with the shadows."

"And how's that supposed to work?" Poet asked. "I couldn't tunnel into the void. I had to die."

"I'm listening," Merrick said in an amused voice. Poet ignored him.

Imani crossed her arms over her chest. "I know you're not powerful enough, but we considered that. That's why we got you back up."

"You did?" Alan asked first. He didn't seem to be in on whatever plan the Dream Walkers put together, and if that was the case, Poet knew to be worried.

"Sorry," Merrick said to Alan, taking out his revolver and holding it at his side. "We didn't want to spoil the surprise." Merrick looked over his shoulder, and Poet and Alan followed his direction. A Dream Walker appeared from a warehouse with Callum in tow.

For his part, Callum was wrecked: cut up, bruised up, beat up. A heavy chain was wrapped around his arms, and his hands were linked behind his back. Samantha gasped, but as she moved forward, Poet reached out to take her elbow to stop her. It was clear the Dream Walkers weren't screwing around.

"Told you we shouldn't have involved them," Poet murmured to Alan.

"What's this about?" Alan asked, stepping forward. "You didn't tell me you had a poet."

Merrick laughed. "Why would we? Look, kid—you're great. Truly. But this isn't a neighborhood game of stickball." He walked over and put the revolver to Callum's temple, and the British poet sighed as if he found it tiresome.

"Poet Anderson," Callum stated calmly. "Can you please tell these mongrels that I can't open a tunnel into the void either? And then, if you wouldn't mind, please tell them to fuck off and die."

Merrick's hand quickly darted out and he smacked Callum in the head with the gun, a hard thump that immediately began to swell up into a knot. Callum tightened his jaw, but didn't react otherwise.

"He's right," Poet said to Merrick. "We can't tunnel into the void. How do you expect—?"

"You leave that part to us," Merrick said. "Everything will be in place, and at the last minute, you and your buddy here will open a tunnel and pull REM's dead body through, trapping him in the void. Otherwise he'll regenerate."

Poet tilted his head. "What do you mean?"

"You didn't know?" Merrick laughed, and looked around at the other Dream Walkers. "God, this kid." He turned back to Poet and nodded along with his words as if he were talking to a child. "REM is a creature of nightmares," Merrick continued. "Unless the Waking World unfucks itself, the nightmares will keep coming. REM will regenerate. He keeps coming back. We want to end that permanently. His consciousness needs to leave."

It made sense, especially when Poet thought about the balance of the universe. He wouldn't destroy REM completely, only trap him. He wouldn't grow stronger, and he wouldn't destroy the entire Dream World either. It could work.

"You're going to take him down?" Poet asked the Dream Walker doubtfully. "Have you ever faced REM before?"

Merrick scoffed. "Kid, I've been battling REM since you were in diapers. You just be there at the last minute. And don't do anything stupid." He put his revolver back in the holster on his hip. "Or I'll kill your brother," he added.

Poet flashed with rage, but Alan held him back. The Dream Walkers took Callum by the arm and led him over to the middle of the street, planting him there. Poet glanced around, noting that this part of Genesis was unusually empty. The streets were deserted, no cars or people in sight. Poet thought about the siren—how she told him he'd destroy the Dream World. REM had said something like that to him once.

What if they were right?

"Poet Anderson," Callum called, on his knees in the middle of the street. "Have you seen Maeve? I'd love to say goodbye."

The Dream Walkers turned to watch Callum as he spoke, but they must have decided it wasn't all that important because they began a quieter discussion between themselves. Callum's eyes flashed with mischief, and Poet felt some relief at this. He didn't want to see a poet be a prisoner of anyone.

"I think she's home, washing her hair," Poet said. "Maybe she'll meet us for a drink tonight."

Callum smiled, and closed his eyes. "Maybe."

There was a rumbling in the distance, the sound of engines. Sam's posture stiffened, and she backed up, bumping into Poet as they stared toward the horizon. The sound was unmistakable: airbikes. The Night Stalkers were coming, and that meant REM was coming too.

The Dream Walkers quickly separated, and while Imani went to stand next to Callum, Merrick headed toward Poet.

"The three of you get out of sight," Merrick said. "I doubt it will matter, he can probably feel you already, but let's give it a shot."

"I don't understand. What about Callum?" Poet asked. "What's your plan?"

Merrick smiled and glanced over his shoulder. "Oh, you mean the bait? Yeah, he'll be fine. You just wait until I obliterate REM's Halo, then you swoop in and save the day. Got that?"

"I...really don't like you," Poet said, narrowing his eyes.

"Luckily for you, the feeling is entirely mutual." Merrick sniffed a laugh, and jogged to take cover in an abandoned building, posing himself just inside the door.

"Come on," Alan said, taking Poet's arm. Samantha followed, looking over her shoulder at the oncoming lights. Poet couldn't see how many airbikes there were, but it seemed like a lot.

In the road, Imani patted Callum's shoulder, and left him there, and Poet couldn't help thinking Callum looked young. Of course, he wasn't—he was older than any of those Dream Walkers—but confined like that, beaten up, it wasn't right. Poet wished he'd done this all differently, stayed away like the poets had asked him.

Poet, Alan, and Sam ducked behind a parked car, and Poet closed his eyes, willing into his hands all the power inside of him, and then all the power he could absorb around him. His umbrella appeared first, and when Poet opened his eyes, the electricity came off them in snaps. Overhead, thunder clapped. Sam looked up tentatively, and then at Poet.

"It's going to work," she said, almost like she wished he'd been the one to say it.

Storm clouds gathered in the sky of Genesis just as REM came into focus, walking among the dozens of air-bikes. Night Stalkers were suited up, helmets down, looking ready for war. Since Poet had seen him last, REM looked bigger. Badder.

Callum opened his eyes as he was surrounded, but he only stared straight ahead, as if he didn't care one way or another. Poet, however, had his heart in his throat. They had put a poet in touching distance of the creature of nightmares. It was too dangerous.

"What's this now?" REM called, surveying the scene. He made a wide circle around Callum, eyeing him carefully. "They'd really give me their strongest poet?"

"Flattery will get you everywhere," Callum said winningly, continuing to stare ahead.

"Ah, yes. I never grow tired of the poet tongues. Perhaps I'll rip yours out for a souvenir. Now why are you here, boy? I have need of a poet, and you'll do nicely, but I'm not stupid."

Callum scrunched up his nose, and finally looked directly at REM. "I don't know," he said, like he was thinking it over. "I'd say your intelligence is…well, below average, if I'm being honest."

REM's hand shot out, and he punched Callum hard enough to knock him back on his ass, sending blood gushing from his nose. The poet's hands were still tied behind his back, leaving him utterly defenseless.

And then it occurred to Poet that maybe Callum wasn't just bait. Dream Walkers hated poets—wouldn't it be better for them if they destroyed the poets right along with REM?

"Shit," Poet cursed under his breath, and Alan looked over, alarmed.

"What's wrong?" Alan asked.

"The Dream Walkers," Poet whispered. "I don't think REM is the only one they're trying to kill."

Alan furrowed his brow, but Sam seemed to understand more quickly. She gritted her teeth and turned her steady gaze toward the street. "I won't let that happen," she said.

Poet had to smile and agree. He really didn't want to die today.

"This is too easy," REM said out on the street, rounding Callum once again. "I'm not sure if there was a plan, but it ends now. It ends with you. And for that, I must say thank you."

REM reached out, took Callum by his jacket lapel, and dragged him to his feet. Once standing, the poet pulled from his grasp, and stumbled back a step. Behind him, a few Night Stalkers approached, but REM held up his hand to stop them.

"Before I devour you," REM said, stepping closer to Callum. "Tell me what you know about the shadows."

Callum laughed, and then turned to spit out blood. "That's not really how a bargain works, mate. What exactly do I get out of this deal?"

"I won't use you to enter the Waking World."

This seemed to stun Callum, and he narrowed his eyes. "I don't believe you."

"It's true," REM said. "There will be other ways, but the most pressing issue is—"

As if on cue, one of the Night Stalkers threw his sword, and REM's Halo quickly shot out and knocked it aside before going back to loop around REM protectively.

REM growled and lifted his arm. His armor split, and a gun appeared. He fired repeatedly, blasting the Night Stalker off his feet. REM walked toward him, continuing to fire until the helmet blew open, and the Night Stalker's head was mush.

REM lowered his weapon and turned back to Callum, who watched in what looked like amusement.

"They have infected my army," REM said, his voice tight. "The shadows have quickly gone from a nuisance to a problem. I'm willing to make a deal for your life if you help me. I offered this same deal to Poet Anderson, but he—"

Callum's eyes drifted in Poet's direction, and REM, in a movement so sudden Poet couldn't prepare, spun around, and began firing in his direction.

"Down!" Alan yelled as lasers hit the car repeatedly, making it catch fire.

The heat flared up quickly, and Poet took Sam's hand and pulled her back.

"Come out, Poet Anderson," REM called, the rage in his voice barely controlled. "We have business, you and I."

"Stay here," Poet murmured to Alan and Sam. Sam tried to grab onto his coat to stop him, and Alan whispered for him to stop, but Poet stood up and glared over the burning hood of the car toward REM, the scene wavy in the heat.

"Ah, yes," REM said. "Come here, my boy. Surely you wouldn't let your friend die. I'm a little surprised. I didn't take you for the heartless type."

Poet swallowed down his fear and settled into himself as he walked toward REM. Poet was more powerful now. He wouldn't get beaten down like last time.

"Ay, Poet," Callum called. "When did you get here?" He smiled, blood coating his teeth.

"Help me defeat the shadows," REM called out to Poet. "And then we can decide what comes next. But you and I both know they are destroying all the realities. They must be stopped."

"There are a few things that should be stopped," Poet murmured. Out of the corner of his eye, he saw a flash of movement. He quickly held up his umbrella and used it to blast electricity to knock down a shadow-possessed Night Stalker that rushed them. The creature started to get up, and Poet shot it again, killing it.

Poet ran his eyes along the rows of Night Stalkers, wondering if more of them had been possessed by shadows. He had no idea how many shadows there were, but part of him wondered if REM was right. That thought didn't last long, though.

A rush of air blew over him, and Poet squinted his eyes and saw Maeve walk out of a tunnel. She took one look at Callum, and before Poet could even blink, she pulled out a gun and pointed it at REM.

CHAPTER TWENTY-EIGHT

MAEVE FIRED WITHOUT HESITATION, but REM's Halo blocked the shots. Maeve cursed and dropped her weapon, only to create a newer, bigger gun. She backed up until she was next to Poet Anderson, and squeezed off a dozen shots, each of them refracted by the Halo.

"I see your friend's here again," Maeve said to Poet. "You and REM star-crossed lovers or what?"

"Seems so," Poet said, lowering his head, ready to battle. "And we're about to break up, so expect some water works."

Maeve snorted a laugh, then dropped her gun and created a long sword, the end glowing with electricity. "Batter up," she murmured, and walked toward REM, her sword out protectively.

REM didn't wait for an invitation. The gun came out of his suit; he pointed it and fired. Maeve grunted as she swung her sword from side to side, blocking the lasers from hitting her.

Poet glanced over to the building where the Dream Walkers were waiting, but he didn't see them anymore.

This was supposed to be their plan. Why weren't they doing anything?

Callum was still in the middle of the road, watching Maeve with admiration. They'd lost two of their own, all because they came back to the Dream World for Poet. He owed them.

Poet swung his umbrella by the handle, and when it made it all the way around, it was a long-barreled gun. Poet caught up with Maeve and together they fired on REM.

REM's Halo was able to block the lasers, but the poets were driving him backwards, his Halo swinging so quickly his own shots couldn't get out. For the first time in a while, Poet felt in control. This would end once and for all.

"This is for Marcel," Maeve said, holding her sword in her right hand while her left created another gun and she fired. REM's Halo was hit, and flew off to the right.

REM's robotic eyes flipped in that direction, but then he aimed his gun at Maeve. She was already running, though, and jumped up to kick him in the stomach, knocking him back. She swung around, elbow to the face, and shot him close range in the chest. His armor deflected it, and he was able to push her back.

Poet fired twice, striking REM and knocking him to his knees. The creature growled, but Poet smiled. Thunder clapped again; lightning flashed above.

A piercing scream cut through the air, and Poet gasped, looking back to where Sam and Alan were. But it wasn't Sam. Maeve, also distracted, turned toward the building where the Dream Walkers had been waiting.

There was a scuffle, and then suddenly Merrick, Imani, and several other Dream Walkers darted out, weapons drawn on whatever was inside. Merrick fired first at something unseen, as he backed up.

Poet watched, confused, as several of the Night Stalkers closed in, surrounding them and drawing their weapons when the Dream Walkers came out into the open. And then, with a stumble, one of the Dream Walkers stepped through the doorway of the building, blood splattered on his face. Poet's gut turned.

The Dream Walker—helmet back and gun out—had black eyes and wisps of dark smoke coming out of his nose and mouth. He flinched once, and then seemed to gain control of his body. The man was possessed by a shadow. They now had one less Dream Walker on their side.

"Draper!" Merrick yelled. "Stand down!"

"That's not Draper anymore," Poet said. "It's a shadow."

Merrick looked back at Poet, seemingly angry at him. "How do we get it out?" he demanded.

"You don't. You kill him before he wakes up."

Merrick's eyes flashed, and then he turned back to Draper. Merrick tilted his head from side to side as if weighing out his options, and then he cursed and fired his gun, blowing off the top of Draper's head. The Dream Walker fell backwards and hit the ground in an uneremonious heap.

Merrick didn't miss a beat before spinning and pointing his revolver at REM, the original plan of a surprise attack now thwarted. Poet followed his lead, but gasped when he saw that REM was no longer where he'd been.

REM had his metal arm wrapped around Maeve's neck as he stood behind her. She struggled, even as REM's other hand seemed buried in her side.

"Let her go," Poet Anderson said, the energy inside him growing white-hot. The sky above erupted in anger, splitting open in flashes of red and midnight blue. "Take me instead."

REM laughed. "You're done making deals. You want her? I want those shadows gone."

Poet shook his head. He had no idea how many shadows there were. He looked at Callum and found him watching, his eyes blazing white.

"Fourteen left," Callum said. He paused. "The next one will take the female Dream Walker."

He only had a moment. Poet spun and pointed his weapon just as a shadow crawled out from a wall and headed directly for Imani.

"Watch out!" he yelled, and Imani moved quickly, grabbing a Night Stalker off his airbike and using him as a shield. The shadow quickly devoured the Night Stalker's Halo, and then the Night Stalker's helmet slid back, and the shadow raced into him. The Night Stalker convulsed.

Imani let go of him, pushing him away with her boot before shooting him point blank in the face. He dropped.

Callum turned. "Third Night Stalker on the left," he said, half in a daze. He was digging into his talent to take REM's deal. He was trying to save Maeve.

"We don't have time for this," Merrick growled, and from the inside of his jacket he pulled out a blue-glowing grenade and threw it into the assembled Night Stalkers. It exploded, blowing several of them off their bikes, while blue mist began to stretch over them.

The Dream Walkers turned back to back, all of their Halos circulating to protect them—including Merrick's Halo, which had been hidden. They began shooting the Night Stalkers, the other soldiers now disoriented by the mist.

Poet joined in the chaos, knowing they were outnumbered. REM backed up, still with Maeve in his grasp. Callum was absolutely still.

Alan and Sam came out from where they'd been hiding behind the car, and Alan pointed a gun he must have gotten from a Dream Walker, firing while taking cover. Sam was a better shot, cocking her head to the side as she took out Night Stalker after Night Stalker.

"Three left," Callum said. "The Dream Walker on—" But he wasn't fast enough this time. One of the Dream Walkers fell to his knees, both hands pressing on the side of his helmet as if his head hurt. His Halo turned black and then crumbled into dust.

Imani cursed, ready to fire, but Merrick kicked the Dream Walker over and shot him. "Two," he said for Callum.

The Night Stalker numbers were dwindling, and there were only four Dream Walkers left. Poet had to get Maeve now and leave the shadows to the others.

Poet changed his weapon back into his umbrella. He swung it around once and reached up toward the sky. Thunder, lightning, and then the rain started. It poured down in blue sheets, hot to the touch.

Rather than looking worried, REM actually smiled. "You can do better than that," he said, baiting him. Behind him, Callum's eyes went back to normal, and he steadied a serious gaze on Poet.

"Stop," Callum said. "Stop now before you lose control."

"I'm not going to lose control," Poet said, but Callum grimaced. Poet wondered if it was a premonition. Callum shook his head slowly, turned to Maeve and called her name.

REM swung her around, and when Callum saw her face, he smiled. He had the lost sort of expression he often got when using his premonition. But this time, his expression was tinged with deep sadness.

"You know I'll always be at your side?" Callum called out to her, misery in his voice. "Here, or...wherever we end up."

Poet watched as Maeve's posture sagged, maybe realizing he meant more. Had seen more. She nodded.

"You were the worst platonic boyfriend I ever had," she said back, tears brimming. "But we had some good times. See you on the other side?"

"Have the whiskey ready," he whispered and closed his eyes as if he couldn't bear to watch any longer.

Poet was confused for a moment, but then Maeve screamed in agony. Her eyelids fluttered.

"Come now," REM said near her ear. "It doesn't hurt that badly." But his eyes blazed brighter, and the arm that was around Maeve's neck was now over her heart. He was absorbing her soul. Maeve gasped for breath, and REM only held her tighter.

"No!" Poet yelled, running toward them, ready to fight off the Halo to get close enough to free Maeve before REM could take her over and get a free pass into the Waking World.

The Halo swung out at him, more powerful than before, and knocked Poet back with its force. Poet fought it valiantly, his whole self fighting to get to Maeve. It would be too late—he saw her fading. Her eyes locked on his, her one ghost eye now a dim gray.

"Maeve!" he screamed, his voice echoed in thunder. The ground shook.

A shot rang out, and as Poet watched, a hole tore through Maeve's forehead, splattering her blood over REM's face as his suit absorbed the impact of the hit. REM, startled, pulled his hand from Maeve, and her lifeless body collapsed onto the pavement.

Sam cried out from the other side of the street, and Poet slowly turned and saw Merrick with his revolver still raised. He looked at Poet and shrugged. "Can't let him out, kid. I'm sorry, but—"

But Poet raged and sent strikes of electricity from his umbrella, knocking Merrick and the other Dream Walkers off their feet.

Merrick *killed* her.

He killed Maeve, and he would do the same to Poet and Callum when he got the chance.

Poet started toward them, feeling irrational and, yes, out of control. The rain turned into sparks, and fire began to fall from the sky. It landed on roofs of buildings, and set them ablaze. Genesis was beginning to burn.

Another swing of the umbrella, and one of the Dream Walkers screamed as his leg was severed with a flash of light. Cracks began to form in the pavement from each of Poet's steps. His entire existence was a live wire, ready to decimate all of them. Everything. It felt like darkness was pouring in, and Poet welcomed it.

"Poet, stop!" Sam called, running toward him, only to be stopped by Alan, who held her back. Poet's skin was beginning to glow blue, an aura of destruction around him. Maeve's power was being absorbed, making him feel unstoppable.

"Brother," Alan said, his voice the calm in the storm. "*Jonas*. You have to get control."

But as he said it, the overturned airbikes on the street began to levitate, trash cans and metal pipes floating. Gravity was shifting.

The Dream World was dissolving.

"Jonas, look at me!" Alan shouted. The anger in his voice was so unexpected, that Poet turned. "Get us out of here," Alan said, his jaw clenched.

Poet's gaze shifted to Sam, who was still struggling to get to him, to stop him. But he couldn't stop. The siren had been right: Poet Anderson would destroy the Dream World. He would do it with darkness because it was the only way to defeat REM.

With a swift swipe of his hand, Poet threw open a tunnel next to Alan and then continued his onslaught on the Dream Walkers. They had moved, taking cover behind one of the cement barriers. Poet quickly blasted through it, sending chucks of concrete in every direction.

"Hey, kid," Merrick said, standing with his revolver held to the side. "Eyes on the prize here. Look, I'm sorry I shot your friend, but—"

Poet's anger flashed, and the ground shook, splitting open wider. The Dream Walker quickly darted to one side so he didn't fall in the crevasse it created.

A Night Stalker ran toward Poet, weapon out, and Poet turned to him and held up his umbrella, transforming it into a gun before shooting him.

"One," Callum whispered, and opened his eyes.

Poet turned to him, just as Callum pulled his hands free and tossed the chains aside. He would have absorbed Maeve's power as well, and was quite possibly the strongest creature in existence in that moment.

But Callum didn't look powerful; he looked...grief-stricken. Devastated. For a moment, Poet thought it was for Maeve, but then it struck him that the poet's premonition powers would have grown too.

Poet turned to REM, but it was too late. The monster of nightmares had a sword extended from his suit, and in one swift movement, he swung around and slashed it across Callum's chest, cutting through his suit and slashing his skin.

The poet fell back a step, blood pouring down in a red river over his shirt. Stunned, Callum raised his hand to fight back, but REM launched himself, and was on him before he could act. They tumbled to the pavement.

On the street, Callum writhed in pain as REM tore open his chest and reached inside. Gruesome. Cruel.

Poet leapt forward, running as hard as he could toward them, but there was a crack, and Poet felt a sharp pain in his chest. For a moment, he thought REM had him too. He fell, his cheek skidding on pavement, before he rolled to a stop.

He put his hand to his chest and when he pulled it back, his palm was covered in blood. He looked down and the burn mark in his shirt, the red blooming of blood. He'd been shot.

Poet choked on a breath, the air becoming harder to take in. He turned to see Merrick, his gun still aimed after firing on him. The Dream Walker lowered his weapon, and then he and the Dream Walkers ran for REM and Callum.

Poet's pain was excruciating. He tried to get to his hands and knees. He felt like he was drowning, and he gasped. Sam and Alan were immediately at this side, trying to help him up. Alan's face had gone white. Sam used her hands to try and cover the wound, tears streaming down her cheeks as red pulsed between her fingers, flowed down her forearms.

"You have to wake up," she said. "You'll die."

"Not yet," Poet said, his breath rattling in his chest. He looked at her. "Why didn't you go in the tunnel?"

"Because I can't leave you," she said. "Now open another one and we'll go together."

Poet watched her, feeling his power drain, and knowing he couldn't heal himself quickly enough to survive this wound. But he wouldn't abandon the fight either. He smiled sadly to let Sam know it was his decision, and she cursed and pressed harder on his wound, making him wince.

"What's the plan here, Poet?" Alan called, turning his back to his brother as he surveyed the scene. Several Night

Stalkers were heading toward them, while the others were racing to protect REM. The Dream Walkers were firing, trying to stop REM from absorbing Callum's soul, but his Halo was impenetrable.

Black dots began to appear in Poet's vision, and he blinked them away. He wouldn't die a coward. Poet gently took Sam's hand off him, blood spurting out the minute he did. He nodded at his brother, and then he knelt down on one knee, bloodied hand to the pavement.

Poet closed his eyes, and found every store of power he had. He willed it, and the ground rumbled and split. The crack raced toward the Night Stalkers and exploded up in a flash of white so bright it temporarily blinded everything. The Night Stalkers were knocked off their feet, and just as the last shadow began to devour one of them, Imani turned around and shot it six times.

The shadows were gone, at least from the Dream World.

Poet tried to get to his feet, stumbling forward. The color of the world had begun to drain from his vision. Everything was black and white.

"I'm dying," he said simply, almost curiously, as Sam came back to hook his arm over her shoulder, holding him up.

"I know," Sam responded, and covered his wound again.

They watched, Poet unable to help, as the Dream Walkers got to REM. There was an explosion of bullets, and the fire in the sky turned to rain as Poet's power continued to drain away.

The Dream Walkers had to stop REM. There wasn't another choice.

Poet's legs gave out, and he faltered, taking Sam down to her knees as she tried to hold him up. She called for Alan, and he was there, telling Poet to wake up. To hurry and wake up.

Poet held up his hand, and found he was too weak to make a tunnel. Instead he rested against Sam, and she brushed his hair from his bloody face. He had no choice but to watch REM continue to devour Callum. Poet was dying, and he faltered, and fell to his side on the pavement. Sam was murmuring something worriedly, but she sounded far away.

As they both lay on the ground dying, Poet's eyes found Callum's across the road. It was clear the pain was excruciating—his teeth were bared, and bloody tears leaked from the corners of his eyes. But he held Poet's gaze, his insides being turned black with REM's madness, and Poet knew that Callum had foreseen this. That was his goodbye to Maeve. He knew how this would end.

Poet licked his dry lips, and lifted his hand once again. He tried to send electricity to stop REM's Halo, to save Callum, but a tunnel started to open, wind gusting and blowing debris across the road. The cars that were levitating got sucked into the tunnel first.

"What are you doing?" Sam asked, but Poet lowered his arm.

"It's not me," he murmured.

Callum's eyes were closed, his body still. Poet didn't feel a rush of power like he had when Marcel and Maeve died. The power wasn't there. It had been absorbed by REM.

"Get down!" Merrick screamed to his Dream Walkers, and they ducked as a car flew past them, nearly knocking them into the tunnel.

Poet could see to the other side—it was downtown Seattle, barely dusk. The cars from the Dreamscape crashed onto the busy streets, and people were screaming and running. REM's soldiers held up their weapons and raced toward the tunnel, toward the Waking World.

"Oh, my God, he did it," Sam said, her voice catching. "He's going to take over the Waking World."

Poet didn't respond. His lips felt cold, his fingers numb. The Dream Walkers scrambled, trying to take out every Night Stalker they could before they could charge into the Waking World, but there were too many of them now. Reinforcements had arrived. The Dream World and the Waking World were colliding with violent force.

Fires began to tear through the buildings of downtown Seattle. People were lying dead in the street from the destruction. And when the first Night Stalker crossed over, it fired at will. The nightmares had been unleashed on the Waking World. It was an invasion.

Poet looked at Callum's body, which was still and empty on the ground. He hadn't realized it, but REM was gone. And then, to Poet's horror, Callum opened his eyes. They were black orbs.

He sat up in a jerky movement, and held up his hands, looking down at them admiringly. Then REM, dressed in Callum's body, turned to Poet. The creature of nightmares smiled, stiff and unnatural, and then he got to his feet.

There was still a slash in Callum's chest, but slowly, it began to close.

"Fuck," Alan murmured, and tried to pull Poet up from the ground. "We have to go," he said shakily, dragging Poet to his feet with Sam's help.

REM didn't come for him, though; instead he turned toward the tunnel, the hole in the veil. REM swiped his hand across the sky and tore the hole bigger. His power was greater than anything the Dream or Waking Worlds had ever seen.

Alan led Poet to the building where the Dream Walkers had been hiding, and ducked him behind the doorway. He set him on the floor, and then Alan waited with his gun out, shooting at Night Stalkers if they came too close. Sam knelt beside Poet.

"I should have destroyed it all," Poet said, his voice weak.

Sam watched him, and then reached to put her palm on his cheek. He leaned into it, missing her. Missing himself.

Poet Anderson had failed. REM was now free to destroy the Waking World. It was the beginning of World War III, and it wouldn't end well.

He'd failed again.

"Hey," Sam said, leaning closet to Poet. "Jonas," she whispered sadly.

And when he looked down, he was Jonas Anderson again. Jeans and a T-shirt, blood still soaking through. No suit. No hat. No umbrella.

"I'm sorry," he murmured. "I never—"

"Shh," Sam said. "There's no time. We need you."

"I can't."

She nodded. "You can still save the world, Poet Anderson," she said as tears dripped on her cheeks. "Callum told me as much while you were gone. He told me what you had to do to get your full power."

Jonas stared at her, flashes of light and echoes of explosions coming in the doorway next to him. The world was literally ending, but all Jonas wanted was to be with Sam. The two of them, alone in a dark room. At peace. Free of destiny.

But he knew that would never happen. And maybe it was never supposed to—that was the cruelest thought of all. He knew what he had to do if he wanted the power.

"Let go," she whispered, her voice cracking. "Let us go, Poet. Become who you have to be to save us." She leaned in, and pressed her mouth to his. The hum of electricity clung to her lips, and Poet couldn't help but fall completely and helplessly under her spell. Sam pulled back first, and put her forehead against Poet's. His sharp black suit raced over his body, and his umbrella appeared next to him.

"You can't love me anymore, Poet," she murmured. "It'll kill us all. Let go, and then go kick REM's ass."

Poet's flinched, wanting to hold her to him. Hold on to who he was, who he could be with her. But Sam pulled back, wiping the tears off her cheeks. She looked at Alan, and in return, the older Anderson brother smiled at Poet.

"I'll be all right," Alan said. "I'll be all right because of you. Now power up."

But Poet's grief was palpable. There would be no coming back from this—once Poet let them go, untethered himself to the Waking World, he would be powerful, but he would never feel the same. He might not feel at all.

He would be darkness. He would be war.

"Poet?" Sam called, and Poet realized his eyes had closed. He was moments from death. Then it would be too late.

Poet forced his eyes open to look at both Samantha and his brother. Alan nodded for him to go ahead, and Poet turned to Sam.

"I love you, Samantha Birnham-Wood," Poet said, his voice barely a gasp. "I love you so fucking much."

Sam bit down on her lip. "I love you too," she murmured, and leaned in to hug him, clinging to him. Her touch, her smell, everything so familiar and painful.

And then Sam put her mouth next to Poet's ear, and whispered, "Now devour that love and fill it with power. Do it now."

Poet hitched in a pained breath, his fingers in her hair, and he cried as he did just that.

As if in a fast rewind, he sped through their past—through their time at the Eden Hotel, fighting REM in the woods. He saw them eating dinner in the Dream World, going to her house and avoiding her father. He saw himself borrowing a pen in English class.

He saw his whole relationship with Samantha, even glimpses of the future they could have had. And then, like a Polaroid that didn't develop, the entire frame began to fill with darkness, blotting out their life together. Erasing it. Devouring it.

The empty space left behind stung for only a moment, and Poet pulled back and looked at her—this girl. Samantha stared at him with bright green eyes, a worried expression. She whispered his name.

And he felt nothing.

Suddenly, a flood of power rushed inside Poet, filling him to the brim with electricity as it shot from his eyes to the sky, shot from his fingertips. The pain was excruciating and exhilarating at the same time. It was everything. It was boundless.

And then Poet Anderson roared, and the entire Dreamscape shook.

THE END

EXPLORE MORE POET ANDERSON AT TOTHESTARS.MEDIA